Shadow Riders

OTHER FIVE STAR WESTERN TITLES BY LES SAVAGE, JR.:

Fire Dance at Spider Rock (1995)

Medicine Wheel (1996)

Coffin Gap (1997)

Phantoms in the Night (1998)

The Bloody Quarter (1999)

The Shadow in Renegade Basin (2000)

In the Land of Little Sticks (2000)

The Sting of Señorita *Scorpion* (2000)

The Cavan Breed (2001)

Gambler's Row (2002)

Danger Rides the River (2002)

The Devil's Corral (2003)

West of Laramie (2003)

The Beast in Cañada Diablo (2004)

The Ghost Horse (2004)

Trail of the Silver Saddle (2005)

Doniphan's Thousand (2005)

The Curse of Montezuma (2006)

Black Rock Cañon (2006)

Wolves of the Sundown Trail (2007)

Arizona Showdown (2008)

The Last Ride (2008)

Long Gun (2009)

SHADOW RIDERS

A WESTERN DUO

LES SAVAGE, JR.

FIVE STAR
A part of Gale, Cengage Learning

Detroit • New York • San Francisco • New Haven, Conn • Waterville, Maine • London

GALE
CENGAGE Learning

Copyright © 2009 by Golden West Literary Agency.

The Acknowledgments on page 243 constitute an extension of the copyright page.

Five Star Publishing, a part of Gale, Cengage Learning.

Set in 11 pt. Plantin.

Printed on permanent paper.

LIBRARY OF CONGRESS CATALOGING-IN-PUBLICATION DATA

Savage, Les.
  [Trail of the lonely gun]
  Shadow riders : a western duo / by Les Savage, Jr. — 1st ed.
    p. cm.
  ISBN-13: 978-1-59414-799-9 (hardcover : alk. paper)
  ISBN-10: 1-59414-799-X (hardcover : alk. paper)
  I. Savage, Les. Shadow riders. II. Title.
PS3569.A826T72 2009
813'.54—dc22   2009013085

First Edition. First Printing: August 2009.

Published in 2009 in conjunction with Golden West Literary Agency.

Printed in the United States of America
1 2 3 4 5 6 7 13 12 11 10 09

CONTENTS

TRAIL OF THE LONELY GUN 7

SHADOW RIDERS 65

101.890

★ ★ ★ ★ ★

TRAIL OF THE LONELY GUN

★ ★ ★ ★ ★

I

When the sound came, Johnny Vickers stiffened, and the lever on his sixteen-shot Henry *snicked* softly to the pull. Moonlight coming in the doorway of the miner's shack fell meagerly across his face, its upper half obliterated by the solid black shadow laid across it by the brim of his flat-topped hat, his long, unshaven jaw thrusting forward in an habitual aggression that drew his lips thin under the aquiline dominance of his nose. The collar of his alkali-whitened denim coat was turned up around the sunburned column of his neck, and his legs were long and saddle-drawn in sweat-stiff Ute leggings with greasy fringe down their seams. Across the gurgle of Granite Creek and on down Thumb Butte Road, he could see Prescott's lights glowing yellow in the soft blackness of the August night.

"Kern?" he said.

"No, Vickers," the man outside answered. "Perry Papago. I'll come in, *si?*"

The half-breed's figure blotted light from the square gloom of the door momentarily, then he was inside, bending forward slightly, as if to peer at Johnny Vickers. In the shadows, Papago's pockmarked face was barely visible to Vickers, the whites of his eyes pale, shifting enigmas above the mobile intelligence of his broad mouth. He wore nothing but a pair of dirty *chivarras* and a short leather vest, and his shoulders were limned smooth and coppery against the dim glow from outside. Vickers marked the three pounds of Remington .44 still in Papago's holster before he spoke.

"You took a chance walking in like that."

"I didn't know it was so bad," said Papago, and his eyes were taking in the acrid rigidity of Vickers's figure. "But I guess I'd be pretty spooky, too, if I'd been hiding out on a murder charge for over a month. They don't give you much peace, do they, Vickers? I hear Deputy Calavaras almost had you last week up in Skull Valley."

"Never mind," said Vickers.

"Why did you really kill Edgar James, Vickers?" asked Papago. "He was such a nice young man. Just because you and him were rival editors . . . ?"

"He was a swilling rum pot who thought he could find out everything that went on in Arizona territory by sitting on his hocks in front of that two-bit *Courier* and. . . ." Johnny Vickers stopped, breathing hard, trembling with the effort of holding all the bitterness of this last month in him. Finally he spoke again from between his teeth. "I told you . . . never mind."

"But I will mind," said Perry Papago. "I always liked you, Vickers. If there's one square man with the Indians in Prescott, you're it. Your editorials stopped more than one Indian war from starting. The Mokis at Walpi won't be quick to forget how the Christmas article you wrote kept them from starving in 'Seventy-Four." His voice had lost its former mockery. "We don't blame you for killing James. He bucked every decent thing you tried to do for the Indians. That's why I'm here, Vickers. Any other man, we wouldn't care, but you always played square with us, and we don't want you to get in any bigger tight than you're already in. We don't want you to do this."

Vickers moved faintly, the Henry scraping against his Levi's coat. "Don't want me to do what?"

"I know you're here to meet Judge Kern," said Papago. "Do you know why he wanted you?"

"I know something's happened to his daughter," said Vickers.

"The Apaches got Sherry Kern," said Papago. "The judge wants you to get her back."

The irony of that almost drew a laugh from Vickers. "Why me?" he said finally.

"Because you're his last card," said Papago. "You know those Indians like nobody else does around here, and you're the only one who might be able to reach them without endangering Sherry Kern's life. They took her off the Butterfield stage between here and Tucson, killed the other passengers, burned the coach. About a week later, Kern was contacted. You know four companies of dragoons were just moved from Tucson up here to Prescott. Kern was given till the end of August to have those troops moved back, or his daughter would be returned to him, dead."

"And Kern thinks it's Apaches?" said Vickers. "What about the Tucson machine? You know how Prescott and Tucson have been fighting for twelve years to see which one becomes the seat of the territorial capital. The legislature's convened in Tucson these past three years, and the Tucson machine's gotten fat on the plum of having it in their town. The movement of these troops to Prescott undoubtedly means the capital's being shifted, too. If the legislature starts convening up here again, the balance of power will shift back to Kern's party, and the Tucson machine will be washed up. You know the machine would do anything to keep that from happening. If they could force those troops back to Tucson, they'd have a big start in keeping the capital there. No legislature's going to meet anywhere in this territory without the protection of the military."

"You're loco," said Papago. "The Tucson machine doesn't have anything to do with this. You know that those dragoons were sent up here by the Department of Arizona as an opening campaign against the northern Apaches. Crook's through with

11

the Tontos, and he's coming up here, that's all. The Apaches just took this way to stop it. Forget the Tucson machine. Forget everything. Just get out of here and don't have anything to do with Kern."

"I'd rather see the judge first."

"You won't leave?"

"I don't think so."

Papago's hand was stiff, now, and he seemed to incline his short, square torso forward perceptibly. "There are other ways of stopping you besides asking you."

Vickers's big Henry lifted slightly till its bore covered the belt buckle of Navajo silver glittering against Papago's belly. "Go ahead," he said, "if you want to."

"I don't have to," said Papago, and his gaze shifted over Vickers's shoulder. "All right, Combabi, you can take his Henry."

"No, Combabi," said someone else from behind Vickers, "you leave his Henry right where it is."

Vickers stood tensely till he heard the movement behind him, then shifted so he could see without taking his gun off Papago. There was no rear door to this old miner's shack, but the roof above the room had caved in, pulling part of the log wall in with it. Combabi must have slipped through the opening while Papago and Vickers were talking; it would have taken a full-blooded Indian to do it without Vickers's hearing. Combabi crouched there now, surprise in the tension of his body, if not in the dark enigma of his hook-nosed face. There was something frustrated about the way he gripped the big Dragoon cap-and-ball in both dirty hands. The man above Combabi on what was left of the decaying log wall had pulled the tails of his pin-striped cutaway up about his lean shanks in order to get there, and a hairy old beaver hat sat like a stovepipe on his head. The faint glow from the town's lights caught his snowy sideburns and luxurious mustache.

12

"Kern," said Vickers. "Looks like we have a pot full tonight."

"Getting right spry in my old age," grunted Judge Kern, lowering himself gingerly from the wall with the four-barreled pepperbox still very evident in one slender hand. He waved the ugly little gun at Combabi. "Put away your smoke box and get on inside."

Combabi moved like a snake, without apparent effort, or sound. He shoved the Dragoon back in its tattered black holster and got to his feet and moved around Vickers sullenly till he stood near Papago, his shifty eyes glittering in the light of the moon filtering into the shack.

"Sorry to be late, Vickers," said Kern, pulling his coat back to stuff the pepperbox in a pocket of his white marseille waistcoat. "Guess it's just as well, though. I saw this here Indian sneaking in through that hole at the back and decided I'd better see what the arrangements were. He just sat there listening to you talk, so I thought I might as well hear a little of the confabulation, too. Oddly enough, Papago was right about this not being the Tucson machine. I'll admit it fits in with their aims rather fortuitously, but I've had an investigator in Tucson a long time now, and I'd take his word on it. He says no."

Judge Kern stopped, something coming into his eyes as he stared at Vickers. There was a fierce pride in Kern's high-browed, eagle-beaked face that otherwise held him from any display of emotion. It was probably the only evidence Vickers would ever get of what this meant to the judge. He could sense all the hell the old man must have been through these last days. Then the sympathy was blotted out by the other emotions Vickers had felt toward Kern throughout the preceding weeks. Kern saw it in his face and caught his hard arm.

"I know, Vickers, I know. I've hounded you and hunted you and driven you like an animal this last month, and you don't owe me anything. But you know how close I was to Edgar James.

13

He was like my own son. You couldn't blame a person for wanting the man caught who murdered his own son. You don't know what it took for me to contact you like this, and come to you. But you're my last hope. You're the only man with enough friends among the Indians around here to do any good. We can't make a move with the troops. If we so much as sent a vedette out of town, I'd be afraid the Apaches would kill Sherry. I'm not asking you to do this from the goodness of your heart, Vickers. I'll promise you amnesty if you get my daughter back. Enough amnesty for you to come back into Prescott and start your paper again, if you want it. Anything, Vickers, anything."

Vickers turned his lean, mordant face down a moment. "Mogollon Kid?" he said finally.

"I don't know who took her," said Kern, desperation leaking into his voice. "I thought you'd know."

"I don't," said Vickers. "I don't even know who the Mogollon Kid is. Nobody does, I guess, any more than they know who bosses the Tucson machine."

Kern grasped his arm. "You will help me, Vickers?"

"No," said Papago, and Vickers whirled toward him, realizing how engrossed they had become in talking. "Vickers won't help you or anybody." Saying that gave Papago the chance to take his jump, knocking aside Vickers's Henry before he could bring it into line, pulling his own Remington at the same time.

Instead of fighting to get the Henry back on Papago, Vickers let it go and threw himself bodily at the man. They met with a fleshy *thud*, Vickers clutching desperately to turn Papago's gun down as the half-breed cleared leather with it. Behind him, Vickers heard Kern grunt, and thought—*Combabi!*—and then the Remington exploded, jarring Vickers's hand up, the slug hitting earth near enough to Vickers to numb his foot from the impact.

With his free hand, Papago slugged at Vickers's face. Senses reeling to the blow, Vickers stumbled backward and tripped on a body, almost going down. He saw the wide head of Judge Kern at his feet. Fighting to stay erect, still holding Papago's gun hand with one fist, he caught the half-breed by the belt with his other, swinging the man around. Combabi must have pistol-whipped Kern, for he was just straightening above the judge and his gun was rising toward Vickers. Swung off balance, Papago smashed into Combabi that way. He grunted, and the whole shack rocked as Combabi was knocked back against the wall.

Vickers still had hold of Papago by the belt and gun. Papago gasped with the effort of smashing Vickers in the face again with his free hand, lips peeled away from his white teeth in animal rage. Vickers took that blow, and set himself, and heaved, releasing both his holds on the man.

Combabi was reeling groggily away from the wall, trying to line up his Dragoon again. Papago staggered back into him. They both crashed into the wall and fell to the floor in a tangle of legs and arms. Papago rolled free of Combabi, cursing, and tried to rise. Vickers was already jumping for him, feet first. One moccasin caught Papago in the jaw, knocking his head back against the wall, and again the frame structure shuddered, and dirt showered from the sod roof. Vickers's other foot caught Papago's gun hand, knocking the Remington free. Shouting with pain, Papago tried to rise, but Vickers caught him again in the face with a moccasin. More dirt showered down on them and Vickers whirled to catch Combabi before the man could rise. The Indian had dropped his cap-and-ball when Papago fell back against him, and Vickers pulled him up by his long, greasy hair and smashed his head against the wall.

"*Pichu quate!*" shouted Combabi, and his hoarse voice was drowned by the rocking shudder of the building, and then a louder noise. Vickers released the man's hair and jumped backward with earth rattling onto his shoulders.

Just trying to rise from the wall, shaking his head dazedly, Papago was caught in the downpour of sod and timbers as the roof caved in. Vickers saw a rotten beam collapse, one broken end crashing into Papago. Combabi threw himself forward with his eyes shut and his face contorted in fear. They both disappeared in the avalanche of brown earth.

Vickers bent to lift Judge Kern under the armpits and haul him out through the door, then he stopped, realizing the rattling thunder had ceased. Only the far end of the shack had caved in. Kern began groaning and shook his head dully.

"Damned Indian gave me the barrel of that cap-and-ball!"

"Think we ought to pull them out?" queried Vickers.

Kern rose unsteadily to his feet, staring at the pile of earth and timbers at the other end of the room, then glanced at Vickers. His eyes suddenly began to twinkle, and he guffawed. "I guess we better at that, Vickers. Those varmints don't deserve it, but I might lose a night's sleep if I had it on my conscience, and Papago ain't worth a night's sleep to me."

Combabi's arm was sticking out of the dirt, and he was still conscious when they pulled him free, choking and gasping. Papago took longer to reach, and to revive. Even after he came around, he lay there where they had dragged him outside, breathing faintly, staring up at them with his enigmatic eyes. Slowly those eyes took on a smoldering opacity, and, when he finally rose to his feet, his breathing had become guttural and rasping. Vickers punched the shells from his Remington and handed it back.

Papago glanced at the gun, slipped it back in its holster, and his voice trembled slightly with his effort at control. "You're going after Sherry Kern?"

"What do you think?" asked Vickers.

"You're going after Sherry Kern." It was a statement this

time. Papago turned toward his horse, hitched to some mesquite at the site, and Combabi followed him, mounting the roach-backed dun beside Papago's pinto. Papago lifted a leg up, and then, with his foot in the stirrup and one hand gripping his saddle horn, he turned to look at Vickers again, and there was an indefinable menace in his flat, toneless voice. "You're a fool, Vickers. You think you had a lot of men looking for you this last month? It wasn't nothing. It wasn't nothing compared to what you'll be bucking if you do this. Judge Kern didn't have to swear out any warrant for your arrest. You've signed your own. And it ain't just for your arrest, Vickers. It's your death warrant!"

II

Up in the Tortillas the heat struck like this in August, about an hour after sunrise, and there was no breeze to dry the beaded sweat on the hairy, little roan standing there in the coulée where bleeding heart lay crimson against the black lava. Vickers had rolled himself a cigarette and hunkered down with his back against a boulder so he could see both upslope and down, his Henry in his lap. Three days of riding away from Prescott were behind him, and he had unsaddled the weary bronco completely to rest it. His pale blue eyes took on a gun-metal color in his Indian-dark face, moving deliberately across the slope below him, and his lank, blond hair hung in a sweat-damp cowlick down his gaunt forehead. He gave no sign when the rider came into view. He sat motionlessly, waiting for the man to rise through the scrubby yuccas down there.

When the rider would have passed him, going on up, Vickers stood without speaking and waited. The man's head turned abruptly, then he necked his big horse around and dropped into the shallow cut Vickers occupied. He stopped the horse and leaned forward in the center-fire rig to peer, wide-eyed, at Vickers. He was a short, square bulldog of a man with heavy jowls and a mop of russet hair that grew unruly down the middle of his head and receded at his temples above the ears like a pair of pink cauliflowers.

"Vickers?" he said. He descended from the horse with a springy ease to his compact bulk, fishing a cigar from inside his short-skirted black coat. "Webb Fallon. The Apaches told me you'd be hereabouts this morning. You running in Kern's team, now?"

Vickers took a last puff on his cigarette, studying the cold relentlessness of Fallon's opaque, brown eyes, then dropped the fag and ground it out with a scarred, wooden heel. "Kern said you'd picked up a few things on Sherry."

The name sent something indefinable through Fallon's face, and he didn't speak at once. "I'm glad you're in it," he said finally. "The judge told me he'd try and get you as a last resort. I have found one or two things." He got a leather whang from his pocket. It was worn and greasy, about four inches long. "This, for instance."

"Looks like the fringe off someone's leggings."

"That's right," said Fallon, and let his eyes drop to Vickers's leggings. "Sherry Kern had a handful of them. They came off the leggings of the man who murdered Edgar James."

For a moment, their gazes locked, and Vickers could feel the little muscles twitch tightly about his mouth, drawing the skin across his high cheek bones till it gleamed. Meeting his gaze enigmatically, Fallon went on.

"It was one of the pieces of evidence Judge Kern was going to use against you, at the trial. Edgar James must have been close enough to rip it from the murderer's pants. Sherry was the first one to reach Edgar before he died, and he still had this bunch of fringe in his hand. Sherry had kept it in her possession, and, when this turned up, it had some significance for me.

As you know, I've been Kern's agent down here for some time, trying to uncover the Tucson machine. One of the Mexicans I've befriended came into Tucson Sunday before last, said a bunch of Apaches with a woman had stopped at his place for food and remounts. They burned his *jacal* and took what horses he had, but he managed to escape into the timber. I went back to his place with him. Found this by the well."

"You think she's trying to leave a trail?" said Vickers.

"It's like her," said Fallon, and that same nameless expression crossed his face as when Vickers had spoken her name before, only more strongly this time. For a moment, Fallon seemed to be looking beyond Vickers. Then, with a visible effort, he brought his eyes back to the man. "You never knew Sherry, did you?"

"Never saw her," said Vickers. "She arrived at Prescott from Austin the night Edgar James was killed."

"You put it nicely."

"Never mind."

"You can admit it to me," said Fallon. "I'm strictly neutral."

Vickers's voice grew thin. "I said never mind."

Fallon's voice held a faint shrug. "All right. So you didn't murder Edgar James. And Sherry Kern came in the night he was killed, and you haven't ever seen her."

"She look anything like the judge?" asked Vickers, feeling the animosity that had descended between them.

"The pride," said Fallon, and again he was looking beyond Vickers with that same thing in his face. Vickers could almost read it now, but could not quite believe it, somehow, in a man like Fallon. "Yes, the pride." Fallon jerked out of it abruptly, waving his hand in a frustration at having let Vickers see it. "Black-haired, black-eyed," he said matter-of-factly, "five-six or seven. Big girl. Yes, quite a bit like the judge." He seemed to realize he hadn't used his cigar and bit off the end almost angrily, spitting it out. Then he waved the leather whang. "Think this will do us any good?"

"If she's leaving those for a trail," said Vickers, "it might do us a lot of good."

"Glad you think so," said Fallon. "This was just a lucky strike, and it's left me up against the fence. I don't have your touch with the Indians. That gate's closed to me."

"We'll have to do a sight of riding," said Vickers.

"I imagine," said Fallon.

III

The Painted Desert extended three hundred miles along the north bank of the Little Colorado, caprices of heat and light and dust changing their hues constantly, a scarlet haze that splashed the horizon, shifting unaccountably into a serried mist of purples and grays from which warmly tinted mesas erupted and knolls of reddish sandstone thrust skyward. Dust-caked and slouching wearily in the saddles of plodding horses, the two men rose from the brackish water of the river toward Hopi Buttes, standing darkly and lonely against the weird sunset sky. All afternoon, now, Vickers had been scanning the ground, and finally he found what he had been seeking. He halted his horse, dismounted to study the mound of bluish rocks, topped by a flat piece of sandstone upon which were placed a number of wooden ovals, painted white and tufted with feathers.

Fallon removed the inevitable cigar from his mouth. "What is it?"

"Eagle shrine," muttered Vickers. "The ovals represent eggs. Probably made them during the winter solstice ceremony as prayers for an increase in the eagles. Mokis figure the eagle is the best carrier of prayers to the rain-bringing gods. We should find some boys trapping eagles near here for their annual rain dance."

"You really know, don't you," said Fallon.

Vickers mounted his piebald horse. "Where do you think I've been living this last month?"

Fallon moved his animal after Vickers, twisting in the saddle. "Got a funny feeling. Ever get it out here?"

"You mean about being followed?"

Fallon turned sharply toward him. "Then it ain't just a feeling?"

"There was dust on the rim this morning."

"You even got eyes like an Indian," grunted Fallon. "Who do you figure? Apaches?"

"We haven't made a move the Indians don't know about," said Vickers. "It might be them."

"Or someone else."

"You should know about that," said Vickers.

"How do you mean?" asked the man.

"Doesn't the kidnapping of Sherry Kern by the Indians seem a little too fortuitous, when the Tucson machine would give anything to keep the capital from being moved to Prescott?" asked Vickers.

"It does. But why should I know . . . ?" Suddenly it seemed to strike Fallon, and his face darkened. "I don't like your insinuation, Vickers. I've been working for Judge Kern for a long time."

"And you told him it wasn't the Tucson machine that kidnapped Sherry."

Fallon suddenly booted his mare in the flank, jumping it into Vickers's horse so hard the roan stumbled. Then he grabbed Vickers by the shoulder to pull him around and catch at the front of his Levi's jacket. There was a driving strength in Fallon's fist that held Vickers there momentarily, and the man's wide eyes stared into the eyes of Vickers.

"Listen, I want to get one thing straight, Vickers. I still think you're a murderer, and I don't trust you any more than you trust me. But I'm not going to have you insinuating I have any connection with the Tucson machine. Nobody knows who runs the machine any more than they know who the Mogollon Kid is."

It was Vickers who stopped Fallon. He tore the man's hand off his Levi's jacket and shoved it down toward their waists. Fallon gave one jerk, trying to free his hand, and then stopped, held there more by Vickers's blazing eyes than his grip.

"And I'm tired of being called a murderer, Fallon," said Vickers through his teeth, "and, if you still want to do it, you'd better go for your gun."

IV

The Mokis built their eagle traps of willow shoots and deerskin, baiting them with rabbits and concealing themselves inside, waiting to seize the eagles that pounced on the prey. Vickers and Fallon came across a trap on a flat atop Hopi Buttes. Another man might have been sullen or touchy after a clash like the one Vickers and Fallon had experienced, but Kern's agent sat enigmatically on his mare, watching the Indian youth emerge from the trap, no expression in his wide eyes.

The Moki boy was lean and drawn as a gaunted bronco, his black hair cut straight across his brow and hanging to his shoulders behind, wearing no more than a buckskin loincloth and a pair of dirty, beaded moccasins.

"*Buenos días, Señor* Vickers," he said.

"*Buenos días,* Quimiu," said Vickers, answering him in Spanish. "You have grown since I last saw you at Sichomovi."

Quimiu nodded his head in a pleased way without allowing much expression to appear on his face. "You are hunting birds, too?" he asked in Spanish.

"One bird," said Vickers. "A female bird with a black head."

"That is a rare bird," Quimiu told him. "Even more rare if she sheds her plumage in August."

"There was a Hopi down on the Little Colorado who said one of the eagle trappers up here found a feather of that plumage," said Vickers.

Gravely the boy untied a leather whang from his G-string, handing it to Vickers. "You know that I would show it to no other white man."

Vickers passed it to Fallon, and the man compared it with the other whang he had, nodding. "Couldn't miss it. No Apache dyes his leggings like that. First bunch of Ute fringe I've seen in the territory in years." He glanced at Vickers's leggings. "Couldn't miss it."

Vickers drew a thin breath, forcing his eyes to stay on the Indian. "How did the bird fly?"

"Proudly. They must have been riding for days when they passed south of Hopi Buttes, but she still sat straight in the saddle without any fear in her face. Her hair was black as midnight, and long and straight like an Indian maiden's. I saw their dust from here and went down to find out what it was. They didn't see me. There must have been a dozen Apaches"— here the traditional hatred of the Pueblo Indian for the nomad Apache entered his voice—"and the bird you seek rode behind the leader. She must have fought them, for there were scratches on her face, and her hands were tied, but they had not subdued her."

"Nothing could," said Fallon, and his eyes had that far-away look again, and this time Vickers realized what it was. He had not been able to believe it before, in Fallon. But the same thing was in Quimiu's face now, and Quimiu's description had made the picture of Sherry Kern more vivid in Vickers's mind. That picture had been forming for a long time, ever since he left Prescott, part of it gleaned from the judge, and other snatches he found on the way to his meeting with Fallon, some from Fallon himself, and now some from Quimiu. Vickers could almost see her, riding proudly and unsubdued in her captivity, her eyes gleaming fiercely, her statuesque body straight and unyielding after a ride that would have exhausted another white woman to the point of collapse. And something else was beginning to form in his mind, or in some other part of him he couldn't name, and it gave him a better comprehension of her capacity to stir other men, or more than stir them. He turned in his saddle to glance at Judge Kern's agent. Yes, even a man like Fallon. Even a cold, passionless man like Fallon.

Then Vickers turned back to Quimiu. "Do you know where they have taken her?"

Quimiu shook his head. "The eagles have some aeries even the Hopis do not know of. There is a Navajo shaman near Cañon Diablo who knows where the birds sleep when the moon rises. I have caught many eagles on his advice."

"Perhaps we had better go there," said Vickers.

"Perhaps you had better not," said a hoarse voice from behind them. "Perhaps you had better stay right here so I can see what your face looks like when I blow your brains out."

The wind sighing across Hopi Buttes blew coldly against the sweat that had broken out on Vickers's brow. His first instinct had been to pull his Henry up from where he held it across his saddle bows. He had stopped his hand from moving with an effort. Finally his rig *creaked* beneath him as he turned.

Vickers wouldn't have thought a white man could have come up on them like that without giving himself away. This one had. He sat on a rim of the sandstone uplift behind them, a huge, grinning man with a hoary, black beard and a shaggy mane of hair on his hatless head, a ponderous Harper's Ferry percussion pistol in each freckled hand.

24

"Well, Red-Eye," said Fallon, "you selling whiskey to the Mokis now?"

"I sell it to any man which buys," said Red-Eye Reeves. He wore a pair of moccasins and his frayed leggings of buckskin were pulled on over red flannels that sufficed for his shirt, the sleeves rolled up to the elbows of his hairy forearms. He waved a .58 Harper's Ferry at Vickers. "The Tucson machine has a price of five hundred on your head. What would you give me not to collect that price?"

It galled Vickers to have to bargain for his life this way, but there was no alternative with those huge percussions in his face. "How much do you want?"

"I didn't say how much. I said *what*."

"Well."

"You're traveling this country, hunting Sherry Kern," said Red-Eye. "You'll hit a lot of Injun camps. Navajo, Apache, Moki. I got a load of red-eye that would bring fifty dollars the quart from them redskins. I never been able to reach them before. You're the only one who could take me into Tusuyan and bring me back out again with my scalp still above my beard."

"And after they get through swilling your rotgut, they'll have a war dance and pull a massacre somewhere while they're drunk," said Vickers. "The only reason I could take you into Tusuyan is the Indians are my friends. You think I'd do that to them?"

Red-Eye Reeves waved the Harper's Ferry again. "This is your alternative, and it's a sort of jumpy one, so you better decide right quick."

Vickers took a long breath, speaking finally. "We're heading for a Navajo shaman in Cañon Diablo."

"Suits me," said Red-Eye Reeves. "He'll be good for a gallon at least."

They rode westward from Hopi Buttes, Red-Eye Reeves forking

a ratty little Mexican pack mule and leading a dozen others, *aparejos* piled high with flat, wooden kegs of whiskey. All day Reeves kept pulling at a bottle, and it was evident he had been doing the same before he came on Vickers and Fallon. He reeled tipsily in his saddle, mumbling through his beard sometimes. They were riding through a scrubby motte of juniper east of Cañon Diablo when Vickers drew far enough away for Fallon to speak without being overheard.

"You aren't going through with this?"

"I'll get rid of him as soon as I can," said Vickers.

"Be careful," Fallon told him. "He's drunk most of the time, but he's dangerous. I don't think his real purpose in wanting to come with us is the whiskey."

Vickers glanced at Fallon, pale eyes narrow. "Is he from Tucson?"

"He's been there," said Fallon.

It was the shot, then, cutting off what Vickers had started to say. His roan shied and spooked, starting to buck and squeal, and Vickers threw himself from the horse while he still had enough control over his falling to roll and come up running, the back of his Levi's coat ripped where he had gone through some jumping cholla. "Come back here, you cross-eyed cousin to a ring-tailed varmint!" yelled Red-Eye Reeves from somewhere behind Vickers, and Vickers saw a mule galloping away with wooden kegs spilling in its wake from the dragging *aparejo* pack.

Then they were nearly out of earshot for Vickers, once he threw himself into the monkshood carpeting the ground near the edge of the grove. He lay there in the heady fragrance of the wildflowers, peering toward the mesa ahead of them. The slope was gentle at first, littered with boulders and scrubby timber, then steepened to a veritable cliff, channeled by erosion. Vickers jumped at the movement behind him.

"Never mind," said Fallon, and he crawled in with an old

Theur's conversion-model Colt. "It looks like we won't have to worry about getting rid of Red-Eye. He's taking care of that himself."

Still yelling in the distance, Reeves had chased his scattering pack train out into the open beyond them, kicking his scraggly mule after a trio of pack animals that had headed up the slope. He was well onto the rising ground when another shot rang out. His riding mule stumbled, and Reeves went over its head, landing on both feet and running on upslope from the momentum, and both Harper's Ferry guns were in his hands before he stopped.

"Come on out, you misbegotten brother to a spotted hinny and a club-footed jackass! Nobody can treat my babies like that! Nobody can shoot my . . . !"

Reeves's own shot cut him off, and Vickers couldn't help exclaiming, because he hadn't seen anybody up there, and he wouldn't have believed anyone could score such a hit with an old percussion pistol.

"I told you he was dangerous," Fallon muttered.

Higher up, a man had risen out of the rocks where he must have been crouched. Both his hands were at his chest, and he stood there a moment, as if suspended. Then he fell forward, rolling out over the sandstone and coming to a stop against some stunted juniper.

Shouting hoarse obscenities, Red-Eye Reeves charged on up the slope. There was something terrible about his giant, black-bearded figure running inexorably upward, and somehow Vickers wasn't surprised to see a man rise farther on up and turn to run. Red-Eye had raised his other Harper's Ferry when the third figure appeared, much nearer, climbing to a rock and holding both hands up, palms toward Reeves.

The drunken whiskey drummer shifted his pistol with a jerk till it bore on that third man. Fallon must have realized it about the same time Vickers did, because he jumped out of the monks-hood, shouting: "Reeves, don't, can't you see he . . . ?"

Vickers's shot drowned his voice. The pistol leaped from Reeves's hand, and he yelled in agony, taking a stumbling step forward and pulling the hand in toward him. Fallon turned back to Vickers, his mouth open slightly, and Vickers realized it must have taken a lot for Fallon to show that much emotion.

Reeves was holding out his bloody, shattered hand when they reached him, studying it with a speculative twist to his pursed lips. He looked up and grinned at them. "I didn't think those old Henrys could go that far," he said.

Vickers looked for guile in his face, unwilling to presume the man held no anger at him for shooting the gun from his hand, but he could find none. "Didn't you see that man wanted to surrender?"

"What do I care?" said Red-Eye, bending to pick up his gun and stuffing it in his belt. "The only good Injun's a dead one, to me, and I don't care how my lead catches them, with their hands up, or wrapped around a gun."

Fallon looked at Vickers, then shrugged. "You go and get him. I'll see what we can do for Red-Eye's hand."

"The hell with that," growled Red-Eye, wiping his bloody hand against his shirt the way a man would if he had scratched it. "Think one of them damn' Henry flatties can do more'n pink a man? It takes one of these babies"—he patted his pistol—"and you'll see what I mean when you find that varmint I pegged higher up. I'm going to get a drink."

He walked off toward where a group of his mules had finally stopped, up on the slope. The Indian who had surrendered was making his way down to them, a gnarled ancient in tattered deerskin, covered with dung and other filth till his stench preceded him a good dozen yards. His watery eyes took some time to focus on them, out of the seamed age of his face, and then he held up a palsied claw of a hand. The single word relegated them to their station, holding neither contempt nor respect.

"*Pahanas*," he said. "White man."

Vickers realized this must be the shaman Quimiu had spoken of. "There was a youth of the *Hopitu-shinumu* named Quimiu in the eagle-trapping ground of Hopi Buttes who told us of a wonder worker at Cañon Diablo who was in communion with the Trues," said Vickers.

The Trues were the gods of the Pueblos and, although nothing showed in the shaman's face, there was a subtle change in the tone of his voice. "You must be blessed by the Trues. Quimiu would not have sent white men to me otherwise. I shall then thank you for saving me from the two Apaches who were holding me."

He waved his hand toward the Indian Red-Eye had shot. The second one had disappeared over the lip of the mesa, and, as Vickers moved up to examine the dead one, Reeves came in leading his pack animals. The ball had taken the Indian through the chest, apparently killing him instantly. He wore a pair of Apache war moccasins, made of buckskin, boots really that were hip-length, turned down until they were only knee-high, forming a protection of double thickness against the malignant brush of the Southwest. About his flanks was a G-string and a buckskin bag of powder and shot for his big Sharps buffalo gun. Squatting over him, Vickers saw the odd expression catch on Reeves's face.

"Know him?" said Vickers.

Reeves nodded, his drunken humor suddenly gone. "That's Baluno. He rode with the Mogollon Kid."

V

The shaman's *hoganda* was up on the mesa, overlooking Cañon Diablo, which formed the other side, a deep chasm of Kaibab sandstone, yellow at the top and fading into a salmon color as it descended. Vickers had borrowed one of Reeves's mules to round up his spooked roan, and he dismounted from the skittish horse now, loosening the cinch to blow the animal.

"What were those Apaches doing here?" he asked the Navajo.

"Holding me hostage," said the shaman. "They still held enough fear of the shamans not to kill me, but they would not let me leave my *hoganda*."

"But why were they holding you?" asked Vickers. "Is there something they didn't want you to get away and tell?"

"I come up here before the summer Rain Dances for a moon of fasting and praying," said the shaman evasively.

"He'll never tell you anything unless you get him inside that *hoganda*," said Red-Eye, "and you know they won't let a white man in their medicine house."

Vickers held out his hand so the scar showed across his palm. "I am blood brother to Abeïto, the house chief of Walpi."

"You *must* be the one who saved him from the *pahanas* near Tucson last year," the shaman said enigmatically.

Vickers shrugged, seeing it had done no good, as Abeïto was a Moki and this man a Navajo. "The white men blamed him for something Apaches did."

Red-Eye put his good hand on the butt of a Harper's Ferry. "We ain't getting nowhere thisaway. Look, you dried-up old. . . ."

"Never mind, Reeves." Vickers hadn't said it very loud, but it stopped the man. Then Vickers moved closer to the shaman, speaking softly. "I know of *Shi-pa-pu*."

It was the first expression the shaman had allowed to enter

Indians from the other pueblos and from the Navajo camps to the east had been passing up the trail to Walpi all day, raising nervous flurries of gray dust over the fields of corn and squash near the village.

Knowing it would be suicide to go out the door of the shaman's hogan there above Cañon Diablo, if anyone was outside, Vickers had unlashed some of the deerskins at the back, crawling out that way, only to find that both Red-Eye Reeves and Fallon were gone, with all the animals, including his roan.

He had trailed them on foot, but, being mounted, they soon outdistanced him. He could read sign of someone on the roan driving Red-Eye's mules, but could find no other horse prints, and concluded Fallon had not left the *hoganda* with Red-Eye.

A week after Cañon Diablo, Vickers was plodding up the trail toward Walpi behind a party of Apaches on wiry little mustangs. Ordinarily the Apaches and Navajos were enemies of the Pueblos, but, during the Snake Dance, hostilities were suspended and other tribes were allowed to view the ceremonies. The houses atop the mesa were built three stories high, each story set back the length of one room on the roof of the lower level, forming three huge steps, with rickety ladders reaching each roof from the one below. What passed for the streets and courtyards in front of the houses were filled with a milling crowd of Indians, Moki women in hand woven *mantas* holding dirty brown babies to their breasts, tall, arrogant Navajo men with their heavy silver belts and turquoise bracelets, a few shifty Apaches who were like strange dogs, standing apart in their little groups and bristling whenever they were approached, turkey-red bandannas on their greasy black hair, perhaps a Sharps hugged close.

Stopping near the entrance from the trail to the mesa top, Vickers was aware of their suspicious eyes on him, and an ineffable sensation of something not quite right filled him. Then a

Navajo stumbled through the crowd toward Vickers, pawing at a big Bowie in his silver belt, and Vickers knew what it was.

"*Pahanas*," growled the Navajo, shoving a Moki woman roughly aside, and Vickers could see how bloodshot his eyes were. A pair of Moki braves moved in from where they had been standing beneath an adobe wall, and they were drunk, too. As Vickers opened the lever on his Henry, he saw the Mexican rat mule standing in a yonder courtyard, its *aparejo* pack ripped off and laying at the animal's feet, empty kegs strewn all about the hard-packed ground.

"*Pahanas, pahanas!*" It was a shout, now, coming from a bibulous Apache, running in from the other side. Vickers had waited till the last moment but, just as he was about to raise his Henry up to cover them, someone else shouted from the rooftop of a nearby building.

"No, not *pahanas*! *Hopitu-shinumu*! He is my blood brother!"

It was Abeïto, house chief of Walpi, swinging onto one of the rawhide-bound ladders and climbing down with a quick, cat-like agility. He was a small, compact man in white doeskin for the coming ceremony, a band of red Durango silk about his black, bobbed hair. The Mokis stopped coming at Vickers, and the Navajo moved grudgingly aside, still clutching his knife, to let the Abeïto through. Vickers embraced the house chief ceremoniously, as befitted a blood brother, but he saw it in the house chief's eyes as Abeïto pulled him through the milling crowd toward his own dwelling.

"Reeves is here?" he said to Abeïto. "Why did you let him sell that whiskey to your people, brother? You could have stopped it."

"He didn't sell it," said the house chief, pulling him urgently toward the ladder.

"But he must have," said Vickers, trying to understand the evasive darkness in Abeïto's eyes. "The Mokis never take things

36

his face, and it caught briefly at his mouth and eyes before he suppressed it—awe, or reverence, or fear, Vickers could not tell which. Then, without speaking, he turned and stooped through the low door of the *hoganda,* a conical hut of willow withes and skins, beaten and weathered by the winds of many years on top of this mesa. As Vickers bent to follow, Fallon caught his arm.

"What was it you told him?"

"*Shi-pa-pu,*" Vickers murmured. "The Black Lake of Tears, from whence the human race is supposed to have arisen. It's so sacred the Indians rarely say it aloud."

"And no white man is supposed to know about it?"

"I never met another who did," said Vickers. "At least the shaman knows I've been inside their *hogandas* before. That's all we care about."

The inside was fetid and oppressive with the same odors the shaman emanated, and Vickers shied away from a *kachina* doll dangling above the door, dressed and beaded and feathered to represent one of the gods. The shaman indicated that they should seat themselves about the flat *walla pai* basket, woven from martynia that reposed in the center of the *hoganda.* Then the medicine man seated himself and stirred the coals of the fire before the empty basket until they glowed, lighting a *weer* he produced from a buckskin bag at his belt. This sacred cigarette he passed around, and, while each of them puffed on it, he began murmuring incantations over the dying light of the coals. It was almost pitch black inside the hut when the buckskin thong appeared, and Vickers couldn't have sworn how it got there. The shaman continued muttering, three feet away from the basket, but Fallon drew in a hissing breath, reaching toward the piece of rawhide fringe now reposing in the bottom of the flat basket. Vickers caught his hand, pulling it back.

"Quimiu had such an object, also," said Vickers. "A feather, he said, dropped from a black-headed bird who shed her plumage in August."

"A goddess, rather," murmured the shaman, and Vickers could feel something draw him up, because he sensed it coming again, and his breathing became audible, and swifter. "A goddess sent by the Trues to prove to the Apaches what coyotes they are. Nothing they had done could subdue her. Their leader himself wished her favor, but she bit his hand when he tried to touch her. Even the dust and sun and weariness of the long ride could not hide her beauty. Her eyes were not as black as her hair, and once, when she turned fully to me, it was as if I had stared into the swimming smoke of a campfire, and another time, when she looked at the leader of the Apaches, it was as if I had seen lightning. Other of the Dineh' have seen her, and, as long as the sacred *weer* is smoked in the *hoganda,* it will be told how the goddess rode through our land, leaving signs to the favored ones."

From the corner of his eye, Vickers could see Fallon bending forward that same way, his mouth parted slightly, his wide eyes rapt. Suddenly he seemed to feel Vickers's gaze on him, and closed his mouth, leaning back, glancing almost angrily at Vickers.

"How did you get the sign?" said Vickers, motioning toward the buckskin whang in the basket.

"The Apaches were apparently expecting to find water in the Red Lake, but it had been dry for a moon and there was none. They would not have revealed their passing to me unless they were desperate for water. They forced me to show them my sacred sink on the mesa, where the sun cannot reach the water that the rain gods have brought and dry it up. Then they left the one named Baluno and his companion to guard me and keep me from telling of them until they were safely away."

Fallon's eyes were on Vickers now, in a covert speculation, as he spoke: "The Mogollon Kid?"

The shaman sat, staring into the basket without answering Fallon. The fire had died completely now, and the light from the smoke hole was rapidly fading as night fell outside, enveloping the interior of the *hoganda* in darkness. Vickers could barely see Red-Eye Reeves across the basket. He saw the man glance at him now, and there was that same speculation as Vickers had seen in Fallon's face. Vickers felt his hands tighten around the Henry across his knees. In a few moments it would be so intensely dark that none of them could see the others.

"I thought the shaman feared none but the Trues," said Vickers, and his body was stiffening for the shift.

The shaman's voice came abruptly from the gloom, almost angrily: "How do I know if it was the Mogollon Kid?"

"I have heard the Indians feared the Mogollon Kid as much as their own gods," said Vickers. "He must have the power of the Trues if he can shut a shaman's mouth." Even that failed to elicit any response from the shaman. "If you can't tell us who it was," said Vickers, "perhaps you can tell us where they are bound."

Vickers had seen the incredible legerdemain of these wonder workers. Once he had seen a shaman make corn grow in the bare dirt floor of a *hoganda,* and it had convinced and amazed even his Occidental realism. But this came so unexpectedly that it held him spellbound as it occurred. A faint blue glow descended from the smoke hole of the hive-like structure, until their four figures were bathed in an eerie light, faces drawn and taut with a sudden tension. The piece of buckskin fringe was revealed momentarily in the basket, shifting like a small snake with a life of its own till it pointed due north. Then the light was extinguished abruptly.

In the following blackness Vickers recovered enough from the sight to do what he had planned. Still sitting in the cross-legged position they had all assumed, he placed his hands on either side of him and shifted himself about twelve inches to the right with his legs yet crossed, speaking as he did to mask any sound. "The sacred sign points to Tusuyan."

"Yes," said the shaman. "The Dance of the Snake is being held at Walpi this year. . . ."

The shot thundered, rocking the *hoganda,* deafening Vickers. He sat rigid with his back against the willow frame of the hut, his Henry cocked across his lap, waiting for whoever came for him. There was a shout, a muffled struggle in the utter darkness, then the *hoganda* shook violently. Outside, the animals had been spooked by the shot, whinnying and nickering and shaking the ground as they tore up their picket pins and galloped back and forth before the door. Vickers knew what a target anybody would be going out that door, and he sat there till silence had fallen again. Finally the spark from a flint and steel caught across the hut. He jerked his Henry that way. It was the shaman, throwing fresh juniper shavings on the dead coals. He lit the fire and shuffled across the room to where Vickers had risen. There was no one else in the *hoganda.*

The shaman fingered the bullet hole in the hide wall. "It would have killed you if you'd been sitting one *paso* to the left," he muttered. "I wonder why they wanted you dead?"

Vickers turned toward the door. "I don't wonder why, so much, as which one."

VI

For centuries the region in northeastern Arizona Territory had been known as the province of Tusuyan, and the Pueblos living there as Mokis, or Hopis, from their own name for themselves, *Hopitu-shinumu.* Walpi was one of these pueblos, perched atop a sombrous mesa, a giant block of sandstone reaching up from the flatlands about it, the tiered mud houses on its top barely visible from below. It was the month of August, and groups of

Indians from the other pueblos and from the Navajo camps to the east had been passing up the trail to Walpi all day, raising nervous flurries of gray dust over the fields of corn and squash near the village.

Knowing it would be suicide to go out the door of the shaman's hogan there above Cañon Diablo, if anyone was outside, Vickers had unlashed some of the deerskins at the back, crawling out that way, only to find that both Red-Eye Reeves and Fallon were gone, with all the animals, including his roan.

He had trailed them on foot, but, being mounted, they soon outdistanced him. He could read sign of someone on the roan driving Red-Eye's mules, but could find no other horse prints, and concluded Fallon had not left the *hoganda* with Red-Eye.

A week after Cañon Diablo, Vickers was plodding up the trail toward Walpi behind a party of Apaches on wiry little mustangs. Ordinarily the Apaches and Navajos were enemies of the Pueblos, but, during the Snake Dance, hostilities were suspended and other tribes were allowed to view the ceremonies. The houses atop the mesa were built three stories high, each story set back the length of one room on the roof of the lower level, forming three huge steps, with rickety ladders reaching each roof from the one below. What passed for the streets and courtyards in front of the houses were filled with a milling crowd of Indians, Moki women in hand woven *mantas* holding dirty brown babies to their breasts, tall, arrogant Navajo men with their heavy silver belts and turquoise bracelets, a few shifty Apaches who were like strange dogs, standing apart in their little groups and bristling whenever they were approached, turkey-red bandannas on their greasy black hair, perhaps a Sharps hugged close.

Stopping near the entrance from the trail to the mesa top, Vickers was aware of their suspicious eyes on him, and an ineffable sensation of something not quite right filled him. Then a

Navajo stumbled through the crowd toward Vickers, pawing at a big Bowie in his silver belt, and Vickers knew what it was.

"*Pahanas,*" growled the Navajo, shoving a Moki woman roughly aside, and Vickers could see how bloodshot his eyes were. A pair of Moki braves moved in from where they had been standing beneath an adobe wall, and they were drunk, too. As Vickers opened the lever on his Henry, he saw the Mexican rat mule standing in a yonder courtyard, its *aparejo* pack ripped off and laying at the animal's feet, empty kegs strewn all about the hard-packed ground.

"*Pahanas, pahanas!*" It was a shout, now, coming from a bibulous Apache, running in from the other side. Vickers had waited till the last moment but, just as he was about to raise his Henry up to cover them, someone else shouted from the rooftop of a nearby building.

"No, not *pahanas! Hopitu-shinumu!* He is my blood brother!"

It was Abeïto, house chief of Walpi, swinging onto one of the rawhide-bound ladders and climbing down with a quick, cat-like agility. He was a small, compact man in white doeskin for the coming ceremony, a band of red Durango silk about his black, bobbed hair. The Mokis stopped coming at Vickers, and the Navajo moved grudgingly aside, still clutching his knife, to let the Abeïto through. Vickers embraced the house chief ceremoniously, as befitted a blood brother, but he saw it in the house chief's eyes as Abeïto pulled him through the milling crowd toward his own dwelling.

"Reeves is here?" he said to Abeïto. "Why did you let him sell that whiskey to your people, brother? You could have stopped it."

"He didn't sell it," said the house chief, pulling him urgently toward the ladder.

"But he must have," said Vickers, trying to understand the evasive darkness in Abeïto's eyes. "The Mokis never take things

36

without paying. They are not Apaches. What's happening here, Abeïto? You're still house chief, aren't you?"

"Yes, yes," said the Moki. "We can't talk here, brother."

Abeïto glanced nervously at a group of Apaches standing near the ladder. One of them, with a Colt stuck nakedly through a cartridge belt about his lean middle, had a keg of whiskey. They were watching Vickers, shifting back and forth restlessly, talking in sullen tones, and Vickers caught the name as he reached for the ladder, and stopped.

"Is that it?" he asked Abeïto.

"Please, don't stop out here. Is what it?"

"You heard what they said."

"Brother, for your own good. . . ."

"Are you afraid of him, too?" Vickers asked. "There was a youth at Hopi Buttes too afraid even to speak his name, and a shaman at Cañon Diablo. If the shamans are afraid of him. . . ."

"I am house chief of Walpi," said Abeïto, drawing himself up, "head of the Bear Clan. Never did I expect to hear such an insult from my blood brother."

"Then is that it?"

Abeïto hesitated, glancing about him, face dark. "The Mogollon Kid," he said finally.

Vickers clutched at his coat. "Is he here? The Kid. Who is he, Abeïto?"

"I did not say he was here," said the Moki, grabbing Vickers's elbow. "Brother, if you value your life, get up that ladder into my house. We can't talk out here. Only their respect for my position holds them now. They have known of your coming for days. I sent a runner out to turn you back, but he must have missed you. Please. . . ."

The spruce ladder *popped* and swayed beneath Vickers's weight. On the first terrace an eagle was fluttering in an *amole* cage, one of the birds trapped at Hopi Buttes and brought here for the rain ceremonies, to be killed after the last *kachinas* came in July, the Indians believing the eagle's spirit would carry prayers for rain to the Trues. Abeïto shoved aside the heavy *bayeta* blanket hanging over the doorway leading into the rooms on the second level, allowing Vickers to go in first. A squaw was sitting on the floor inside before the cooking stone the Mokis called a *tooma*, mixing blue cornmeal with water to form a thin batter for *pikama*. Vickers spoke their language to some extent but, when she looked up and saw him, she said something so fast he couldn't catch it.

"He is my blood brother," the house chief told her. She said something else, rising from the *tooma*. Abeïto took an angry breath and motioned toward the door. "Get out," he told her. "Get out."

When she was gone, he turned to Vickers. "You see how it is? You can't stay here. I am violating all the laws of hospitality now, but it is for your own good, brother. For weeks we have heard of your search for the black-haired woman. I knew you, and I knew sooner or later you would arrive here. She is not here, believe me."

"Then who is?" said Vickers. "What's happening? Why have you so little control over your people? Surely it was not your wish that they took Reeves's fire-water. You know what will happen with everyone drunk like this. You have a hard enough time maintaining peace among your people and the Navajos and Apaches as it is. Why were they talking of the Mogollon Kid? Where is he?"

A man shoved aside the *bayeta* blanket in the doorway, stepping inside. "Here he is," he said.

Vickers had lived and traveled among the Indians long enough to acquire some facility at hiding his emotions when it was necessary, but he felt his mouth open slightly as he stared past Abeïto's white doeskin shoulder at the man swaggering in the doorway, one hand holding aside the curtain to reveal the Apaches behind him, the other hand hooked in his heavy cartridge belt near enough to the big, blued Remington .44 he packed. His lean, avaricious face was scarred deeply from smallpox, and the whites of his eyes were pale, shifting enigmas above the thin, mobile intelligence of his broad, thin-lipped mouth.

"Perry Papago," said Vickers emptily.

Papago grinned without much mirth, moving on in, and Combabi followed him on silent, bare feet, shifting black eyes unwilling to meet Vickers's gaze, and the other Apaches blotted out the light from the door behind, the bores of their Sharps rifles covering Vickers.

"This is why your blood brother has so little control over his people, Vickers," said Papago, tapping the short buckskin vest covering his bare chest. "I've taken over. It's for their own good. Four troops of dragoons in Prescott and more coming up as soon as the Department of Arizona can shift them. If the Indians don't organize now, they'll be wiped out. The Navajos and Apaches are all ready. All we need are the Mokis, and we'll have them as soon as the Snake Dances are over. I tried to talk some sense with Abeïto, but he wouldn't listen. Get his people drunk enough and they'll listen. There are half a thousand warriors in the seven pueblos of Tusuyan, Vickers. What do you think your bluecoats can do when I add them to my Apaches?"

Vickers was bent forward, his voice intense. "You've got the girl?"

Papago's eyes raised slightly. "Girl?"

"You know, Papago. You're the Mogollon Kid? You've brought her here to this. We found your man, Baluno, at Cañon Diablo." Vickers was trembling. "Don't try and deny it, Papago. What have you done with her? What have you done with Sherry Kern?"

Papago pursed his lips; something mocking entered his voice.

"I didn't know you felt that way about her, Vickers. She must be a beautiful woman."

"Papago. . . ."

"Brother!" Abeïto caught Vickers as he lunged forward at Papago. Then he turned to the half-breed. "Let him go, Papago. He has always been our friend. Even your friend. Take me in his place. Whatever you were going to do with him, do with me."

"No," said Papago, and lifted his hand off his cartridge belt to motion at his men, and they began slipping in and moving around behind Papago and Combabi, dark, menacing Apaches, the whites of their eyes shining in the semi-gloom. "No, Abeïto. I tried to stop Vickers from this at the beginning, but he wouldn't listen. As you say, he has been our friend, and I didn't want him mixed up in it. But now, he has come too far. Take him!"

This last he called to his men, and there was the abrupt scuffle of feet across the hard-packed floor. Vickers tore loose of Abeïto, trying to bring his Henry into line and snap down the lever all in one action. He saw Combabi go for his cap-and-ball, whirled that way, already seeing he would be too late, because the Indian's Dragoon was free even before Vickers heard the metallic *click* of his cocked Henry. Then a white figure hurtled in front of Vickers, and the thunder of Combabi's shot filled the small room. Vickers pulled his gun up in a jerky, frustrated way, till it was pointing at where Combabi had been, hidden now by the other man. Stunned, Vickers watched the man in white doeskin sink to the floor in front of him, and Combabi was visible again, his cap-and-ball dirtying the soft gloom with a wreath of acrid, black powder smoke. Perry Papago stood to the other side, and he was looking at Abeïto, sprawled on the floor. Then he lifted his eyes.

"You better drop it, Vickers. My Apaches got their Sharps rifles loaded now. You haven't got a chance."

All around him, Vickers was aware of the Indians, standing with their muzzle-loaders trained on him. He dropped the Henry, butt plate striking first, then the long barrel, and went to his knees beside Abeïto. It was then he became aware of the hubbub outside. The *bayeta* blanket was torn aside and a Moki brave thrust into the room, followed by a pair of *principales,* white-headed dignitaries of Walpi's governing body. They stopped when they saw Abeïto, and other Mokis crowding in from behind stumbled against the *principales.* Lifting his head toward them, Vickers did not know what he was going to say, when he saw the gun in Papago's hand. It was Combabi's cap-and-ball, still reeking of the black powder.

"*Pahanas,*" said Papago, waving his hand toward Vickers, then holding the gun up. "Your house chief found the *pahanas* with one of your women."

"No!" Vickers was surprised to hear Abeïto's voice. He lifted the man's head higher, and Abeïto shuddered in his arms, trying to get the words out. "He cannot . . . my blood brother cannot . . . have done that," said the house chief incoherently. "The Trues sent him. He is the only one who ever befriended us. The Trues sent him."

Abeïto sighed deeply, and his body was a sudden weight in Vickers's arms. Then the fetid smell of sweat and buckskin gagged Vickers, and rough arms were pulling him off Abeïto. He was still staring at the dead house chief, a thin pain somewhere inside him now. They had known a lot together. It was odd he should remember that time he had caught his hand between the bed and the platen of his first press. He had wanted to cry then.

"You wanted to see the girl?" It was Papago's voice, entering Vickers's consciousness. "You'll see her now, Vickers. You thought it was the Tucson machine? That's funny. I'm sorry it had to be this way, but you were on the wrong horse from the beginning, I guess, even about the machine. We tried to stop

41

you, didn't we? Other men had been sent out to find her, and I didn't go out of my way to stop them. I stopped them, but I didn't go out of my way to do it. I wouldn't have ridden from here to Prescott to stop them the way I did you. But I knew what a mistake it would be to let you get started, Vickers. I'd already gotten here with Sherry when I got word Kern had contacted you to meet him there in that miner's shack outside Prescott. You almost made it anyway, didn't you? You came farther than anyone else ever did. You're the only living white man who knows I'm the Mogollon Kid."

They were hauling him roughly past Papago and the other Apaches. The strange, dazed emotion of seeing Abeíto dead had held it back, but now the full comprehension of what had happened struck Vickers, filling him with the first impulse to struggle since Papago had told the Apaches to get him. Vickers threw his weight against the Mokis, managing to halt them momentarily, and turned enough to see Papago's Indian *segundo*.

"Combabi," he said, and perhaps it was the utter lack of any vehemence or emotion in his voice that made the Indian's face pale slightly. "I'll kill you for that."

Somewhere outside, the big medicine drums they called the *tombes* had begun to beat. Vickers knew what that meant. The Snake and Antelope fraternities had conducted their secret rites in the *estufas* for eight days, fasting and purifying themselves, and now the *tombes* were heralding their readiness for the public dance.

VII

The floor was hard and rough beneath Vickers as he sat up. They had taken him to the eastern end of the mesa and thrown him into one of the ceremonial *kivas,* a room dug out of the solid rock and roofed over about a foot above the level of the ground, a ladder leading down into it from above. There was an air hole in the roof. His eyes had been accustoming themselves to the semi-gloom when he realized there was someone else in here. At first, it was only a dim, unrecognizable figure, standing against the wall on the far side. Then he saw it was a woman and realized she had been standing there like that, watching him, ever since he had come in. And, finally, he recognized her.

It was like a physical blow. He felt his breath coming out audibly between parted lips. He had tried to prepare himself for it, all the way from his first knowledge of her, telling himself preconceived notions were always wrong. Yet no preconceived idea he had formed could match this, now. They had given her a split Crow skirt of buckskin to enable her to ride, and it only seemed to delineate the tall, statuesque lines of her body. What had Fallon said? The pride? Her white linen blouse had been smudged by dirt and torn by chaparral, but it still shone palely in the dusky light.

"Who are you?" she asked. "Why do you stare at me like that?"

He had no right to let it catch him like this, with the grief of knowing Abeïto was gone still so fresh in his mind. Yet he could not help it, and he knew, somehow, that Abeïto wouldn't mind. He was still gazing at her, hardly conscious of his actions as he fished the three whangs of fringe from his pocket.

"I had a handful of them," said the woman, seeing what he held. "Several people know that I possess them. I tried to leave a trail. I thought if they found them, somehow, they could follow me." She motioned with her hand. "You . . . ?"

"It began to be like I was following someone I'd known all my life," he said. Then he was leaning toward her, still on his knees, something urgent crossing his lean face. "It can happen, can't it? I mean, without ever having seen you, it can happen, to a man, that way?"

Her bosom moved faintly beneath the soiled blouse, and her eyes were still held to his. "What can happen? What way?"

"I wouldn't have believed it could happen," he said, getting to his feet. "Not without knowing you. Not without even seeing you. I tried to tell myself I was a fool. At night I'd lie there in my blankets and think about it and laugh at myself, or try to. I couldn't really laugh, because it was happening, whether I believed it or not."

Suddenly there seemed to be an affinity between them. Perhaps it was the way they were gazing at each other, perhaps something less physical than that. Vickers saw a growing comprehension in the woman's eyes, and she bent forward slightly, searching for something in his face, her voice barely audible, as if she feared to break a spell.

"Believe what? What was happening?"

"It started so long ago," he said. "Do you think I'm crazy? In Prescott, I guess, when the judge told me. . . ."

"My father?"

He had hardly heard her. "I'd known of you, of course, but only vaguely. The judge didn't tell me much. Just what you meant to him. Not even a description. But it must have started, even then. Later, it was more than that. Do you think I'm crazy? A man named Fallon. He told me some. Your pride? It was like getting a glimpse of you through a window. Not much. Not enough, but enough to want more. Then an Indian boy. He told me the way you rode. About your hair. It was the way he told me. They have a sensitivity to something like that no one else possesses. Just at that age. You know?"

She must have understood what he was trying to say now. She wanted to smile, and couldn't. Staring at him, her eyes were soft and smoky, and her brows were drawn together in a strange, intense way, as if she were groping to define some emotion within herself.

44

"I know," she conceded, at last, almost whispering.

"After that, a shaman," said Vickers. "An old man. Too old for anything like the boy. And yet, even him. Telling me about your eyes. And after I left him, I wasn't even trying to laugh at myself any more. It can happen, can't it, that way? Do you think I'm crazy?"

She was still gazing at him, lost in it, like a child enraptured by a storyteller, and she moistened her lips, speaking almost dreamily. "No," she said, and drew a quick, soft little breath, as if faintly surprised at her own words. "No, I don't think you're crazy."

"Well," said a rough voice from the dark corner, "now that you've told the fair maiden of your undying love, maybe you'd better let her know who you are."

Both the girl and Vickers stiffened, as if snapped from a trance. Then Vickers turned to see the big, bearded man in the long-sleeved red flannels sitting cross-legged against the far wall.

"Reeves," said Vickers stupidly.

"Yeah, little old Red-Eye himself," said Reeves. "I guess I should have waited for you to come with me and help sell that rotgut, shouldn't I? Those damn' Apaches took my goods and dumped me in their calaboose. What was all that shooting in the shaman's diggings at Diablo?"

"I think you know," said Vickers.

"Do I?" said Reeves slyly. "What happened to Fallon?"

"He ran out the same way you did."

When Reeves spoke, the woman had turned toward the bearded man. Now she was looking at Vickers again. "Mister Reeves said you were going to introduce yourself."

"I'll do the honors." Reeves grinned. "Johnny, this is Miss Sherry Kern. Miss Kern, meet Johnny Vickers."

All the blood seemed to drain from her face at that instant.

"Johnny Vickers!" she said, and there was a loathing in her voice. "Johnny Vickers," and she spat it out the second time, pulling a handful of fringe from the pocket of her shirt, holding it out in front of her for him to see. "I was at the Butterfield station on Union Street when I heard the shot. It was just around the corner, right in front of the *Courier.* I was the first to reach him, and he was still alive. 'Get to Johnny Vickers,' he said, and this was in his hand. . . ." Her fingers closed on the handful of fringe spasmodically, and then opened as she flung it at Vickers, taking a step backward, her mouth twisting as she wiped her hand down her skirt. " 'Get to Johnny Vickers,' he said, and then he died."

Vickers held out his hand, something chilling him suddenly. "You think . . . ?"

"You know what I think," she said, the words torn from her in a hollow, bitter way. "Why do you suppose I'd come to Prescott that evening? Edgar James and I were going to be married the next day!"

VIII

The darkness trembled to the incessant rhythm of the *tombes* now, and beneath the hollow, muffled beat, the other sounds had begun, as the Mokis and Navajos and Apaches gathered toward the end of the mesa for the dance. Vickers hunkered in bitter silence against the wall opposite Red-Eye Reeves, looking neither at the bearded man nor at Sherry Kern.

Sure there were hunks missing out of his fringed leggings. Every man who wore leggings cut the fringe off at some time or another when he was without any other kind of lashings to repair his saddle or tie his duffel or a thousand other things they could be used for. So there were hunks cut out of the fringe on his pants. And no other man wore Ute leggings around here. All right. So the Utes dyed their fringe differently. All right. And so Edgar James told them to get Johnny Vickers. The hell with it! He shifted angrily, running his tongue across dry, cracked lips. This was what he'd come for. He should have known it from the beginning. Not the way a Moki boy looked when he described her, or the way Fallon lost himself when he talked of her. Not any of that. This!

Vickers wanted to spit and didn't have enough saliva in his mouth to do it. His head rose abruptly at the scraping noise from the direction of Reeves. The bearded man had stiffened; he rose to his feet, turning to face the wall, backing off toward the center of the room. The walls were curtained with red *chimayo* blankets, and one of these was thrust aside. The room being sunk into the earth this way, it had never entered Vickers's head that the blankets might conceal a doorway. The portal that opened behind the blankets was a heavy oak piece, set in the solid rock, and a man stood there with one hand holding the *chimayo* blanket back. His face was painted black to the mouth and, from there down to the neck, white. The rest of his body, naked to the waist, was a light red. About his square belly was a dancing skirt of wool, with fox skins dangling behind, rattles tied to his naked ankles.

"Your fate has been decided, Vickers," he said in English. "It seems Abeïto tried to tell them you were sent by the Trues before he died. Otherwise they would have killed you outright. As it is, the *principales* have been debating, and their decision is that, if you were really sent by the gods, you can survive the Snake Dance."

Vickers was on his feet, staring at the man, and it had struck him by now. "Fallon," he said. "Webb Fallon."

Fallon shut the door quickly behind him, coming forward to be surrounded by the three of them, forgetting their hatred and bitterness in this moment enough to come together. Fallon caught at Vickers's arm.

"Not much time for explanation now. I rode away from Cañon Diablo. Came across one of these Antelope men out getting rattlesnakes for the dance. Knocked him on the head and took his outfit. That Navajo shaman said the Snake Dances were being held at Walpi, and the buckskin thong in the basket was pointing north. I took the chance that implied Sherry had been taken here. Climbed the cliff on this south side during the night, hunted till daylight for her without success. In this monkey suit, I could move around the pueblo pretty free as long as it was dark. Had to hide in one of their *estufas* during the day. I don't speak their language. But neither do the Apaches. Some Moki was talking to an Apache in Spanish outside the *estufa*. The court where they're going to hold the dance is on a lower level than the upper part of the mesa. Guess you know this. It's where this door leads. It's how we'll escape."

"But it's a sheer cliff on the south side of the court," said Vickers. "We'll have to go through the whole pueblo to get out."

"I don't mean that way," said Fallon. "They'll let you all go if you survive the Snake Dance."

"That's impossible," snapped Vickers. "There's over a hundred rattlers in the ceremony. A white man wouldn't last a minute in that court."

"It's the only way. You can't fight your way through a thousand drunk Indians without even a pocket knife in your hands." Fallon turned toward the door. A *tombe* had begun thumping out there. He spoke swiftly. "They're starting. This has to be fast. When I heard what the *principales* had decided and knew you were in here, I managed to get inside that cottonwood booth where they keep the snakes in a big buckskin bag. I let one out, stepped on its tail before it could coil, closed the bag on the others. Then I grabbed it behind the head and extracted the fangs. Did the same with four others. Sweat made this paint on my body wet enough to daub a circle of it around the tail of each snake. You can't miss it. Whatever they make you do with those snakes, pick the ones with the paint on them."

"But there'll be others," said Vickers. "They have a dozen at a time crawling around that court."

"I'll see that they don't bite you," said Fallon.

The girl's face darkened. "What do you mean?"

Fallon left without answering her. Vickers could feel sweat dampening his face as he stood there with the girl and Red-Eye. The fight going on inside Sherry was evident to him in her rigid body, her set face. He didn't blame her. He felt a fear growing in himself. There was something ghastly about the thought of that courtyard out there full of writhing, hissing snakes. Vickers reached out and touched her impulsively, and then let his hand slide off as she turned toward him. He didn't know whether the look on her face was for him or for the snakes.

The door was thrust open, and a pair of braves in the same costume as Fallon had worn entered, carrying the sacred rattles known as *guajes*. One of them told Vickers in sonorous tones of the sentence imposed on them by the *principales,* then nodded his head toward the door.

Vickers took a deep breath and stepped out, followed by Sherry. A deep sighing sound went up from the crowds lining the tops of the houses on the west of the courtyard, and then a shout, as the Apaches saw the girl following Vickers. There was no ladder from the housetops into the courtyard, but Perry Papago dropped off the first roof, landing like a cat, running out to the captain of the Antelope Society where he stood with his dancers by the sacred cottonwood booth called the *kee-si*.

"There is no reason for the girl to be tested," he told the Moki, and Vickers realized Papago feared her death would leave him with no hold over the troops in Prescott. "*Pahanas* Vickers is the only one on trial."

"They are all *pahanas,*" said the captain. "If they are sent by the Trues, they must prove it. This is the judgment of the *princi-pales*."

"No!" shouted Papago. "Combabi, Assaya, Jerome . . . !"

At his call, his Apaches began surging toward the edge of the roof, pushing through the other Indians. Combabi dropped off a house into the court, pulling his cap-and-ball. Then he stopped, with the gun held there in both hands. At the signal of the captain's hand, one of the Antelope men had swung aside the curtain of the *kee-si* and reached in to unlace the top of one of the buckskin bags holding the snakes, and the first rattler slid out, hissing and writhing. Instinctively Papago jumped back against the wall, and another big, ugly diamondback rattler slithered from the *kee-si*. Combabi backed up, a twisted revulsion on his face. Perhaps it was the very primitive horror of the slimy death in these creatures that held him from firing, or perhaps because he knew how sacred the snakes were to the Mokis and how the whole pueblo would mob him if he dared shoot.

Behind him, Vickers heard a strangled sound. At first he thought it was Sherry, and looked toward her. But she was standing rigidly beside him, a white line about her tightly shut lips, staring wide-eyed at the half dozen huge snakes writhing across the floor of the courtyard. It was Reeves.

"Vickers," he said hoarsely, "they ain't gonna make us dance with them snakes. Not white men. Not rattlers like that."

It surprised Vickers. He hadn't expected it from Reeves, somehow; he remembered how Reeves had gone out to get those Apaches at Cañon Diablo, and how he had reacted to the gunshot wound.

"You heard Fallon," said Vickers. "He's fixed some of the snakes. It's our only way."

"No." Reeves's palms were spread out against the rock on either side of him as the Antelope man let out another hissing snake. "No, Vickers, you're the only one on trial. Papago's right, you're the only one on trial. Ain't no reason the rest of us have to dance with those snakes. I don't see any with paint daubed on their tails. They're real, Vickers. I seen a man bit by one of them diamondbacks last year. He swelled up like a balloon." Sweat was streaking the grime in Reeves's face now, leaking down into his beard. "Tell them I don't have to do it, Vickers. Make up some excuse. You can. You know them. Tell them I got a special chit from these Trues or whatever they are. I just come along. Tell them, Vickers. . . ."

The girl was still standing there like that, and a faint line of red showed across her chin, and Vickers could see now how her teeth were clamped into her bottom lip, and the sight of Reeves disgusted him suddenly. He grabbed the man's arm.

"Come on. You'll spoil it all. If we were sent by the Trues, we wouldn't act like this. They'll get suspicious, and it'll be all over. You've got to trust Fallon."

"No!" Reeves tore from Vickers's grasp, a glazed look in his eyes, falling back against the stone. "Please, Vickers, get me out of this. I'll do anything else. Man or devil. I've fought 'em all in my time. Injun or white, black or yellow, man or beast. I fought a grizzly once. See? See the scar on my chin? But not this, Vickers. You can't just walk in there and start playing with them diamondbacks. They'll have you bloated like a Cimarron carcass in five minutes. Please, Vickers. Anything. I'll do anything. Tell them, Vickers. . . ."

"Shut up!" Vickers slapped him across the face, knocking his head back against the wall. The Indians were watching them now. "If you spoil our only chance here, I'll kill you myself. Now get up like a man and take it. I thought you were a man. Down at Cañon Diablo I thought I hadn't ever seen that kind of nerve before."

"This ain't the same." Reeves was huddled back against the

51

wall, his lower lip slack and wet. "Snakes, Vickers, snakes. It ain't the same. There's something special about them. Anything else, Vickers. I told you. Anything else. Not snakes, Vickers. I seen a man bit. Anything but snakes. I didn't come for this!"

"What did you come for then?" Vickers had both hands buried in his shirt, shaking him savagely. "What did you come for?"

"To get the gal. You know that. Get me out and I'll tell you. Get me out. I'll do anything, Vickers."

Vickers shook him again. "It was you who took the shot at me back in the shaman's *hoganda* at Cañon Diablo?"

"Yeah"—Reeves wiped his slobbering mouth, struggling against Vickers's grip—"yeah, I had to wait till you found out from him where the gal was. I knew he wouldn't tell right out. That ain't an Injun's way. When he said the Snake Dances was being held at Walpi, I knew. Still can't figure how I missed. You must have moved. I placed you dead center before it got too dark. You must have moved."

Vickers shook him again as he started babbling anew. "Who sent you? The Tucson machine?"

"Yeah, yeah." He glanced wild-eyed at the snakes again. "Get me out, Vickers, get me out. The machine. I'll do anything. You promised. The machine. Papago'd worked for us before. We got him to hook the girl so we'd have control over Judge Kern till the elections were over, and we were strong enough to keep the capital at Tucson. Only Papago switched ends on us and brought Sherry here for his own purpose."

"How did you get that handful of fringe from my leggings?"

"Your apprentice printer." Reeves's breathing sounded like a crazed animal's, hoarse, broken. "He cut off a handful when you were sleeping after a bulldog edition. Edgar James had found out about this plot to get Sherry Kern, and had to be eliminated. I guess that's what James meant when he told Sherry your name. You'd been claiming all along the Tucson machine was behind all the trouble in the territory, and James had always laughed at you. It was only then that he knew you were right."

Sherry had turned toward them, a dazed comprehension seeping through the other emotions twisting her face. "You mean Vickers didn't murder Edgar? Why should they try to implicate him at all?"

"I guess you haven't been in the territory long enough to know how Vickers was fighting the Tucson machine," said Reeves. "I guess you don't know how hard they've been trying to get rid of him."

"They've tried it before?" Sherry's voice held doubt.

"I've got a slug in my shoulder for one time," said Vickers in a flat tone. "There's a dead triggerman buried on Caliente Hill for another. I guess they got tired of trying it that way. This was a sort of two-birds-with-one-stone deal, wasn't it?" He jammed Reeves back against the rock wall viciously. "Who was it?"

Reeves's glazed eyes rolled up to him. "When we knew James had to be killed, we paid your apprentice to cut a handful of fringe off your leggings. Everybody knew how you and James hated each other. He made it even better by saying your name at the last. . . ."

"Who was it?"

The utter savagery of Vickers's voice made Reeves recoil. "Papago," he gasped, staring at Vickers. "We'd hired him other times. Papago burned James down." Then he was staring past Vickers. "They're coming. Vickers, you promised. Get me out. Get me out! I can't dance with any snakes! For God's sake!"

Vickers sensed the dancers moving in behind him, and he almost shouted the last, jamming Reeves against the wall. "Who's the top saddle in the machine, Reeves? Who runs the whole thing? You know. Tell me, tell me. . . ."

"No, Vickers, no!" Reeves began fighting with a sudden,

bestial fear, screaming and writhing against the rock wall, tearing at Vickers's face, lurching out of his grasp. "Don't let them, Vickers. I ain't going to dance with no snakes. No, Vickers, no . . . !"

Vickers was torn aside from behind, and two Antelope men caught Reeves, pulling him to his feet. Reeves was a big man, his fear giving him a violent strength, and he surged forward with a scream, fighting loose. Another pair of Mokis caught him, and the four dancers shoved the shouting, fighting, man out toward the snakes. When they were near the writhing mass of reptiles, they gave Reeves a last shove. He stumbled forward, unable to catch himself till too late. Already, three of the snakes were coiled. The *thump* the first one made, striking, carried clearly to Vickers. Reeves's scream was hardly human. Kicking the snakes away, he whirled blindly, but another diamondback whirred and struck. The big man jerked with that hammer blow against his thigh. He tore at the bullet head, whirling and bawling in a frenzy of fear.

"Vickers, get me out! You promised, damn you, promised! Get me out! I ain't going to dance with no snakes! Vickers, Vickers, Vickers!"

The words ended in a crazy scream as another snake hit him. They were all about him now, hissing and rattling and coiling, and he turned this way and that, kicking wildly with his feet, roaring in a terrible fear. Vickers was held spellbound by the ghastly spectacle, filled with a wild impulse to rush in and drag the man out of it, repelled by a growing horror of the snakes. Twice he made a spasmodic move toward Reeves, and the Antelope men caught his arms. Sherry was watching with terrified eyes, bosom rising and falling violently beneath her blouse.

"Vickers, please, Vickers, Vickers." Reeves's shouts became weaker, and he made a last attempt to turn away from the snakes, arms held across his face, and other rattlers struck him, almost knocking him over. He sank to his knees, his cries hoarse, pitiful, shaking and blubbering. He tried to crawl out on his hands and knees. Another snake coiled before him, hissing, rattling. Reeves let out a last, hoarse scream, rising almost to his feet. Turning wildly away, he shuddered at its blow, falling down again.

He sank onto his belly, his soft blubbering becoming incoherent, finally stopping, to lie there, a great hulk of a man in his Levi's and red flannels, utterly silent.

Two Antelope men walked out to get him. A rattler struck at one of them, and he kicked the snake away casually, stooping to lift Reeves. They carried him back past Vickers into the room from which they had come.

Vickers caught himself abruptly, moving over till Sherry was against his side, catching her cold hand. "You've got to trust Fallon. It's our only chance, Sherry. It was the panic that got Reeves. Not the snakes. A man doesn't die that fast from their bite. Maybe fear makes the venom work faster. I don't know. All I know is you can't let it affect you like that. Fallon said he'd get us out. Do you hear me, Sherry?"

"I hear you, Vickers." Her voice was small, shaky. She was trembling against him, and her fingers dug into his palm till the nails brought blood. Then a *tombe* began to beat from the nearby rooftop.

In front of the *kee-si* was a pit dug in the ground, supposed to represent *Shi-pa-pu,* the Black Lake of Tears, and the twenty men of the Antelope Society began circling this, shaking their *guajes.* Then a huge *tombe* on the rooftop nearby began to beat, and the men of the Snake Society emerged from the sacred *estufa* at the north end of the court. The captain of the Snake Society, upon reaching the first snake, tickled it with a feather as it started to coil, making it stretch out, then snatched it behind the head and put it between his teeth. A man of the

Antelope Society placed his arm around the snake man's shoulders, and together they started in the peculiar hippety-hop toward the sacred rock at the south end of the court. Each snake man in turn took his snake, and was joined by his Antelope partner. As the third pair left the *kee-si* together, an Antelope man emerged from the booth behind them, so close that Vickers was sure he alone saw it, the Indians on the rooftops probably not even aware the man had not been there all the time, the dancers too busy with their rituals to notice where he came from. There were seventeen of the Snake Society, and twenty of the Antelope, and, when they had all paired off, it left three Antelope men to gather up the snakes as each pair of dancers rounded the sacred dancing rock and came back, each snake man dropping his reptile with a twist of his head. The snakes were writhing furiously in the Mokis' mouths now, trying desperately to strike the Indians, all their leverage for striking dissipated by the position in which they hung. The captain of the Snake Society had already rid himself of his first snake and, standing by the *kee-si* with his partner, rattled his ceremonial *guaje* at the whites, calling something.

"What did he say?" Sherry's voice was hoarse.

"He's ordering us to pick up a snake and dance with it in our mouth," said Vickers.

Suddenly the girl's body was shuddering violently. Her teeth showed whitely against her red lower lip, drawing blood, and her voice shook with the terrible effort she was making to control herself.

"I can't do this," she said. "I can't. I can't!"

"You've got to," said Vickers tensely. The Antelope man who had come from the booth was separating a big diamondback from three other reptiles on the courtyard floor. He reached in with both hands to grab the snake behind its head before it could coil. Vickers saw a smaller one coil and strike, and saw

56

the man flinch and grit his teeth.

Fallon. Dressed in the bizarre costume, he moved toward them, holding the leaping diamondback, two red dots on his right hand. Sweat was streaking the black paint on his face.

"Take it," he told Sherry under his breath. "It's the one I fixed. Take it."

Sherry stumbled backward, her hands out in front of her, face pale. Vickers clamped his teeth shut and grabbed the snake behind the head, just beneath Fallon's grip, tearing it from him. He caught Sherry by the arm, pulling her violently to him, then caught her abundance of black hair and held her head rigid, her body against him, and jammed the seven feet of writhing serpent against her face. She screamed, and for that moment her face was twisted in utter horror. Then he felt her stiffen against him, and her eyes were staring widely and suddenly free from fear into his, and it was as if she took the strength from him.

Her mouth opened and he forced the snake between her teeth, and she bit into the smooth, diamond-marked hide so hard the tail and head leaped into the air, the circle of paint Fallon had daubed on its body near the rattles gleaming wetly. An Antelope man put his arm around Sherry and guided her toward the dancing rock in that strange hippety-hop.

Fallon had already chosen another marked snake for Vickers. Vickers felt a moment of sick revulsion and closed his eyes as he took the snake from Fallon's hand, jamming it into his mouth. It tasted wet and acrid and sandy all at once, and he almost gagged on it. The fetid arm of a sweating Antelope man was thrown around his shoulder, and they hopped toward the dancing rock. The snake beat against him, sending waves of nausea through his whole body, and he knew an insupportable desire to vomit. But, as he turned the dancing rock with the stinking partner, he saw the real danger was ahead of them. The snakes that the other pairs had dropped were slithering across the courtyard between the rock and the *kee-si,* and, although the three Antelope men relegated to that job kept picking them up and putting them into the cottonwood booth, there were always some snakes left on the ground.

Sherry and the Antelope man who was dancing with her were almost to the *kee-si* when she dropped the snake from her mouth. It slithered away, and she tried to disengage herself from the Antelope man. Vickers could see it now, and almost upset the man hopping with him as he tried to reach Sherry. One of the diamondbacks had freed itself from the writhing mass on the floor within the circle of dancers, slithering directly toward Sherry and her partner, and it had no paint daubed on its tail.

Vickers dropped his own snake, fighting free of his partner, leaping toward her, as the diamondback reared up, and coiled. Sherry screamed, scratching the face of her partner, but he caught her hand, ignoring the coiling snake to pull her toward the *kee-si* to get another serpent. A sob escaped Vickers as he saw that he would be too late. The diamondback's head disappeared in a blur of movement. Vickers shouted in a hoarse, cracked way, still running forward. Then he saw what had happened. Somehow, another Antelope man had gotten in between Sherry and the snake in that last instant, and the serpent fell back from striking the man's leg.

"Fallon," gasped Vickers between his teeth, and suddenly understood what the man had meant back in the *kiva: I'll see that they don't bite you.*

Again the Mokis made them take snakes in their mouths, and again it was Fallon who managed to be the one handing them each snake, picking out the ones marked with paint. This time Sherry took it herself. She was sobbing and her hands were shaking, but she took the ugly reptile, making a choked sound as she forced it into her mouth, and started dancing toward the rock again. Fallon caught a snake for Vickers, staggering toward him. The man's face was turned muddy by the sweat mixing with the black paint, and he fell against Vickers, gasping.

"We're doing it, we're doing it. If only she can hang on one more time. Three times around, see. . . ."

After the third time to the rock and back again, after casting aside the writhing snake, Vickers asked him: "Why, Fallon?"

"My job, isn't it?" panted Fallon, shoving him. "I'm all right. Got hold of some of that tea they call *mah-que-he*. Antelope men drink it to give them immunity. Kern sent me out to get her, didn't he?"

"This isn't your job," said Vickers, fighting with the writhing snake in his grasp. "A man wouldn't do this just for a job. You knew what it meant. You knew that *mah-que-he* wouldn't give you immunity. These snake men train all their lives. They've been drinking that tea eight days now. You knew what it meant. Why, Fallon?"

Fallon whirled to face him fully, those wide eyes meeting his, a little crazy now. "You know why! You came for the same reason. Even when I met you there in the Tortillas, it had already happened to you. Just hearing about her. I knew her, see. You just heard about her, and it happened to you. I knew her. That's why."

The *tombe* stopped. A hush fell over the throng on the walls, and the sweating dancers halted, drawing together in front of the *kee-si*. The captain of the Snake Society held up his *guaje*, turning toward the four quarters, then bowing to Vickers.

"Abeïto spoke the truth. No *pahanas* has ever passed the ordeal before you. The Trues have sent you."

Vickers had a chance to speak with Fallon, grabbing his arm when they passed him going out. "You're coming with us. If you can't get away now, we'll wait for you below."

"Don't be a fool," said Fallon. "I can't leave till the dance is over. They'd suspect something."

"Fallon. . . ."

"No!" The man jerked away, his face twisted. "This tea's about through working in me anyway. You know that. What's the use of risking your life for a dead man? I did this for her. You get her back. Promise me that."

Vickers drew a heavy breath. "I promise you that."

"Now, get the hell out of here."

They gave Vickers his Henry back, and the roan Reeves had taken at Cañon Diablo, and another horse for Sherry. The Mokis watched them pass down the street, sullen and silent, and Vickers could see how many of them were still drunk on Reeves's whiskey. He was practically holding Sherry up, and, as they neared the start of the trail down, leading their horses, he felt her grow taut against him, and he saw it, too.

They were strung out across the trail, a dozen or more, with their narrow, drunken faces and glittering eyes and .50 Sharps, and Papago stood out in front of them. "You aren't taking the girl, Vickers. Hand her over and you can go."

"I'm taking her, Papago. You heard the decision of the *principales*. You'll be bucking more than me if you try to stop us."

"The Mokis won't interfere," said Papago. "You see how drunk they are. They'd just as soon see you dead as not, after the way you messed up their Snake Dance. Now, hand her over."

"It won't stop with me," said Vickers. "There's still the Tucson machine. Do you think Reeves will be the last man they send up here?"

"As a matter of fact," said Papago, "I do."

"You're dreaming," said Vickers.

"No," said Papago, "you wanted to know who sat the top saddle in the Tucson machine? A strong man, Vickers. The kind of man who could get out and do something himself when his men failed."

60

The implication of that shocked Vickers enough to take him off guard, and his incredulity was in his voice: "Are you trying to say that Reeves . . . ?"

". . . was the head of the Tucson machine! He'd sent half a dozen of his men out to find the girl before he finally got impatient and came himself. He was that kind, Vickers. Almost as dangerous as you. And now that he's gone, Kern won't have much trouble shifting the capital back to Prescott and smashing the machine for good." Papago shifted impatiently. "I'm through talking. Come on alone, and we'll let you do it standing up."

"You're bluffing, Papago," said Vickers. "You don't dare defy the edict of the *principales* if you want them to help you against the troops. We're coming through."

He put one hand behind Sherry's back, guided her forward, but, with his first move, Papago went for his gun. "This is how we're bluffing, Vickers."

Vickers had not really believed they would try it, here. He could have brought his own Henry up and cocked it about the same time Papago got the Remington out, but that would have left Sherry in the line of fire. With a grunt, he threw himself against the girl, not even trying for his own gun, and the two of them went down, rolling into the dark doorway of the adobe house on this side, the roar of gunfire echoing down the street as Papago and the Apaches opened up.

The wall cut him off from most of the Apaches, but he could still see two of them out there. He snapped the lever of his Henry, and it bucked in his hand, and one Apache yelled and doubled over, dropping his Sharps. A new volley of gunfire rocked the narrow way, and bullets made their deadly *thuds* into the mud walls all about Vickers. But there were only one or two Apaches beside Papago with six-shooters, and the others had those old, single-shot Sharps rifles. The sudden cessation of gun sound told him they had emptied their rifles and had to take that moment for reloading, and he knew it would be his only chance.

"There's only one way to finish this," he muttered.

"Papago?" said Sherry.

He turned to see her face, pale and drawn in the dim light, staring up at him. "Indians are like that, Sherry. Get their leader and all the sand will go out of them."

"Vickers, you can't go out there. . . ."

"I can," said Vickers. "While they're busy with me, you get out of here and back down the street to the *principales*. They'll keep their word about letting you go."

"Vickers. . . ."

But he was already throwing himself out the door with his Henry held across his belly, an adamantine cast to his lean, burned face, his mouth twisting as he saw the first Apache skulking down the wall across the street, and fired. The man jerked against the wall, still trying to jam a fresh load down his Sharps, then fell forward onto his face. A figure loomed on the roof of the first level across the street, and Vickers realized they had been trying to come up on him inside the house that way. The man had a six-gun and began firing wildly, with both hands, and only then did Vickers recognize him. The Henry made its single hollow *boom*.

"I told you, Combabi, I told you!" shouted Vickers, still going forward down the street, as Combabi pitched head foremost off the roof, and then Vickers's eyes swung to the man farther down in the middle of the street. He had been trying to work down next to the wall while Vickers was inside, but as soon as Vickers showed, he had moved into the center. It was some distance, and Papago did not fire as most Indians would have. He moved toward Vickers, increasing his speed, bent forward a little. Vickers was still turning from firing at Combabi, and he snapped the lever home hard, and the gun bucked hotly against his belly. Papago did not jerk, and Vickers knew he had missed. Then Papago's Remington spoke.

Vickers had been shot before, and the hammer blow against his leg was no new sensation. The street seemed to drop from beneath him and he found himself on his belly with the Henry pinned beneath him. A terrible, swimming pain robbed him of all volition. Through a haze he saw Papago still coming forward, lining up the gun for another shot. Then it was Sherry's voice.

"Vickers!"

Something inside him grew taut and hard and clear. He pulled the gun upward till the barrel lay beneath his chin, snapping the cylinder out sideways beneath him. Papago saw it and tried to stop him, firing sooner than intended. The hard earth kicked up in a puff of acrid, blinding dust before Vickers's eyes. He squeezed the trigger that way.

When the dust fell and the stunning force of the bullet striking earth so near to Vickers left him, he could see Papago lying on his belly down the street. The Apaches were already beginning to gather about their leader, forgetting Vickers. One of them had a surprised look on his face. Then it was Sherry's hands on Vickers, soft, cool, somehow, lifting him up. The pain in his leg made him dizzy.

"Help me on the roan," he said between gritted teeth. "We've got to get out. It's all over now."

She helped him up against the horse, her arms about his body. "In a way it's over, Vickers, but in another way it's just begun," she said. "I told you I didn't think you were crazy, back in that room. You were right. It can happen, that way, to a man"—and her eyes were soft and smoky, meeting his—"or a woman."

★ ★ ★ ★ ★

SHADOW RIDERS

★ ★ ★ ★ ★

I

When he had finished washing, Morgan Banning took the hotel towel off the rack and went to the window. They were on the second story, and he stood to one side so he could see the street without being visible from below.

"Is he down there?" Eddie asked.

"Big as life," Morgan said.

The bed *squeaked* as Eddie swung off and came to the window. Morgan caught his arm.

"Keep to one side, kid. . . ."

"Why?" Eddie asked impatiently. "We know he's following us and he knows we've seen him."

Morgan dropped his hand off his younger brother's arm. Eddie was still looking out the window, and a sudden grin crinkled up the corners of his eyes.

"Skinny yak, isn't he?"

"That Colt's tied down."

"I've seen a lot of dudes with their guns tied down."

"He's no dude."

Eddie chuckled and turned to clap Morgan affectionately on the arm. "OK, mother hen. I'm not worrying. Long as I have my big brother around to pull me out of bogs. Let's get dressed. I'm starved."

Morgan remained at the window, gazing down at the man who stood in the shadow of an overhang across the main street of this Wyoming cow town. At last Morgan went back to wiping his hands dry, the deliberate movements bunching up heavy muscle across his shoulders and at the base of his columnar neck. This was the only place he carried any weight. The rest of him was saddle-spare, flat through the middle, and long through the legs. His face was strongly framed, with a high forehead and broad, flat cheek bones against which the sun and wind and weather had worked for twenty-nine years, till the flesh was Indian-dark and had the graining of some fine wood. It was a sober face, composed of patience and watchfulness; it would have been somber but for the hint of droll humor in the curl at one tip of the lips.

Finally he went back to the washstand and hung the towel carefully on the rack, shrugging his shoulders to get the kinks out. They had been three months on the trail, driving a herd of feeders north from Texas, and he did not yet feel completely rested.

Eddie showed none of the effects of the two hard nights in town. His blue eyes were bright and eager as a kid's, and his swift, grinning movements gave no hint of his wild drunk the night before. At twenty-two, he was still slim and lithe as a whip, with deceptive strength to the light frame of his body. After dressing and using the cracked mirror to comb his hair carefully, he put a Texas crease in his immense Stetson and set it jauntily on his head. Morgan slipped into his denim ducking jacket and put his own hat on, and they left the room.

Morning sunlight struck them a brazen blow when they stepped out of the moldy lobby. When his eyes had accustomed themselves to the brightness, Morgan could see the man who had been watching their window from across the street. He was six feet tall and narrow enough to take a bath in a shotgun barrel. He leaned against the support of a wooden overhang, rolling himself a cigarette, and the brim of his hat cast his cadaverous face into deep hollows of shadow.

Another man with a Texas crease to his Stetson angled across the street to meet the two brothers at the curb.

"Oakland hit town yet, Will?" Morgan asked.

Will Hyatt was one of the trail crew, gangling and raw-boned as a Texas steer. "Oakland's at the bank now," he said. "Told us he'd pay off over at the Hoof and Horn." He finally noticed Morgan's half-lidded attention on the cadaverous man beneath the overhang. "What's the matter?" he asked.

"Ever see him before?" Morgan asked.

"Can't say so. He on the prod?"

"Been watching us since Saturday night," Eddie said impatiently. "We oughta. . . ."

"Never mind," Morgan told them. "Let's hit the saloon."

From the hotel, the main street of Chinook went westward four blocks, and then ran against the first steep slopes of the mountains and stopped abruptly. The wind of the high country was already beginning to stir dust from the wheel ruts, lifting its acrid tang to mingle with the scent of sage that crept in from the southward flats. A man in rolled-up shirt sleeves and a soiled apron was perched on the cracker barrel in front of the general store, spitting idly at tobacco-stained cracks in the sidewalk and gossiping with a pair of townsmen in blue jeans. Their voices broke off sharply as the three Texans approached. Morgan sent them a narrow glance as he went by, trying to define the tension pinching in their faces.

"Gives me a creepy feeling down my neck," Hyatt said. "Don't this town like newcomers?"

"It's more than that," Morgan muttered. "I've felt it ever since we came here."

The wind banged a loose shutter somewhere. Its hollow echo ran down an alley and died. A pudgy man in a soiled frock coat hurried down the walk across the street, checked himself before the harness shop to peer at the three Texans, then wheeled and ducked in the door. Eddie spat grit from between his teeth.

"Damn," he said. "What do they all want?"

Neither Morgan nor Hyatt answered him. They were almost to the Hoof and Horn when they saw the spring buggy coming down toward them from the bank. Harvey Oakland was driving. He had a leonine mane of white hair that made his head seem too big for his body. His Prince Albert had satin lapels and his marseille waistcoat was of white padded silk, but these marks of affluence could not hide the rough heritage in his weather-seamed face. The woman sitting beside him drew a low whistle from Eddie Banning.

"That," he said, "is silver-plated."

Oakland halted the buggy with a flourish, touching the tip of his whip to an immaculate hat brim. " 'Morning, boys. Like you to meet my daughter, Nora. This is Morgan Banning, Nora. Trail boss for that herd they brought us."

Nora smiled at Morgan, and at the others, as Oakland introduced them. It was an infectious smile, tucking in the corners of her full lips with a hint of puckish humor. An amused twinkle filled her dark eyes as they met Eddie's grin, filled with its frank and wondering appreciation. She was hatless, the wealth of her auburn hair done in an upsweep. Even in this harsh light, the flesh of her face was flawless satin. The fullness of her underlip, the deep curve of breasts in the tight bodice gave the sense of something at the peak of its ripeness.

"Sorry I didn't have enough room in my bunkhouse to put your crew up, Banning," Oakland said.

"I think they wanted to hit town anyway," Morgan told him. "That advance you gave us was just about enough to cover a high-heel time."

"I didn't expect you so soon or I'd've had the whole amount on hand," Oakland said. He climbed out of the rig with a genial grunt and bent to get a bag out of the buggy. "You'll excuse me a minute, Nora, while I pay the boys off."

Oakland started into the saloon, squinting at each *squeak* of his boots. "Damn these new Justins. Get 'em bench-made and they still bind."

The woman nodded. Her eyes were on Morgan, and the puckish smile had faded. It was as if she had changed from a little girl to a woman. There was a searching quality to her dark eyes that disturbed him.

The trail crew was lined up at the long cherry wood bar. A couple of them had bandages on their heads and one was holding a beefsteak to his eye. It drew a grin to Oakland's lips. Morgan saw how much it was like Nora's smile, with that puckish amusement hiding slyly at the tucked-in corners. After paying the men off, Oakland turned to the brothers.

"Heard you boys were making inquiries at the Land Office," he said. "Plan on settling here?"

"The agent took us up yesterday to see that Doubloon place," Morgan said.

Oakland glanced at Morgan sharply, then turned away. But Morgan had seen the sudden darkness filling his eyes. He started moving toward the front door, and Morgan saw the same pinching tension in his face he had seen in the men at the general store.

"What's the matter with the Doubloon?" Morgan asked.

"Nothing." There was a quick defensiveness in Oakland's voice. He stopped, with one hand on top of a batwing door. "It's been in litigation so long I don't know whether you'd ever be able to buy it."

"The land agent told us the Eastern heirs are coming to a settlement," Morgan said. "We've been working on a stake for a long time. We only need a couple of hundred to swing the deal."

Oakland frowned at Morgan, as if studying him. "That road herd was ten pounds heavier on the average than any feeders

71

I've ever gotten," he said. "If you're that good with cattle, I could use you. Knowing the herd, you can be a big help getting them up to summer pasture. Why not sign on with me till word comes from the East? Your wages should just about make up that couple of hundred."

Eddie grinned out over the batwings at the girl in the buggy. "Man talks sense, Morg," he said.

Morgan was looking at the traces of that strange tension that still clung to Oakland. "We'll think it over," he said.

As Oakland pushed the door open and swung out, Morgan saw that there was a man standing by the buggy. He was tall and broadly framed in his blue broadcloth suit, and his flat-topped hat was as black as his hair, cropped closely against his copper-colored temples. When he turned his face toward Oakland, it was devoid of expression. " 'Morning, Harvey," he said.

Oakland nodded without smiling. "Charlie," he said, "this is Morgan Banning and his brother Eddie. They brought the trail herd up. Charlie King, boys. He owns the Double Arrow east of here."

Charlie King's eyes passed across Eddie and settled on Morgan. It gave Morgan a definite sense of impact. They were strange eyes, black as ink. Somewhere deep within them little lights seemed to flare and die and flare again.

"Staying in Chinook long, Banning?" he asked.

"Haven't decided yet."

King did not smile. His features were boldly sculptured, with cheek bones high and sharp as arrowheads, and a narrow bridge to his nose that gave the whole face a strong arrogance.

"The winters are extremely cold up here . . . for a man from the south," he murmured.

Oakland grunted with the effort of stepping into the buggy. "Don't let Charlie kid you, Morgan. He just has a prejudice against outsiders. He's half Sioux and thinks the whole country should be given back to the Indians."

King turned slowly away from Morgan till the full weight of his glance settled on Oakland. But Oakland was leaning forward to flip one of the reins straight in a terret. Morgan saw a little pulse begin to beat in King's swarthy neck.

"I was asking Nora if I could help her with her shopping this morning," he said.

"I'm helping her this morning, Charlie," Oakland said, still not looking at King. "I guess one man's enough."

Nora put a hand on Oakland's arm. "Dad. . . ."

"Some other time, Charlie." Oakland snapped the whip. "Thanks anyway."

King stood with his shoulder to Morgan, watching the rig *clatter* away. Those tawny little lights in his eyes seemed to be glowing more brightly. The sidewalk began trembling with the unhurried passage of another man, coming toward them. He halted by one of the poles supporting the saloon's wooden overhang, and started to build himself a cigarette. Morgan saw that it was the same one who had been watching their hotel window.

King finally seemed to remember Morgan, and wheeled back to him. "Did Oakland offer you a job?" he asked.

"Sure did." Eddie grinned. "If that gal comes with the outfit, I mean to sign on."

King's face tightened. "I wouldn't advise you to."

"Is that why you've had your heel dog scouting us?" asked Morgan.

"The name is Law," said the tall man, idling closer. "Tom Law."

Morgan sent his cadaverous face a close glance, seeing how deceptive his gauntness was. It was the heavy bluntness of his cheek bones that made his face look sunken beneath them. His wrists had that same massiveness, and the fingers pinching his cigarette were splayed flat at the tips and scarred by a lifetime of rope work.

Morgan let his eyes move back to King. "Do you really think the land belongs to the Indians?"

King's voice sounded thick. "Oakland makes poor jokes."

"Then why has Law been tailing us since Saturday night?"

Law had a voice like an undertaker's. "The town's free."

"You were following us and you know it," Eddie told him hotly. Then he wheeled back to King. "Maybe we better get this straight. No half-breed outfit is telling us where we can stay and where we can't. Next time I see one of your heel dogs peekin' through our window, I'm going to shoot his marbles out."

"Take it easy, Eddie," Morgan said.

All of King's weight seemed to have thrust forward against the balls of his feet. For a moment he hung that way, with the little lights playing savagely through his eyes. The batwings *creaked* as a couple of trail hands pushed through, drawn by Eddie's loud voice.

"Something wrong, Morg?" Hyatt wanted to know.

"Nothing wrong, Will," Morgan told him.

A spasmodic pucker of muscle ran through King's swarthy cheek. He settled back slowly. More of Morgan's crew drifted out, some of them still holding beers, banking up behind Morgan and Eddie. Tom Law dropped his half-smoked cigarette without bothering to put it out. King's eyes were hooded now.

"You aren't going, then?" he asked thinly.

"We haven't made up our minds."

King's boots scraped against the sidewalk. It was a raw little sound in the moment of silence. He let his eyes pass over the men behind Morgan.

"I've seen a lot of trail crews hit this town," he said. "Drunk a week, gone as soon as their money is spent. What then, Banning? Just you and your brother? Won't you feel alone?" He took a quick little breath. The tip of his tongue darted slyly across his upper lip. "Shall we see?"

II

There wasn't really much to do in a town like Chinook. A card game started in the Hoof and Horn about noon. Eddie got $20 of his pay from Morgan to sit in; Morgan watched a while, but grew restless. He wandered out of the back room for a beer at the bar. There was only one other man out here, standing at the other end of the bar and drinking steadily. Morgan recognized him as the foreman of the Keyhole, Oakland's outfit.

"Hello, Drift," he said. "That trail herd minding?"

The man turned drink-glazed eyes to him without answering. He was taller and heavier than Morgan, with a look of violent strength to the great shoulders hunched over the bar. His blond hair was cropped short on a square head, and old scars made an ugly mottling across his raw cheek bones. After that one blank look, he turned back to his drinking. Morgan lost his desire for a beer. He went out past Drift into the street. It was filled with the hot emptiness of early summer. Wind was the only movement. It was like a rat worrying the newspaper wedged against the curb at Morgan's feet. It filled the air with the smell of scorched dust.

The pudgy man in the dirty frock coat came from the harness shop across the way, stopped for a strange glance at Morgan, turned down the sidewalk at a hurried walk. After he was gone, it was only the wind again, stirring the dust to little eddies in the street. There was something desolate to it that darkened the restlessness in Morgan. He realized he had not eaten yet, and turned toward the café. Before he reached it, he saw Oakland's spring buggy standing before the general store on the other side of the street. He went on into the café and took a table near the window. He had just begun eating when his brother appeared at the corner. Eddie seemed headed toward the café when he saw the Keyhole rig and turned that way instead. Morgan saw a pair of men across the street watching Eddie closely as the boy paused before the store, then turned in through the door.

After a while, Eddie came out of the store with Nora Oakland. He was holding an armful of packages and sunlight made a bright flash against his teeth. Morgan saw the girl reacting to that smile, the way he had seen so many others react. There was an excited flush to her face and her eyes danced beneath their dark brows. Eddie put the packages behind the seat, and then helped Nora in. It left him leaning against the side of the rig with his face close to hers. He said something in her ear, and Morgan saw a shocked surprise widen her eyes. Then she burst out laughing, and Eddie joined her, and they were like a couple of kids.

The food suddenly tasted flat, and Morgan pushed it away. Absently he rolled a cigarette with one hand, as was his habit, wondering at the sour irritation in him. He had never denied to himself that he envied Eddie's easy way with women, but it had always been an indulgent envy, almost the attitude of a father toward his son. Now, somehow, there was a vague resentment. Why? This girl, perhaps, was more beautiful than the others. But aside from that she was no different.

He was drawing deeply on his cigarette when Will Hyatt and two other hands came across the street and into the café, war bags under their arms.

"Barkeep told us you come down this way." Hyatt grinned. "Looks like Eddie's at it again."

"Wherever there's a girl," Morgan said. "You aren't trailing out already?"

"I want to keep some of my money," Hyatt said. He glanced

around the room. "Looks like you been thinking deep again. This place is full of smoke rings."

Morgan glanced ruefully at the circles of smoke disintegrating above him, realizing for the first time what he had been doing.

"I guess so." He smiled wryly.

"Why don't you come with us?" Hyatt said. "This ain't no country to settle in. My horse gets plumb seasick on these hills."

"Eddie likes it," Morgan said.

"When're you going to quit thinking of that kid and light your own smokes?" Hyatt said. He clapped Morgan on the shoulder. "You got that restless look in your eyes already. This town won't hold you much longer. I'll bet you catch us before we hit Cheyenne."

Morgan watched them go, the tall, booted silhouettes filling the door for a moment, laughing and swaggering and giving him a nostalgic stab of homesickness. At the same time, he saw Oakland getting into the spring wagon and driving it away, with Nora casting a laughing glance over her shoulder at Eddie.

The younger Banning yelled good bye to Hyatt and his men, and then crossed toward the café. He must have had a lot of beer, for his face was flushed and his walk wasn't too steady, and, before he reached the door, Morgan could hear him singing his song.

> *My pa he drowned in the Pecos,*
> *My ma's at the Pearly Gates,*
> *My brother got killed in a big stampede,*
> *Now I've drawed aces and eights.*

He came through the door, blinking in the gloom. Then he saw Morgan and veered toward him, raising one hand in a gay salute.

"How about another twenty, Morg, I had a bad streak."

"You promised there wouldn't be any more."

The humor left Eddie. "It's my own money."

"You want to be a thirty-and-found rider all your life?"

Eddie started to speak angrily, then he checked himself, grinning sheepishly. "You're right, Morg. You keep it. I'd shoot the whole roll in a day."

"Let's ride out and take another look at the Doubloon."

The boy sighed restlessly. "We've seen it once. If we do any riding, why don't we head for the Keyhole? I'm for taking Oakland's offer."

"Eddie, what's the point in deliberately making enemies?"

The boy frowned. "How do you mean?"

"It's obvious King and Oakland walk on different sides of the street in this town. From what I gathered, they're the two biggest men in Chinook Basin. I don't see any reason to get in King's bad book just for a couple of months' wages from Oakland."

"If there's any trouble here and we stay, we're gonna have to take sides anyway," Eddie said impatiently.

"How do you know Oakland's the right side? There's no point in making trouble before it comes, Eddie. Admit it. The only reason you want to sign on the Keyhole is Nora Oakland."

Eddie's eyes shone like a kid looking at candy. "I never saw one like that, Morg . . . silver-plated."

"That's what you said the last time," Morgan said. "We could have had that outfit down below the border if you hadn't gone after that Mexican girl."

"This is different, Morg. . . ."

"It's never different. It's always a girl and it's always trouble. Don't spoil it this time. The Doubloon is something that only comes once in a cowman's life, Eddie."

The boy's face grew surly. "You ever going to stop being the mother hen? I can live my own life."

"And stomp up more trouble over one girl than a bull in a thunderstorm. Give us a chance this time, kid."

"You give me a chance. I'm going to the Keyhole."

Morgan came up out of the chair as Eddie turned, catching his arm. "Kid. . . ."

Eddie twisted away. "Let me go. I'm tired of being towed around behind an old mare."

Morgan sat heavily in the chair after Eddie left, an unsmoked cigarette in his fingers. An old pattern was beginning to take form before his eyes. It set him to looking back down the long trail. It seemed he had always been riding herd on Eddie. Their parents had been killed when Eddie was nine and Morgan sixteen. There had been no relatives to help raise the kid, no one to turn to. It would have been hard enough for a boy of sixteen to keep himself alive in the rough border country; the added burden of a kid Eddie's age had made it a thing of pain and hardship and unremitting labor.

There had been jobs in a stable and jobs in a general store, and a shanty on the edge of town, with Eddie getting a haphazard education at country schools and picking up the rest of his knowledge in the streets of San Antonio or Dallas or whatever town they drifted to in their constant search for the barest necessities. Later on it had been punching cows on one spread or another and Eddie in his early teens living in a bunkhouse or a cow camp and picking up the things he shouldn't have learned till he was a man. It was not a good life for a kid, but it had been the best Morgan could do.

The uncertainty of their existence and the freedom he had known since he was so young seemed to have intensified Eddie's innate recklessness. The responsibility and the never-ending struggle to live had developed Morgan in the other direction, deepening his tendencies to caution and to a suspicious search for the dangerous issues hidden beneath life's surface.

Eddie's attraction for women had begun to enter the picture about five years ago, when the boy was seventeen. It was an early age for something like that to appear so dominantly, but his hard life and the worldly things he had learned so young gave him the *savoir faire* and polish of an older man. It was really no more than a handsome boy's unique talent for romance. Yet it had grown, insidiously creating a pattern that had gained a destructive place in their lives. Sometimes, when he found himself thinking along these lines, Morgan wondered if he weren't as much to blame as the boy. Was he really nothing more than a mother hen? Had all those years of painful toil and responsibility molded into him the palsied prudence of an old man? And yet he could not help looking back to the countless times Eddie's involvement with a woman had caused them dangerous trouble.

Morgan shook his head, up against the same wall he had reached so many times before. It didn't particularly matter who was at fault. He didn't want to leave the boy completely. They had gone through too much together. Their dreams of putting down roots were mutual dreams.

Morgan left the café finally and strolled back onto the main street. He could hear what was left of the trail crew whooping it up in the Hoof and Horn. There was a crash of furniture. The batwings slammed open, a man came staggering out to pitch off the curb into the street. He rolled over, groaning, and came to a sitting position.

"Now, Marv," he complained. "You know a looloo beats four aces."

Morgan walked on to the Chinook bank and deposited their money, then he went to the hotel and found that Eddie had not returned. He left word for the boy that he would be back in the evening, and headed toward the stable.

A block before he reached the big barn he could hear the

clang of the blacksmith's hammer. He was across the street from the store, but he could see the storekeeper and the same pair of idlers by the cracker barrel. They had stopped talking, but would not meet his gaze directly as he looked over toward them. When he was a few paces beyond, he looked quickly back over his shoulder and surprised all three of them staring at him intently.

He was beginning to react to the strange suspicion of the town. He felt tension pinch at his own eyes when a man opened a door farther down the street and stepped out. Boots made a sudden *clatter* on the planks behind him and he could barely keep himself from wheeling around. Then the man stepped off into the street and the *clatter* stopped. It left an eerie hole of silence. Morgan did not understand it at first. Then he realized the blacksmith had stopped hammering.

He dropped off the end of the sidewalk and saw that the big sweating man before his anvil was staring at him, hammer still upraised. Morgan walked across the compound, trying to keep a rising irritation from his voice.

"My brother been here?" he asked.

The smith lowered his hammer without answering. A bucolic withdrawal tucked his eyes in behind beefy cheeks. Morgan drew an impatient breath.

"A kid with a big white Stetson, forks a silver-plated saddle, you remember."

The smith took a long time to answer. "He rode out."

Morgan had expected that. He lounged against a hitch rack, studying the smith. "What's wrong with this town?" he asked. "Gives me the creeps."

The sweating man glanced obliquely at him, then dropped the finished horseshoe he had been working into a box. "You got caught between Charlie King and Oakland this morning," he said. "You oughta know what's wrong."

"It's more than that," Morgan said.

He saw something furtive shuttle through the smith's face. The man stooped to pick a rough shoe from another box and laid it on the anvil. His eyes touched Morgan and fluttered away, swinging around till they were staring at the westward mountains. They held the same haunted darkness Morgan had seen in Oakland's eyes when he had first mentioned the Doubloon,

"I guess it is more than that, ain't it?" the smith said. "Maybe what's going on between King and Oakland doesn't have much to do with it. You've heard of. . . ." He broke off suddenly, as his eyes snapped to a point across the street. He quickly began to work the bellows again, hooking the shoe with his tongs to thrust it in the fire.

Morgan looked across the street. Tom Law stood with one shoulder tipped against the scabby siding of the Land Office.

Morgan looked back to the smith. "You didn't finish."

The bellows were coughing so hard the smith's voice was hardly audible. "You better get your horse, mister."

Morgan was staring at Law again. "I don't want to cause you trouble."

"You won't cause me trouble, mister. Just get your horse."

The hostler was in the barn, but Morgan saddled up himself. Then he stepped aboard the pied bronco and rode out.

Law still stood by the Land Office, meeting Morgan's gaze insolently from the cavernous sockets of his eyes. Morgan had the impulse to rein his bronco over there, but checked himself. He did not think he could get any more out of the man than they had this morning, unless he made an issue of it, and there was really nothing to make an issue of.

The wind stirred little dust devils against Pie, causing the bronco to spook and fiddlefoot all the way out of town. Morgan felt his own nerves kinking up in sympathetic reaction and was glad when the road lifted him from the confinement of the buildings into the mountains beyond.

Around the first shoulder, the road forked three ways, and he took the middle one, riding westward a few hundred yards till he reached a spot from which he could climb onto the shoulder, pushing the bronco up a steep boulder-strewn slope to the top. Here, screened by a clump of twisted junipers, he could see the town.

A great flare-boarded grain wagon was just pulling into the main street at the other end. Tom Law was just riding out of the main street at this end. He disappeared behind the shoulder, where the roads forked.

Morgan turned in the saddle, holding a tight rein on his fiddling bronco, waiting for Law to reappear on the middle road. But it remained empty. After a few minutes, Morgan shifted his position on the slope till he overlooked the other two forks. They, too, were empty.

He slid his horse down through the rocky slope to the middle fork again, filled with the sense of something ugly going on just beyond his reach. Several times more he pulled off the road and waited, or cut around to watch his back trail, but he saw nothing. Finally he gave up and pushed straight into the mountains.

Grassy slopes dotted with gnarled cedar ran up to rock-shod rims that glowed redly as blood in the sunlight. Serviceberries were fat and purple with high summer along the road and raspberries made a crimson stippling against the tawny mantle of curing buffalo grass higher up. The peaks gained height and closed about him and the timber became pines ranked file after file like some army marching from the beginning of time to its end with wind a million years old stirring ceaselessly at their pointed green helms.

Finally it made Morgan draw rein and stare at the peaks. The pressure of the mountain country was bringing itself to bear on him, telling him of titanic things that had happened here before man was on the earth, of worlds dying and new worlds coming into being, of life and death on a scale too gigantic for him to comprehend. It filled Morgan with awe, and with something else, a poignant sadness he could not define. He was still sitting there, gripped by it, when he heard the *rattle* of a wagon.

It was coming fast, beyond a turn in the road, so he pulled his horse off to one side. The rig came hard around the curve, skidding and flinging dirt and rocks against the boulders at the far side. It was a long mountain wagon with a red rack bed and a yellow keyhole painted on the side. The woman driving hauled up so sharply it took the horses back on their haunches, squealing and tossing their heads. Then they gained their balance again, stamping and fretting at the tight rein she held on them.

Her body was maturely curved beneath a simple calico dress. Her yellow hair was braided around her head in a coronet, wisps of it whipped out by the wind to curl playfully around her ears and brush the back of her neck. There was a fresh and earthy vitality to the whole picture that stirred Morgan. With one hand she shaded deep-blue eyes against the sun.

"You're new around here."

He touched his hat brim. "Morgan Banning."

She nodded. "The trail boss that came up with those feeders. I'm Janice Wickliffe. I keep house for the Oaklands. Where are you bound now?"

"Piece of land out here I'd like to look at."

He saw a shadow darken her face. "The Doubloon outfit," she said. Her eyes seemed focused beyond him a moment. Then she shook her head, as if trying to dismiss it, and looked at him again. "Your brother's out at the ranch. He's started fireworks already."

He leaned toward her. "Anything bad?"

"Some kind of argument in the bunkhouse. It didn't come to anything. Are you signing on, too?"

He frowned. "I don't know."

"Don't do it, Banning. Get your brother out. He's headed for trouble."

"Seems to me he doesn't need to stir up any."

Her body straightened a little on the seat. "What are you talking about, now?"

"I think you know." He settled his weight forward in the saddle, hitting her hard with his glance. "What's the trouble in this town, Miss Wickliffe? In this whole basin. I've seen it ever since I've been here."

It was like a cloud covering the sun. The smile dropped off her face and she lowered her hand, leaving her eyes squinted against the strong light. The booming of the wind through the pines seemed to grow louder.

"Charlie King is a half-breed, isn't he?" Morgan said. "Is that it?"

She gave a little shake to her head that might have meant anything. "You know how folks look down on anybody with Indian blood. A 'breed isn't rated very high around here."

He nodded slowly. "It's pretty bad on the border, too. The men will play poker with him in town, but few of them will invite him to their homes."

"That's about it," she said. "King's background makes it worse. His father had a name up here. It's worked against King. He hasn't helped it any."

"I got the impression it was something special between Oakland and King," Morgan said. "Is it Nora?"

She dipped her head. "King's got his eye on Nora. Oakland won't have that. They've had several run-ins over it."

"But that isn't the whole trouble here," he said. "The blacksmith started to tell me something else when Tom Law scared him off."

She studied him a long space, then turned in the seat, pointing to the highest ridge of mountains in the west, a mauve silhouette of rough peaks and shaggy saddles lying against the misty blue sky.

"That's the backbone of the Absarokas. Beyond it lies the Yellowstone country. It was made into a national park in Eighteen Seventy-Two. But that didn't change things any. The country's as wild, as little known as it's ever been. You could camp on the Yellowstone a year and never see anybody. You won't find a man in Chinook who's ever been many miles into it. The Indians are about the only ones who know anything about the park and they won't talk. A lot of things could happen over there and nobody'd ever know the difference."

She continued to look toward the west, a haunted expression on her face. He studied it a long time before getting the implications. His saddle made a mournful *creak* beneath his shifting weight.

"And that's where the trouble comes from?" he said.

She turned back to him and her voice grew husky. "You've met Drift, Oakland's foreman. Almost two years ago, he and a hand named Laramie followed a cut of Keyhole cattle that had wandered over into Yellowstone. Somewhere up near the lake, Laramie was shot to death. Drift's horse was killed, too, and he barely made it out alive. To this day he doesn't know who did it or why."

Morgan frowned at her. "The land agent told me the owner of the Doubloon disappeared. It wasn't over there?"

She nodded. "The same way. Dodge went over into Yellowstone after some of his Doubloon cattle that had drifted into the park. He hasn't been heard from since."

"How about rustling trouble?"

"If you're thinking it's some gang hiding out there, you can forget it," she said. "We cleaned the last bunch of rustlers out of

Chinook Basin six years ago. We haven't had any trouble like that since."

"But you're trying to give me the impression somebody doesn't want anyone going into Yellowstone," he said.

"I'm not trying to give you any impression," she said. "I'm just telling you what has happened. A person can't tell it in words. Just to say a couple of men followed some cattle over into Yellowstone and got killed doesn't mean much. It's something you can't put your hands to. Most of the men in Chinook Basin are afraid to follow any drifting cattle beyond the Absarokas, now. A couple of smaller outfits have lost so many steers that way they've had to close their books. Even the bigger outfits are beginning to suffer. That's why Oakland brought you north with that new bunch of feeders. It's affecting everybody. The town depends on the cattlemen for its existence. If they go under, it goes under. Yet not a one of us really knows what it is." She sighed, settling resignedly against the seat. "There. I swore I'd never try to tell anybody again. You don't understand it any more than before I tried to tell you."

"Maybe I do," he said. "Chinook is a frightened town. I've seen that."

"If you have the eyes to see that, you should have the wisdom not to involve yourself in its troubles, Banning. You should get your brother and leave as soon as possible."

She looked at him a moment longer, then clucked her tongue, snapped her whip. The horses bolted, then settled into a hard run that took her rattling down the road to skid around the next turn with a *clang* of iron tires and a *squeal* of brake shoes. The dust furled out behind in a tawny smoke that swept against Morgan and settled grit in his eyes and ears. Yet he did not turn away, watching the wagon disappear through squinted lids and grinning thinly. He had never seen a woman drive so impetuously. At last he lifted his reins and put Pie back onto the road.

The road led upward; the air grew thinner. He crossed a brawling stream and climbed a shelving road to a cut-off. A post had been planted in the earth here with a slab of wood nailed to it. A keyhole had been burned into the slab with a branding iron. For a moment he had the impulse to ride to the ranch. But he still did not want to sign on, and he knew any fresh attempt to get Eddie away would only deepen the boy's stubborn resolve to stay. So Morgan kept going along the main road. It dipped into a cañon with basalt walls so black and polished they seemed to drip darkness. The dank shadows were thick with the reek of ancient earth and damp granite. The sun's warmth was a welcome thing when Morgan finally emerged into view of the real peaks beyond. They towered above him in rock-ribbed grandeur, mantled with glaciers and ice fields that gleamed like marble in the bright light.

The road petered out as it climbed the first shoulder of these patriarchs, becoming no more than a game trail. His horse was shining with sweat from the hard pull, and laboring in the thin air. He pulled up to let it blow, turning for a backward look. The basin was out of sight behind. There was nothing but the hoary undulations of timbered ridges that stretched away one after the other like the restless waves of a vast sea. It gave him the eerie feeling of being transported in time and space and swallowed up by the ageless enigmas of the mountains. There was something poignantly sad about the land. The endless files of trees looked as if they had stood here for eternity, waiting for something that never came. The wind whispered through their ruffled tops like a lost soul. It filled him again with that feeling of sadness he had known just before meeting Janice Wickliffe. Only now it was stronger, more fully realized. Somehow, it was not unwelcome. It seemed to give him affinity with the sadness of the mountains, making him a part of the bleak rocks and the black earth and the mournful passage of wind through the pines, bringing him closer to the land than he had ever been before.

Held in the spell, he turned his horse on. The trail became a narrow shelf on a rock-littered slope, cutting up near the first glacier. It was strange to see pink bitterroot and wild flax painting the ground almost to the edge of the ice fields. Finally he rounded the last jagged shape of the shoulder and came into view of the Doubloon. It lay in a shallow valley, surrounded on three sides by the towering peaks.

The wind moved through the bluegrass and wild hay and alfalfa that covered the valley's bottom till it was all ruffling like a miniature ocean. The house lay snugly against a timber-sheltered slope; there was a substantial look to the hip-roofed barns, the solid corrals. Morgan had the same feeling he had experienced with his first sight of this place. It filled some deep need in him. It stilled the restlessness and the vague longings and pervaded him with a sense of great peace. It was as if the raw, wandering years, the loneliness, the growing need to find some place to stop had all been directed toward his first sight of the Doubloon. Then Pie began fretting beneath him and *crunch-ing* on the bit, and finally tossed its head to whinny. He swung down and went to its head and tightened the buckle on the noseband to keep it from whinnying again. He was remembering Law, following him out of town.

He hitched Pie to some buckbrush and got his Henry from the saddle boot and started working back through the trees toward the glacier. He passed a pine deeply scarred by a moose rubbing velvet from its antlers. A woodchuck heckled him from somewhere and then stopped abruptly. It made him pull up against the cover of a tree.

The only sound was the melancholy whine of wind across the ice. The countless perfumes of the summer forest surrounded him, turned tart by the chill breeze. The vague sweetness of serviceberries swept fitfully against him; the timber swam with the tang of pine needles. He was beginning to think he had made a mistake, when he heard the first noise. It was small and crunching.

Tension brought out latent somberness in his face. His lids drew close till his eyes were mere silvery lines and the square Banning jaw seemed to gain belligerence. The little sounds grew larger and in another moment a rider appeared on the trail. Morgan knew surprise that it was not Tom Law. The man was a stranger to him, big and black-headed, with a bold face roughened to the texture of old leather by a lifetime of weathering. He sat heavily on his California sorrel. A sullen indifference to the land around him lay in the thick grooves about his mouth and in his half-lidded eyes. His clothes were as rough as his face, a red wool shirt with sleeves rolled to the elbows, a pair of greasy leggings slick and malleable as a second skin from use.

Morgan meant to let the man ride by. Before he had passed, however, someone spoke from the trees behind.

"Drop both your guns, Banning, and then don't turn around."

Morgan felt his hands grow tight on the rifle. At the same time, the rider in front of him pulled the sorrel up, looking toward Morgan without surprise.

At last Morgan let his Henry slip to the ground, and took out his six-shooter and dropped that, too. He heard the resilient *crunch* of pine needles beneath heedless boots, then a soft grunt. After a moment there was a sharp metallic *rattle*. He guessed the man behind him had thrown his guns on down the slope.

The pine needles began their muted crackling again, and Tom Law moved around in front of Morgan. He stood there a moment, a Ward-Burton bolt-action cuddled in one arm. Finally his mouth formed a pursed-lip smile that dug seams like claw tracks about his mouth.

"We thought it might distract your attention to have something keeping you busy at the front," he said. Then, without turning, he called the other man: "Come on down, Rideout!"

The horseman brought his animal sliding down over the talus lip of the shelving trail into timber. He drew up within a few feet of Morgan. There was a heavy protest of leather as he swung off. He tucked rope-scarred thumbs into his heavy gun belt and stood regarding Morgan with that half-lidded glance.

"Who are you, Banning?" Law said at last.

"Talk sense," Morgan said. "You know about the trail herd."

Rideout pushed his thumbs against his belt till it *creaked*. "Trail bosses generally head back where they came from."

"Yeah." Tom Law sent a squint-eyed look to the valley below. "Trail bosses don't generally have the kind of money it takes to buy an outfit like that."

"No money," Rideout said. "No outfit."

"You might learn something new about trail bosses," Morgan said.

Those claw tracks dug into Law's face again, but it was not from a smile now. "King told you to get out," he said.

"Maybe I like the country."

"Then we'll make it so you don't like the country," Law said. "Make it, Rideout."

From the corner of his eye, Morgan saw Rideout draw his gun as he stepped forward. Morgan wheeled and threw up an arm to block the attack. The gun hit his wrist a stunning blow, knocking his forearm down. This left his face open for Law, who stepped in from the other side, pulling his six-shooter.

Left arm numb, Morgan tried to twist away from this second blow. But Law's gun slashed downward across his face. He felt the tip bite through flesh and strike bone. The flashing pain robbed him of will. He could not keep from going down.

Even as he fell, Rideout struck again. The shock of it was like a great explosion at the back of Morgan's head. It knocked him flat to the ground.

He seemed to be spinning. That and the pain were his only sensations. For a long time he seemed to be spinning and to be hurting. Then, somewhere from a vast distance, he heard Tom Law's funereal voice.

"I hope you get out of the basin now, Banning. Next time we won't even stop to talk it over."

"No questions, no answers," Rideout said.

The blood was thick and wet beneath Morgan's face now. He heard the protest of rigging as Rideout swung back on the horse. He heard the *squeak* of pine needles as Law walked away.

He got to his hands and knees at last and dully watched the blood drip from his face to the ground. The pain was eating through his daze. It burned like fire across his cheek, throbbed dully behind his neck.

He got his neckerchief off and dabbed at the wound in front, trying to clot the blood. It had bitten through to bone all across his cheek, and the sharp pain kept his eye twitching.

The haze of early evening was gathering in the timber, a mauve twilight that was as thick and textured as cotton beneath the trees. He was sick at his stomach with anger, but he knew there was nothing he could do now. He finally got heavily to his feet and started down the slope, hunting his guns.

A night hawk began whimpering in the sky. The wind moaned down over the glacier and filled the world with loneliness.

III

Night came quickly in the high country. It couldn't have been much past 6:00 when Morgan reached the stream he had crossed earlier in the day, yet it was already dark. He felt apprehensive about building a fire, after what had happened, but he knew a meal would make him feel better. He made coffee, strong and black and had three cups of it before he even ate the bacon and biscuits. It cleared his head and put new life into him.

He washed the dried blood off his face and started off again, feeling stronger. His wound still throbbed painfully, but there was little rancor left in him. He was not a man to hold anger long.

The night sounds gathered about him as he groped his way on down the mountains. An owl *hooted* from the dim recesses of the forest. From even farther away a great cat screamed. His horse was nervous with weariness and kept shying at the nearer rustlings of small animals in the brush.

The moon rose at last. Its light descended moltenly through the timber to catch on the foliage and fling the leaf shadows in a black dappling across the lemon ribbon of the road. He was beyond the cut-off to the Keyhole when he saw a rider topping a rise far ahead. He pulled Pie off the road and waited. The rider came on, alternately trotting and walking. Finally the moonlight enabled Morgan to recognize Nora Oakland.

She was on a dainty little bay with jet-black points, and no longer wore her dress. She had a heavy buckskin habit and knee-length boots, and a jaunty pork-pie hat sat precariously atop her auburn upsweep.

Morgan pulled out before she reached him so as not to startle her. She reined up when she saw him, bending in the saddle to try and make him out. Her bay fretted nervously, lifting its hoofs high.

"It's Morgan Banning, Miss Oakland," he said.

"Banning!" It left her in a sharp relief, and she gigged her horse up to him. "I was looking for you in town. I waited all evening at the hotel."

"What is it?" he asked.

She came closer, till she was almost beside him. Her fringed jacket was laced shut, and moonlight left a deep shadow beneath the outward curve of her breasts. She bent forward to peer at his face, eyes widening in a shocked compassion.

"Tom Law and a man named Rideout," he explained.

"Oh"—it hissed from her with intense anger—"they shouldn't have done that, they shouldn't!"

"Is Rideout one of Charlie King's men, too?" he asked.

"Yes," she said disgustedly. "Charlie's a fool to think something like that would make you leave."

He settled in his saddle, silent for a moment, then said: "King told us in town it would be a mistake to stay because of you. I guess he really meant it."

"Because of me?" Her voice was sharp.

"Why else do you think Eddie went out to the Keyhole?" he asked.

She stared at him a moment, eyes wide and blank. Finally they narrowed, and she ran her tongue across her lips, studying him closely. "I had the same feeling when I first met you in town, Banning. You don't like me."

He shook his head. "It isn't that at all."

"Are you a woman hater?"

He found a rueful smile tilting one end of his mouth. "All right. If you insist. It isn't my own feelings toward you at all. It's women in general, and it's Eddie. It seems like he's always getting into some kind of trouble over a woman."

"And he thinks you're an old hen."

He looked at her in mild surprise. "Did he tell you that?"

She seemed to relax a little, that provocative smile tucking in the corners of her lips. "He told me a lot of things. I'd think you were an old hen, too, if he hadn't. But he told me of when your folks died. He didn't actually tell me how hard it was after that. I guess it didn't seem too bad for a kid his age . . . as long as he had shoes and his stomach was full. But I could see what you must have gone through." She paused, a half smile returning to her lips. "When did the women start?"

"Four or five years ago," he said, looking at that smile. "I guess it would be amusing to an outsider. On the surface it's innocent enough. Eddie doesn't mean any harm, and you can't get mad at a kid like him. It would be hard for anybody else to understand how much trouble it's caused."

"El Paso was the last time, wasn't it?" she asked. "He told me part of it. You had a chance at managing an outfit in Mexico with the possibility of taking it over if you made good. He didn't want to go with you because of a girl in El Paso."

Morgan nodded. "I'd been in Mexico two weeks when Eddie had a fight over the girl and shot a man. It was a clear case of self-defense on Eddie's part, but the dead man's family was out to kill him. I got back to El Paso just in time to get him away."

"And lost your chance at the ranch."

"They didn't want a manager who'd get mixed up in that sort of thing."

"Did you want that ranch as badly as you want the Doubloon?" she asked. Again he felt his surprise mirrored in his face. She smiled softly. "Eddie told me about that, too."

"Man gets my age, he wants to stop somewhere," he said.

"I don't think Eddie appreciates just how bad you want to stop." She straightened a little, taking a deep breath. "So you think this is going to be El Paso all over again."

"El Paso, Dallas, Santa Fe, a dozen other places," he answered. "It's always the same. It's started just as innocently so many times before. There's something bad between King and your father. Eddie puts himself right between them by going after you. In a little while it gets ugly. We're fighting half the men in the basin. If we don't get killed for it, we lose our chances for the Doubloon anyway. . . ."

He broke off, realizing how much of the bitterness and defeat of the past years he had let out, embarrassed by having revealed himself so much, withdrawing from the mixture of pity and puzzlement on her face.

"You make it sound bad," she said.

"Hasn't it started already?" he asked resignedly.

She looked at the wound on his face. "Do you think King had them do that simply because of me?"

"Don't tell me you're not aware of how he feels about you."

A pout swelled her underlip. "I'm aware."

But her question had put something in his mind. "Why else would he do it?" Morgan asked. It brought her eyes intently to his own, and he sensed something closing off in her. "Janice told me about Yellowstone," he said. "Is the trouble over there connected with what lies between Charlie King and your father?"

"No." She shook her head. "What's between Charlie and Dad goes back a long way. I don't think it's connected with Yellowstone. But it doesn't help things any." She tossed her head suddenly. "How did we get off on all this? While we're sitting here, your brother's probably getting hurt."

He felt himself lift in the saddle. "Is that why you were looking for me?"

"I wouldn't have come this far if I didn't think it was serious," she said. "He's already had a fight. Two of the men were trying to help him pick out his saddle string. They told him his Texas bronc' wouldn't be any good in these hills. You know how Eddie would react to that."

"Too well."

"He flared up. It started a scuffle. Eddie hurt Tony Raines so he won't be able to work for a week. It turned the whole bunkhouse against your brother. I guess he was only defending himself, but the men still hold it against him. There's something brewing now that's ugly."

Morgan shook his head. "I couldn't get him away from there

now with a team of mules. It would look like he was backing out. He just couldn't take that."

"At least you can try," she said. "You just can't sit back and let it happen."

He met her eyes. "See what I mean?"

Compassion softened the curve of her cheek. "I guess I do, Morgan. Doesn't seem like you can get away from it anywhere, does it?"

He sighed heavily. "Let's go."

She wheeled around past him and he turned to follow, lifting his horse to a canter immediately. The pied bronco was tired, however, and he soon had to break the pace. They reached the fork and turned off past the sign with the keyhole branded on it. Nora pushed the pace to a canter again.

It was all yellow moonlight and velvet shadows to him. No matter where he looked, he was always conscious of the sullen presence of the mountains on his left flank, the rock faces black and somber against the night, the snowfields flashing vagrantly beneath the moon.

He had a poor measurement of the time it took them to reach the ranch. At last the road curled around into a valley that wedged itself back between a pair of spur ridges, and a snake fence began to run with them. They came to a gate in the fence, through which the road led, with the rectangles of lighted windows gleaming softly from ahead.

Nora pulled up before they reached the main house, pointing toward the first cluster of windows. "That's the bunkhouse." She squared herself in the saddle, lips parted expectantly, watching his face. He peered toward the building. Light from the half-open door fanned out across the flanks of two horses stamping fretfully at the corner of the log building. There was the sudden lift of voices from the bunkhouse, and one broke through clearly.

"Damn you, kid, I got a right to see your cards. . . ."

"I bluffed you out, Nations. Why should you see my cards?"

"That's Eddie," Morgan said. "Sounds like there's trouble already."

He booted his horse across the compound, almost ramming a snubbing post in the dark. He cut around it and swung off near the door, dropping the reins. He took those last long strides with the whole scene playing itself out before he reached the door.

Morgan had met the crew when he delivered the trail herd, so he knew all the men. Eddie sat with his back to the side wall, facing across the table to Shyrock, whose shaggy-peaked brows and a red spade beard gave his gaunt face a devilish cast. To Eddie's left was Jinglebob, the immense cook. Beside him sat Drift, the foreman, his eyes still sullen and bloodshot with drink. The fifth one was Nations, a knife-bladed man from Oklahoma Territory, sitting with his back to the door. Tony Raines lay up on one elbow in a bunk, his face still bruised from Eddie's fists, a dirty bandage around his head.

Nations had just reached out one hand to cover the cards Eddie had put face down on the table. But Eddie had grabbed his fingers, pinning them. They were facing each other in that static pose, with cigarette smoke turning to blue haze around the overhead light.

"Make him show his openers," Raines said vindictively.

"Nations quit," Eddie said. "What difference does it make what cards I held?"

"Maybe it was five aces." Jinglebob chuckled.

Eddie's face snapped angrily toward the cook. It took the boy's attention off Nations for that instant. Nations jerked the cards from beneath Eddie's hand. The boy wheeled back and came halfway up from his chair to grab Nations by the front of his shirt and pull him out of his chair and hit him in the face. It spun Nations around to stagger across the room and slam against the wall. Eddie followed him and caught him there, doubling him over with a blow to the belly. Morgan went through the door as Drift shoved his chair back and leaped right over the table at Eddie.

Eddie wheeled away from Nations to meet Drift, who was coming down off the table onto him. At the same time, Jinglebob swept both hands underneath the table and heaved it over into Morgan.

Morgan tried to dodge in that last instant, but the uptilting top smashed its whole surface into him, carrying him heavily back. As he fell, he saw Drift's dive smash Eddie against Nations, who still hung against the wall, incapacitated by Eddie's second blow. But Eddie got his feet beneath him again. He thrust Drift away from him and went with the man as Drift staggered backward.

Morgan was scrambling from beneath the round deal table now. He saw Drift trip and go down, pulling Eddie with him. Eddie tried to rise on hands and knees and smash at the foreman's face. But Jinglebob had jumped up from his chair, and he gave the kid a vicious boot in the rear. It knocked Eddie flat across Drift.

Then Shyrock came from the other side with Drift's chair above his head. As Eddie tried to rise again, Shyrock brought it down on his head.

"Hit him again, Shy!" Raines shouted. "Hit him again . . . !"

The chair had smashed with the blow, and Shyrock tore its pieces away till he was left with one leg. Jinglebob saw Morgan coming in and tried to jump around the men on the floor and block him off. But Morgan threw his whole body into Shyrock as the man was bending over to strike Eddie with that heavy chair leg. The red-bearded man staggered helplessly a couple of steps. Then the sideboards of Tony Raines's bunk caught him knee high and pitched him in on the man.

"I got him, Shyrock!" shouted Jinglebob.

Fighting to free himself from Shyrock's kicking legs, Morgan spun away from Jinglebob's rush. The great tub of a man could not stop himself and went into the bunk post with a shocking crash of wood. His false teeth popped from his mouth and he went slack and slid down the post as limply as jelly. At the same time, Shyrock lunged out of the bunk. Morgan tried to wheel back and meet him. The man's lowered head butted him in the belly, knocking him helplessly backward.

Drift and Eddie were still grappling on the floor. Morgan tripped over them and fell into the smashed table. It slid backward beneath him till its top struck the wall in a slanting position. He saw Shyrock jumping over Drift and Eddie toward him. He rolled off the table and came up to meet the red-bearded man. Shyrock was coming too fast to stop soon enough. He flailed one blow at Morgan and Morgan blocked it and hit him in the belly. Shyrock's own momentum folded him over Morgan's fist. While he was still bent double, Morgan caught him by the belt and heaved him, headfirst, into the wall. Shyrock emitted a stunned grunt and sank to the floor.

Morgan wheeled to see that Drift had rolled over on top of Eddie and was up on his knees, battering at the kid's face. Morgan lunged across the room, tripping in the wreckage, and caught one of the foreman's arms. Drift released Eddie's hair with his other hand and twisted into Morgan suddenly. It took Morgan off balance. He could not help staggering backward. He still held Drift's arm twisted upward and the man had to go with him. They reeled across the room to smash against the wall. Drift's head was buried in Morgan's belly. Before Drift could pull back, Morgan caught him with a rabbit punch.

Drift jerked down, tried to tear his arm free. Morgan twisted it back, holding the man against him with the leverage. Then he

100

hit Drift behind the neck again. Drift grunted sickly. Morgan struck again, shooting his wad. Drift sagged heavily into him, fighting no longer. Morgan released him and the foreman slid down his legs to crouch helplessly on the floor, making small animal sounds of pain.

Only now did Morgan realize how violent it had been. He found that he could not move away from the wall. His ribs ached for breath. He sought more air, gasping like a fish out of water, but it seemed his lungs could hold no more. His legs were like rubber beneath him and his clothes were soaked with sweat. He knew if he left the support of the wall he would go down.

Nations was trying to get up from where he sat against the wall farther down. Morgan turned toward the man, wondering if he had enough left in him to meet it. The movement stopped Nations. He sat back against the logs, a pinched sickness on his sharp face as he held his belly. His black sloe eyes traveled away from Morgan and around the wreckage of the room. Jinglebob was still out cold at the foot of the bunk. Shyrock was huddled against the wall, holding both arms around his head and groaning. Drift was still on hands and knees at Morgan's feet, shaking his head slowly from side to side.

"I saw a twister hit a town once in the territory," Nations said at last. "Looked just like this when it was over."

"You don't want any more?" Morgan said feebly.

Nations licked his lips. "Not tonight, Texas."

"Then get this," Morgan said thickly. His voice gained strength and he was speaking to the whole room. "When you take on a Banning, you're not taking on one man. There's always two of us. Just remember that. There's always two of us."

IV

There was a water trough at the side of the shack. Morgan and Nora helped Eddie around there to wash off some of the blood. Nora rolled the boy's sleeves back, pulling splinters from his hand. Sick and drained from the fight, it was all Morgan could do to dump half a pail of water over Eddie's head. The boy spluttered lustily with the amazing recuperative powers of youth, splashing water like a playful pup. He came up for air, grinning at Morgan.

"That was silver-plated," he said. "We ought to do it every Saturday night."

Morgan had noticed a dim figure hurrying down from the barn. It finally emerged into light from the open bunkhouse door, a short, bowlegged little bantam wearing a plug hat and flowered suspenders.

"What happened?" he said. "Sounded like me old man on Saturday night."

"You missed a fight, O'Toole," Nora said.

O'Toole's greasy-jowled face mirrored profound disappointment. He rammed horny thumbs through his suspenders, snapping them disgustedly against his chest.

"Why do I always have to be somewhere else when there's a fight?" he said.

Jinglebob came out of the bunkhouse door, squinting his eyes like a man with a hangover. He held the broken pieces of his false teeth in one fat hand.

"Look at that now," he mourned. "You've busted them all up. I can't get any more, either. I'll poison your food, that's what I'll do. I'll put arsenic in the huckydummy."

A lantern was being carried down from the big house now, its ruddy light flaring upward over the full bosom of Janice Wickliffe and glinting in the gold of her hair. With her was Harvey

Oakland, his starched shirt front shining like a patch of snow in the darkness.

"Eddie got into a fight with the crew," Nora told them. "Morgan had to pull him out."

Shyrock lurched out the door and leaned against the building, rubbing his shaggy red head. "Damn' bees still buzzing in there," he grunted. He squinted painfully at Morgan. "I won't forget that, Banning. My head's going to be sore a year. That's a long time to remember."

Morgan met the man's angry eyes for a moment without speaking, then turned to Eddie. "You ready to light a shuck?"

Eddie looked surprised. "Where to? I signed on here. I'm not backing out just over a little fight."

"The boy's right," Oakland said. "Make him look yellow if you asked him to quit now. You don't want to tamper with a man's self-respect that way. Why don't you sign on, too, Morgan?"

Before Morgan answered, Drift came out, holding the back of his neck. The lantern light turned the mottled scars of his cheeks chalk-white. Oakland bent toward him, peering at his bloodshot eyes.

"Where were you this afternoon?"

"In town."

"Drinking?"

"That's my business."

"Not if you do it on my time, Drift," Oakland said. "I thought we talked that over."

Drift's eyes dropped to the ground. His massive shoulders seemed to bunch up beneath his shirt, and he did not answer. Oakland finally turned back to Morgan, the humor gone from his face. "It's all settled then," he said. "You're staying."

"If he stays, I go," the foreman said.

"Now, Drift," Janice told him chidingly, "you're a bigger man than that."

Drift's eyes ran to hers for a moment, all the sullen hostility drained from them by some strange expression. That maternal smile was on Janice's face, filled with the same indulgence she had shown Morgan, as if she were treating with a little boy. Only there was something more, something that made her eyes luminous and her lips part faintly. Finally Drift looked at the ground again, rubbing the base of his neck.

"All right," he told Oakland grudgingly. "It's your outfit."

He turned back into the bunkhouse, and they could hear him kick a piece of furniture out of the way. Oakland forced a chuckle.

"Janice is the only one who can do anything with that foreman of mine."

Nora was smiling at Morgan. "Looks like you're trapped, Morgan. It's obvious Eddie can't be dragged away. And if you don't stay with him, he's going to get into trouble again."

Morgan was watching the expression in Eddie's eyes, as the kid looked at Nora. It was the same look he had seen the boy settle on a dozen girls along their back trail. It had lasted a week, a month, and then faded out. The same thing would happen here. If Morgan could only ride it out, Eddie would be willing to leave as soon as he lost interest.

"I guess you're right, Oakland," Morgan said. "If it won't eat Drift too much, I'll sign on."

Oakland chuckled heartily, coming over to clap him on the back. "Turn your horse into that pen up by the barn. I'll see you in the morning and help you get squared away."

Janice turned away with Oakland. Nora was not so quick to move. She watched Morgan as he went for his horse. He felt her eyes on him till he was around the corner of the bunkhouse and out of sight. It cost him a great effort to drag himself aboard the horse.

When he walked Pie back around the corner, Nora and Eddie were already heading toward the big house together. Morgan rode up to the barn, unsaddled in the dark, turned Pie into the pen. All the time he was working, he was aware of Eddie and Nora on the porch of the big house. Their voices came to him as soft murmuring and several times the tintinnabulation of Nora's laughter reached through the quiet night, and once he heard Eddie whistle and say: "Silver-plated."

He found himself filled with the same sour irritation he had known when he was watching Nora and Eddie through the café window. Why should that be? She was just another girl. He had seen this happen with a dozen girls. She was just another one.

In that bleak mood he went back to the bunkhouse. Tony Raines was still up on an elbow in his bunk, and his eyes met Morgan vindictively at the door. Shyrock had rolled in and was already snoring.

Drift and Nations and O'Toole were finishing the game of cards. They had knocked the table back together again, propping a spare chair under it in place of the broken legs. Both Drift and Nations turned baleful eyes at Morgan as he entered.

Jinglebob sat on his bunk, dolefully trying to fit his broken dentures together. "Look at that," he said. "I'll poison your splatter-dabs, that's what I'll do."

Morgan found a bunk unoccupied by gear and dropped his blanket roll and war bag into it. Then he sat down heavily, aching all over from the fight.

"I'm out," O'Toole said, putting his cards down.

Morgan fished for the makings and absently began rolling himself a cigarette. He felt O'Toole's eyes on him, and looked up at the man.

"One-handed," O'Toole said. "Even my old man couldn't do that."

An utter silence had dropped into the room. O'Toole suddenly became aware of all the other men glaring at him. He looked around defensively.

"What the hell. I was just watching."

Morgan lay back with one arm under his head, smoking and staring at the ceiling. He finished his cigarette and ground it out. Then he must have dozed. The next thing he knew a wild shout was raising him violently in the bunk. He blinked across the room to see Shyrock sitting up in his bunk, too, eyes wide and blank.

"I don't work for the Chinese navy!" he yelled. He jumped out of his bunk, staring right through the men at the table. "I never had anything to do with the Chinese navy!"

"Git the water!" O'Toole shouted. "It's the only thing that'll bring him out of it."

Jinglebob jumped up from the table and ran outside. Shyrock had begun to grope his way toward the door. O'Toole grabbed him and started slapping his face.

"Wake up, you cod," he snapped.

"Chinese navy!" Shyrock shouted, trying to tear free. "I never worked for the Chinese navy . . . !"

"Drift, help me hold him!" O'Toole yelled. "He almost broke his neck the last time he got out there in the compound."

Drift was out of his chair now, trying to help O'Toole with Shyrock. Even his great strength was taxed to keep the redhead from getting loose. Nations joined them, and it was all a wild shouting whirl of arms and legs till Jinglebob burst back through the door with a pail of water. He threw it in Shyrock's face, and the struggle stopped abruptly.

The men let their hands slide off Shyrock, as he stood there, blinking stupidly about him. Finally his eyes gained focus, and understanding filled his gaunt face. He shook his head angrily, shaking water off like a puppy. "Can't get one good night's sleep," he said. "Gotta drag me out in the middle of the floor to play their little jokes. . . ."

"You was having nightmares again," Jinglebob said.

"I never have nightmares. Just gotta rawhide a man!"

"You was working for the Chinese navy again."

"I never had anything to do with the Chinese navy. I never even heard of it. Someday you're gonna go too far with this."

He stamped sourly back to his bunk and started unbuttoning his soaked underwear. All of them were laughing now. Even Drift could not help grinning. It peeled his lips back off broken teeth in a grudging way. It was as if all the hostility had been wiped away by this.

Morgan began undressing, too, the tension suddenly gone from him. He slipped into his blankets and stretched out. The wind skittered gravel against the walls of the building outside and clattered a loose shake on the roof. It was the last thing he heard.

There was the acrid tang of wood smoke in the air when Morgan awoke next morning, and the *rattle* of pots and pans mingling with the *sizzle* of bacon that came from the cook house. The men were rolling out, grumbling and tousled, to haul on boots and Levi's. Jinglebob was *clanging* the triangle outside and shouting the breakfast call.

By the time Morgan had finished dressing, the others were gone, and he was alone in the room. As he rose to go, Oakland stepped in through the door, grinning at Morgan. He eased himself down into one of the chairs, taking his weight off his boots with a grateful sigh.

"Won't keep you a minute," he said. "A government inspector has been up looking over them feeders for tick fever and

107

such. I'm going back into Chinook with him this morning. I thought I'd better tell you what's up before I leave."

"I thought the herd was given a clean bill of health at Cheyenne," Morgan said.

"They're just double-checking. You know how scared they are of tick fever. It'd hit this valley worse than an ordinary country. We're so closed off here it'd just about wipe all of us out to find that in the herds." Oakland looked up with a grin. "But there ain't no danger of that. With the herd cleared, I want you to get them up to summer pasture. You can start as soon as you pick your saddle string." He got to his feet, giving a comfortable belch, and rubbed his full stomach. "I hope Jinglebob's hucky-dummy is as good as Janice's cakes. Get to it, Morgan."

After breakfast, Drift took Morgan and Eddie out to the corrals to pick their saddle string. Morgan had seen how his pied bronco played out in the high country yesterday, and knew he would have to give it up sooner or later for the mountain-bred animals if he stayed here. They found O'Toole sitting on the top rail of a pen, watching the wrangler haze some horses in. He pointed to a buckskin.

"That line-back is a good animal for you, Morgan. I just busted him a couple of months ago."

"I never knew a bronc' buster that wore a plug hat." Morgan grinned.

"I never knew a Texan that rolled a cigarette with one hand," O'Toole said. He pulled a piece of rock from his pocket. "I'll let you kiss this if you teach me how. It's a bit o' the Blarney Stone. It'll give you the devil's own luck."

"Haven't got time today." Morgan chuckled. "Let's get to the horses."

The buckskin was shedding its winter coat, and looked pretty ratty, but Drift pointed to the heavy mountain muscles in its broad chest and solid flanks. Morgan was surprised how much vinegar it showed under saddle. It had a beautiful mount that responded to the slightest touch and it could turn on a dime despite its bulk. Pleased with the animal, he lashed his war bag and bedroll on behind the cantle, and then roped out two other animals, which O'Toole suggested, for spares. Eddie showed up still forking his Texas bronco and leading a mare and a gelding.

"You ain't giving Pie up for that pudding foot," he said.

"I had a chance to try Pie in the hills," Morgan said. "You better trade that bronc' of yours for a mountain horse."

"I'd sooner give up my pants than Hell Kitty."

Morgan shook his head ruefully at the boy, and they lined out for the herd. The cattle had been scattered out at the head of the valley, and, while Morgan and Eddie were picking their horses, the rest of the crew had been collecting the herd for the drive.

It was a scene Morgan had known from the beginning of his life, the dusty ranks of cattle spread out across a sage-covered plain with their white faces bobbing like puffs of snow in the darker mass of their packed bodies, and the dust beginning to rise about them like smoke from a fire. Shyrock was to go with them, and was waiting with his spares and a pack horse upon which were loaded their supplies. They put Eddie in the drag with the cavvy of spare animals, while Morgan took the swing, and Shyrock the lead. The rest of the crew helped them haze the herd as far as the mouth of the cañon.

As they passed within sight of the house, Nora rode out to say good bye. She met up with Eddie first, and Morgan could see the kid grinning and making flamboyant gestures. She did not seem to react with her usual humor. When she finally left Eddie and rode up to Morgan, he was surprised at the dark expression of her face.

"Sorry to see the kid go?" Morgan asked.

The dust made her clear her throat. "It won't be for long. Cold weather'll hit pretty soon." She was silent, watching him from eyes that were big and solemn as a child's. "You know where you're going, Morgan?"

"Drift called it Crazy Horse Ridge. He said you ran your stuff into the high country every summer."

She leaned toward him. "Morgan, you'll be careful, won't you?"

He frowned at her. "You want us to be careful in general, or on Crazy Horse Ridge in particular?"

Her eyes grew dark. "The line shack's not actually on Crazy Horse Ridge. It's about a thousand feet below it, on this side. If you climb to the ridge, you'll find you're at the top of the Absarokas. Yellowstone is on the other side."

"I see," he said darkly. For a moment he rode silently, lost in his own speculation. Then he made an attempt at smiling. "Don't worry. I'll bring Eddie back safe."

She leaned farther toward him, putting her hand over his on the saddle horn. The satiny pressure sent a sharp leap of pulse through him.

"I'm not talking about Eddie now," she said. "I'm talking about you."

He could not deny how deeply she stirred him. He had tried to think of her as just another of Eddie's conquests. Now he knew how wrong he had been. He stared at the soft contours of her face, trying to read what lay there.

"Eddie's the one the girls always go for," he said.

"Is he?" she asked softly.

She met his eyes with her quiet search for another moment. Then she took her hand off his and heeled her bay around to drop behind, still watching him. There were many things mingled in her face, and he could not separate or define any one of them, but he knew the expression would remain with him a long time.

By afternoon they had left the valley and had risen into a pass that would take them through the first ridges toward the high country beyond. For a short drive like this, they did not need as big a crew as Morgan had commanded on the trail north, but there was still enough work to keep them busy.

Before evening they reached the crest of the pass and came into sight of the Absarokas. Now it was the great rock-ribbed titans rising like jagged teeth against the sky with their glaciers and snowfields gleaming marble-white in the sun and the timber on their lower slopes so dark it looked black from a distance. Now it was the rock-littered meadows and grassy parks sweeping upward from the valleys and the streams brawling down over boulders smoothed by the ages. Now it was the *clatter* of dancing hoofs in shale as a horse fought to keep upright down a steep slope, or the sound of a dogie calling for its mammy in thick timber, or Shyrock dropping back to borrow a smoke and pointing at a star-shaped cluster of purple flowers in a crevice of granite on the hillside.

"That there's monkshood. Keep the cattle away from it or you'll have a sick herd."

And now it was night camp at a creek in the mouth of a rocky cañon where beaver dams had transformed the descending water into a series of small lakes that glittered shiny as steps of glass in the light of a rising moon. The soft splash of miniature falls dropping over each succeeding dam never ceased. It formed a subdued undertone to the cattle sounds out in the meadows and filled the night with peace.

After the meal, Morgan built himself a smoke and sat with his back to a tree, staring off across the meadow at the Absarokas in the distance. Eddie had first shift as night hawk and was throwing his silver-plated saddle on one of his spare animals.

"What's got into you, Morg?" he said. "You ain't said a word since supper. Just sit there and stare off like a man saw a pretty gal."

Shyrock rolled to one side where he lay in his sougan, head pillowed on his saddle. "Country's got him, kid. I've seen it eating at him ever since he hit Chinook Basin. Make you sad, Morgan?"

Morgan glanced sharply at the man, remembering the tenuous sense of sadness he had known on his ride into the mountains to see the Doubloon. As he stared into Shyrock's eyes, a rapport seemed to grow between them. It was as if the antipathy was swept away. It was as if they had been touched by a common truth that let them see the world from the same eyes. Shyrock seemed to feel it, too. His features had lost their Satanic sharpness.

"It's a sad country," he said. "You know that when you hear the wind in the trees. Sometimes it's like a gal crying. Sometimes it's like a lost something, you don't know what, only the sound it makes ain't from this world. It makes you afraid of things you never saw."

Morgan frowned intensely, trying to identify his own reaction. "I don't know. It made me feel sad. But not quite like that. It made me feel nearer to the country. Almost like I belonged."

"Then it's got you, Morgan," Shyrock said. "Them that don't belong, they don't feel it. Them that do, they'll never be happy any place else."

"What's got into you yaks?" Eddie said. "One country's as good as the next. Only thing different is the gals."

He swung up on his horse and turned it out toward the browsing cattle. Before the *tinkle* of his bit chains died, he began to croon. He was tone deaf and had no tempo and the husky off-key melody only lent accent to the mournful sound of the chant.

My pa he drowned in the Pecos,
My ma's at the Pearly Gates,
My brother got killed in a big stampede. . . .

Shyrock stirred restlessly in his blankets, staring out at the drifting sound of the boy's voice. "Kid sings a sad song. Don't know what it is to be sad."

Morgan did not answer, and Shyrock looked at him. The devilish expression was back in the redhead's face. That rapport had gone from between them. Firelight gleamed on the peaks of Shyrock's cheek bones till they were sharp as arrowheads.

"Head still sore, Shyrock?"

"Be sore a year, Banning. I told you. That's a long time to remember." The man stared enigmatically at Morgan for another moment, then pulled his blankets up over him and turned the other way. Morgan slipped into his own blankets. The fire died to a dim red glow. The sound of falling water seemed to grow louder in his ears. Somewhere off a wolf began to howl.

It took them two more days to reach the line cabin, climbing through the pass with the patches of snow beside the trail growing larger and the air becoming thinner and colder at night. It was near evening of the third day that they rose out of the pass into a park of blue root that swept up against the very backbone of the mountains. There was a great cliff, shaped like one side of a bowl, and the cabin was set back in its shelter. They left the cattle to scatter through the meadows while they turned their horses into the pole corral and clumped their duffel in the bunk room.

It was full night by the time they had fixed dinner and eaten. It was full night, and the wolf had begun howling again. Morgan asked the redhead about it.

"Still sounds like he's in higher country," Shyrock said.

"Won't bother the cattle none unless he drops down." He walked to the door and opened it for a moment, staring out into the night. A gaunt expression filled his face. "See what I mean?" he said at last.

"Lonesome," Morgan murmured.

"Sad," Shyrock said. "That ain't a wolf crying. Somebody died a long time ago up there. They're lost. They can't go on and they can't get back. It makes you afraid to die sometimes."

"You're as bad as an Indian," Eddie grumbled. "Let's have a little game of draw."

They drew up chairs and Eddie got a pack of greasy cards from his war bag. They cut for high card and Shyrock drew it. He shuffled and let Eddie cut, and then dealt. Morgan picked up his hand and leaned back in the chair, studying his cards.

"That time Drift and Laramie went into Yellowstone. Did they start from here?"

Morgan saw the cards bend suddenly between Shyrock's fingers. "Why bring that up?" the man asked sharply.

"Laramie got killed and Drift lost his horse and barely made it back alive," Morgan said. "Janice told me it was two years ago. Was Drift a drinking man before it happened?"

"What's that got to do with it?" Shyrock was growing belligerent.

"If he wasn't a drinking man before, and became one after, something must have happened over in Yellowstone to change him. Wouldn't you say?"

Shyrock dropped his eyes gloomily to his cards. "I wish that wolf would stop howling."

"Must have been something pretty bad to make a man take to drink."

"Damn you, Morgan." Shyrock slapped his cards down and skidded his chair back, getting up angrily. "If you're going to ride that kak all night, I'm hitting my sougan."

Eddie disgustedly put down three aces. "Now, Morg, why did you have to go and spoil things when I had a silver-plated hand like that?"

Shyrock sat down on the bunk and tugged off a boot. It made a heavy *thump* against the puncheon floor. Then he sat there, looking morosely at the door.

"I wish that wolf would stop howling."

V

After breakfast next morning they rode southward along a high line to see how the cattle were drifting. For several miles they clung to a trail that followed the shoulder of the mountain, with Crazy Horse Ridge paralleling them a thousand feet above. Shyrock rode in the lead, gaunt and hunched in the saddle, spitting grit whenever they crossed an open space.

"Damn that wind. Think it'd get tired sometime. I been up here twenty years and I never seen it stop blowing."

Eddie rode behind, the silver mounting on his saddle glittering in a strong sun, the brim of his Stetson rattling against his grinning face. Now and then the wind swept snatches of his song up to Morgan.

> *My brother got killed in a big stampede,*
> *Now I've drawed aces and eights. . . .*

They sought a sheltered basin in which to eat lunch, and then pushed on south, till the trail began dropping off into a pass that cut through the backbone of the mountain. Finally Shyrock pointed to some tracks in soft ground.

"There's the wolf. I told you he was high. Looks like a big boy."

"You got cattle sign just above him," Morgan said.

Shyrock's glance snapped higher to where the sharp imprint

of hoofs indented soft earth near a mossy boulder. It looked like a dozen or more head, including a couple of cows and their calves, heading toward the pass. Shyrock sent Morgan one dark glance and gigged his horse, following the tracks. The pass ran east and west here, rising swiftly to the saddle it formed through Crazy Horse Ridge. Shyrock pushed to the top, and then halted.

The pass funneled the wind into a howling malignance. It boomed down through the rocky defile and tore at them with frantic hands. The horses stood with their tails frayed across their rumps and their ears flat against their heads. Morgan was hardly aware of its brutal force. He was taking his first look at Yellowstone. The mountains seemed to drop away from his very feet, falling off into a series of gigantic broken rock faces where nothing grew but a few twisted junipers. It seemed a thousand feet down before a high transverse pass caught up some of the tumbling steps. But it only held them temporarily. Beyond its trough the mountains began to roll off once more, crouching beneath the sky like stooped old men, hoary and ancient in their cloaks of pine and fir. The mass of trees was broken here and there by sweeping meadows or mountain parks, their rich grasses turning them to jade pools in the dark sea of timber. And finally pass and meadow and timber and rock face lost their identity in the tawny haze that covered the floor of the great valley twenty miles away. More mountains rose from the haze on the other side of the valley, like shadowy reflections of the peaks on this side, etching a sullen barricade against the sun-bleached blue of the farther sky. Eddie was staring off into the vast distance, too, and for the first time Morgan saw some of his own awe in the boy's face.

Morgan realized that Shyrock was not looking at the vastness beyond. He was staring at the tracks at their feet. His features seemed to have shed their sharp diabolism. All the doubts and apprehensions and fears that lay beneath every man's surface had risen up to muddy his cheeks, shuttling like shadows across the oblique planes of his face.

"Damn that wolf," he said at last.

"Looks like he pushed the cattle right on down this side," Morgan said. He glanced at the blue root siding the rocky bottom. "That grass usually straightens up in a few hours if it isn't mashed bad. It's still bent a little. That could mean they didn't pass here too long ago."

"Then we might catch them before they hit the bottom of that first valley," Eddie said.

Shyrock shook his head. "Wolf's probably pulling them down now."

"He won't pull down more than one," Eddie protested. "What do you say, Morg?"

Morgan was suddenly filled with the helpless feeling of some inevitable pattern drawing its web tightly about him. He stared westward into Yellowstone, the bottom of its valleys hidden in that mysterious haze, and he was remembering Janice's story of the men who had died over there. He realized he wouldn't be here now but for Eddie's interest in Nora. It was the same old story, and he was getting dragged deeper and deeper into it by the same insidious channels. For a moment he was filled with the nagging need to turn back now, to escape it while there was still time, before another dream was smashed. But he knew he couldn't. He had signed on with Oakland and committed himself to this. He spoke with a heavy reluctance.

"That bunch is worth about four hundred dollars to Oakland. We can't let him lose that much."

Shyrock met his gaze sharply. "Do you know what you're saying? That's Yellowstone country."

Morgan's brows raised in faint inquisition. "What would Oakland say, Shyrock?"

"I don't care." Shyrock shook his head. "I ain't going."

"Down where we come from, a man who won't go to hell for his own brand ain't worth a busted latigo," Eddie told him.

"Talk away," Shyrock said. "I ain't going."

"We'll meet you back at the line shack, then," Morgan said, and heeled his horse on through the pass.

Eddie followed him, huddling against the wind. They had not gone a hundred feet before Shyrock gave his horse a vicious boot and galloped after them. When he came up with them, he shouted against the wind.

"Damn both of you and that wolf!"

One edge of Morgan's mouth curled into his droll smile. Eddie threw back his head and laughed outright. Scowling darkly, Shyrock ran on ahead till he was in the lead, and then pulled up. They were starting to drop down the western slope of Crazy Horse Ridge now.

They were still above timber line, however, at the alpine level where nothing but sedge and mosses could grow and the snow never melted and the ice filled gorges and hollows with glittering alabaster that lasted the year around. Over slide rock and talus the spiny red currant and the dwarfed raspberry struggled up toward summits they would never reach before winter. The wind was never still, howling like a ricochet across bleak rock faces, whipping loose shale against men and horses in stinging blasts.

A mountain sheep appeared on a ledge high above them, aloof and apart, staring at the men with the distant gaze of some god supreme in his domain. With a toss of great curving horns it wheeled and leaped out of sight. The poor footing and prolonged strain of the steep incline showed up in Eddie's bronco first. Already blown from the climb on the other side, it began to shy and balk, legs trembling visibly. Finally mats of willow began to appear in moisture-retaining basins and then stands of stunted juniper were filling the gullies beneath rocky ridges and shedding their alligator bark into flaky heaps that were soon swept away by the wind. At last the men reached timber line and dipped into cool shadows fragrant with the scent of pine needles that had fallen through uncounted ages to pile up in a tawny mat underfoot. Eddie's bronco was shiny with sweat and blowing heavily and stumbling on uncertain footing by now.

"If it plays out that bad downhill, what's it going to do when we have to climb?" Shyrock asked.

"Hell Kitty'll climb any hill that crowbait of yours will," Eddie said angrily.

The cattle had drifted more slowly here than above, for there was more browse to be had, and apparently the wolf had not begun to press them yet. The trail was not hard to follow—the edges of a meadow cropped over, strips of bark chewed off aspen to let the under wood gleam out, sticky and white. Shyrock didn't spend much time on those signs. His head kept twisting and turning as if he were trying to keep every bit of the country in sight. A horse sensed any undue tension in its rider, and the animals were beginning to shy at the sudden appearance of fireweed on the trail, or spooking at the *crackle* of a pine cone underfoot. Now a strange scent began mingling with the ordinary smells of the pine forest. Morgan could not place it at first. Eddie began sniffing the air.

"Somebody's used up all his matches," he said.

"Sulphur pools to the north of us," Shyrock told him. "I never seen them. Wind comes right, you can smell them for miles."

It grew stronger as they descended. The horses began snorting disgustedly at it. The air seemed to thicken as they dropped down, too, and Morgan noticed that the buttery haze filling the valley to the south had taken on a glowing tint.

"We got forest fires, too?" he asked.

Shyrock's voice sounded thin and tight. "Sometimes it dries up so much during the hot spells half a dozen fires break out at once in different places. You're in a helluva country, Morgan. You'll wish you'd never come."

All the way down, the pass had twisted and curled its way between a pair of spur ridges that ran away from the main body of the mountains. Now, with the big valley in sight below, the tracks of the cattle turned abruptly up the slope of the north ridge, climbing steeply toward its top. The animals seemed to have been bunched up and Morgan guessed the wolf was pressing closer, hoping to pull down one of the tired calves.

Shyrock and Morgan lunged their horses at last onto the exposed top of the ridge and halted, waiting for Eddie to join them. They found themselves looking down into the next cañon. This was shallower than the pass they had left, and its bottom was taken up by a plunging mountain stream whose waters filled the gorge with constant crashing echoes.

Shyrock gave Eddie's bronco a disgusted glance as it labored onto the rocky ridge and halted hipshot and trembling. "They're heading for that water," Shyrock told Eddie. "You'd better stay here."

"Damn you," the boy said, and spurred Hell Kitty off the ridge. The bronco slid down talus and caught its balance at the edge of a dense stand of pine. The shadows swallowed Eddie hungrily. Shyrock followed, and they closed softly over him, blotting him from Morgan's sight. Morgan knew a tugging little impulse to keep from following, filled with a vague reluctance to enter the darkness ahead. He had to force himself to slide his buckskin down the talus and into the trees. Pine cones sent up their sardonic crackling from beneath the horse's hoofs and the two-toned cry of a curlew broke lonesomely through the hollow brawl of the water for a moment and was drowned once more. Fifty yards on, sunlight poured like molten gold over Eddie as he broke from the trees and brought his horse up sharply.

Morgan and Shyrock caught up with him to find themselves on the edge of a drop-off. The slopes steepened to veritable cliffs on both sides, a hundred feet above the stream. The only way down was by one of the gullies that erosion had cut through the softer strata. The cattle had taken to one of these cuts, and the three riders followed their trail, slipping and sliding single file down the narrow notch to the sandy beach below. Shimmering white aspen lined the shore and the cutbank was crumbled off into water for a distance of a hundred yards along the stream where the cattle had drunk. Shyrock held his fiddling horse here, staring darkly at the boulders studding the bottom and tearing the shallow water to feathery furrows as it poured over them.

"Ain't letting a few rocks spook you," Eddie said, and put his horse into the water. Morgan followed him. The buckskin was just sliding down the crumbling cutbank into icy water when a picket-pin squirrel dropped off an aspen and ran, chattering, across the narrow beach. The buckskin reared and spun, almost pitching Morgan. It was probably what saved his life.

The *crash* of a rifle slammed against his ears while the buckskin was still in the air. From the tail of his eye he saw sand kicked up to his left, and knew the bullet must have passed through the space he had occupied an instant before.

Now the animal was really spooked. He slacked the reins and beat against its neck with a fist, raking the flanks with his rowels at the same time. The buckskin came on its forehoofs so hard Morgan almost went over the horn. Then it took off across the water. Eddie was fighting his excited bronco in midstream.

"Don't pull up on those reins, kid!" bawled Morgan. "Slack off and give him the spurs!"

There was another shot as Eddie slacked his reins. The high scream of a ricochet filled the air as the bullet caromed off a streambed rock. A horse added its shrill whinny to the metallic howl of the bullet. The hoofs of Morgan's buckskin mingled with the din, crackling across the ledge rock and boulders on the bottom. Then it was lunging up the crumbling bank.

Morgan saw Shyrock angle off through the shallows for the mouth of a gully below the steep bank. He had the impulse to veer that way, but a bullet kicked up sand to his left, turning the buckskin back. Eddie was already charging up the steep shale slope toward the topknot of timber above. The impetus of the run across the beach sent the buckskin leaping up the incline for a pair of spasmodic lunges. Then it had to start fighting for every step. The churning hind legs of Eddie's bronco kicked a rain of dirt and rocks into Morgan's face. Half blinded, Morgan heard the *crack* of another shot. Shyrock shouted from somewhere behind. When Morgan looked, he couldn't see the man.

Eddie's bronco slipped and went to its foreknees. The boy spurred it back on its feet, but the animal was about through. Morgan's buckskin lunged past the struggling horse before he could pull it up. He wheeled it to one side on the steep slope, shouting at Eddie: "He'll never make it, kid! Kick free before he goes down and rolls you!"

At that moment Hell Kitty stumbled again and Eddie had to roll off to keep from being pinned as it spilled. The rifle made another smashing sound and a bullet kicked up shale six feet from Morgan. The buckskin fought to wheel back and finish the climb, but Morgan reined it on around till it was sliding back down the steep bank on its hind legs.

"Grab a stirrup, kid," he bawled, "let's go!"

When he was even with Eddie, he put the reins against its neck again. The talus was so steep the buckskin's hoofs almost went out from beneath it as the animal tried to wheel back up. Morgan gave it a rake with his spurs that sent it into a wild lunge. It was the only thing that saved them. As the horse spun around, hind hoofs digging into the shale, Eddie came to his knees and lunged for a stirrup. Morgan gave it another rake and the horse screamed in pain and fear. He felt its heavy hindquarters bunch behind him as it took off. Eddie was half dragged up the slope, trying to keep his balance. His feet flailed wildly at talus. The gun smashed again. But their movement was so violent and erratic now they must have made poor targets.

Finally, unable to keep his feet, Eddie grabbed the stirrup with his other hand. Morgan felt the buckskin jerk and almost spill aside with the sudden tug of the boy's weight as Eddie's feet went out from under him. He gave it a last desperate jab with the spurs, shouting wildly. The horse let out a wheezing grunt and went over the top in a final lunge, dragging Eddie like a sack.

In the mat of willows, Eddie let go and rolled over onto his belly. Morgan pulled the buckskin up as quickly as he could, swinging off. The beast was dripping dirty yellow lather and trembling like a child in fear. Morgan held the reins, yanking his Henry from the boot. The buckskin reared, snapping the reins from his hand. He tried to catch them, but the horse spun and charged back into the timber.

He ran a couple of steps after it, but the rifle *cracked* from across the cañon again, and a bullet ate off a chunk of cottonwood not a foot from his head. He dropped to a crouch in the cover of willow and chokecherry, and wormed back to Eddie. The boy was lying flat behind the cover of matted juniper growing thickly over a ledge of shale. The boy lifted his head, grinning through the sweat streaking his face.

"Thanks, Morg," he said. "Seems like you're always pulling me out of a bog."

"Where's Shyrock?" Morgan asked him.

"He was heading for that cañon below us the last I saw him," the boy said.

They glanced at each other and dipped their heads in tacit agreement, and began squirming their way down through the buckbrush and crimson fireweed till they reached the head of the deep gully that cut into the slope here. For a moment, Morgan stared down the dark notch without seeing anything. Then he found the fresh hoofprints, leading up through the crusty dun earth past where they lay, to disappear in the bigger timber behind them.

"He got through all right," he said. "His horse has already reached the timber."

"He wasn't on the horse," Eddie said.

The hushed tone of his voice brought Morgan's eyes around to stare back down at the stream. The slope that formed the upper side of this gully ran out to hang over the water in a high point of land. Shyrock had just come into view around this point. He was in midstream, flopping over and over with the current. A studding of boulders caught him and he sprawled there a moment in the shallow water, body draped slackly over the rocks. A stream of blood was trickling from the wound in his ribs to stain the water on his downstream side. His body kept jerking softly with the steady little tugs of the current until it finally tore him loose again. He flopped over onto his back and then lay there on the sandy bottom. The water was so shallow on this shelf that even with his head thrown back, his gaping mouth was still out of water.

It was a grisly scene, that great raw-boned body sprawled out on the glittering sand, the red hair and beard so soaked they looked almost black. The water pushed insistently at him, first swinging his feet downstream a little till they caught against another boulder, then pushing at his shoulders till they began to slide on the bottom.

"Looks like they knocked the dust out of him," murmured Eddie tightly.

Morgan hardly heard him. Some faint movement of Shyrock's chest had caught his eyes. He watched till he was sure. "He's still breathing, Eddie."

The boy's eyes widened with disbelief, but as he stared, he, too, saw it. "They must think he's dead or they'd take another shot, sure."

"We've got to get him before he slides off that shelf," Morgan muttered. "It's deep water a few feet on and he'll drown. You get out on the end of that point and cover me. I'm going down to the mouth of this gulch."

He put the Henry in Eddie's hands. The boy started to say something, then checked himself. Morgan met his eyes for a moment, then turned to squirm down through the best cover he could find into the gulch. Here matted willows and cherry thickets hid him from the opposite slope till he reached the end of the gulch. A beach of bone-white sand ran ten feet across to the water. The redhead was now almost directly opposite the gulch.

"Shyrock," said Morgan. "Don't move. Can you hear me?"

It was silent for so long he thought the man would not answer. Finally, however, the lips moved, shaping a word with great difficulty. Shyrock's voice was so feeble he could hardly hear it. "I'm done, Morgan. Leave me be."

"I'm coming out to get you," Morgan said.

The current moved Shyrock softly into a boulder, flopping him back over on his belly till he lay sprawled across the smooth rock with his chest on its top.

"Don't be crazy." It was barely a whisper from Shyrock. "They're still up on that ridge. They'd kill me if they knew I was still alive. They'll get you for sure."

"Just lie tight and don't fight when I reach you. Eddie's covering me. Hang onto that rock now. I'm coming."

For that last instant, Morgan crouched there, sending a final searching glance toward the opposite ridge. His soaked clothes lay clammy as paste against his body. The shadows were chilly enough to draw a shiver from him. Shyrock lay so slackly across that boulder he must have looked dead from the high land over there. But Morgan could see his right arm hugged around the rock in the effort to hang on. Feathery little furrows of white water streamed from each foot, and they kept jerking faintly with the tug of the current.

Morgan rose to his hands and knees, hung there, lunged out. He ran headlong down the beach toward a point a little above Shyrock. He knew the surprise of his appearance would give him a moment. When he judged that had passed, he cut sharply the other way. The gun *crashed* then, and the bullet kicked up sand where he would have been if he'd kept going in the same direction. He was in the water now, ten feet from Shyrock. Eddie's gun began going from somewhere above him, a methodical *crash* of gunfire that echoed against the opposite ridge until the cañon was filled with the din.

Deafened by it, Morgan changed his direction once more. And once more a bullet struck a rock where he would have been if he'd kept going that same way. The ricochet screamed like a cat in pain, adding its banshee howl to the rest of the crazy sounds. Morgan slipped on the rocks and went to his hands and knees in the shallow water just as he reached Shyrock. He freed his hands to catch Shyrock under the armpits. He lunged to his feet, dragging the dead weight up and back.

Shyrock made one feeble effort to get his feet under him. One of them slipped and his whole weight sagged into Morgan, almost knocking him over. Morgan fought for balance on the slippery rocks. Then his foot sank into sand and he knew he was at the bank. His muscles swelled and bunched in that last effort of staying on his feet. He didn't know how long it took him to drag Shyrock across the beach. His head seemed filled with the wild thunder of gunfire, crashing back and forth like the echo of some giant's hammer on a titanic anvil. Then he was in the willows, dropping Shyrock and going to his belly.

Morgan had known this stabbing need for breath before. It was amazing how drained a man could get in such a short stretch of violence. His ribs swelled till he thought they would burst through his skin, and still he could not get enough air. The struggle made his whole body ache. At last it eased off, and he raised to an elbow to look at Shyrock. "Still with us?"

The big man was sprawled on his back, head thrown back, breathing in shallow gusts. His lids fluttered. He had trouble focusing his eyes. Then he grinned. "Sure am. And you know, Morg . . . my head ain't sore at all any more."

Morgan could not help answering the grin. "I thought you'd get over that. Let's see if we can't get farther back."

It was heavy work. Shyrock was too feeble to help much. Finally Eddie came down through timber from the point.

"He don't answer my fire any more. I think he's moved."

The two of them crouched above Shyrock in the timber, silent for that moment, and then Morgan spoke softly. "We'll do what we can for him here. Then one of us had better round up the horses. It might take some time."

Shyrock sucked in a breath. "It's thirty miles back to the Keyhole. I can't ride it, Morg, I know I can't."

"You won't heal out here," Morgan said. "You need a doctor."

"He's right about a horse," Eddie said. "It'd kill him to ride that far. Couldn't one of us go for a wagon?"

"We'd never get it down here," Morgan said.

"Nearest wagon road is the one that goes to Charlie King's," Shyrock said in a whispering voice. "He's a lot closer than the Keyhole."

Morgan squinted at Eddie. "King?"

Eddie frowned at him. "What's the matter with that?"

Morgan shook his head. "I guess that's about the best we can do."

The stream had kept the wound washed off, and Morgan made a compress of his neckerchief and tied it on with his belt in an effort to stop the bleeding. Then they made Shyrock as comfortable as possible, and Morgan started out after the horses, leaving Eddie with the wounded man. He figured Eddie's animal would not run as far as the others, since it had been so played out, and he picked up its trail.

It took him an hour to come up with the bronco, where it was feeding in the next spur valley. It was still nervous and almost jumped out of its hide when he first showed. He talked to it, moving in a slow circle around the fretting horse, finally closing in and getting the reins.

After that it took less time to pick up the other two. They had run farther, but he got there quicker. It was late afternoon when he brought the three of them back. Eddie was huddled over Shyrock, miserable and shivering in his wet clothes.

"He's passed out," he said. "I wanted to build a fire and dry out but I figured that might bring them down on us again."

"We'd better do it for his sake, before we leave," Morgan said. "Take his clothes off and wrap him in our sougans. I want to check that ridge across the way before we build a fire."

He got off Eddie's mare and pulled the boy's Winchester out for him. Eddie handed him back his own Henry.

"You'd better put some bullets back in," he said.

Morgan extracted the tubular magazine and began ramming .44s from his belt loops against the spring. When he had fifteen shells in, he slid the magazine back into the stock, and put the Henry in its boot on the buckskin. Eddie was pulling Shyrock's soaked clothes off now, and drying his big frame with one of the

128

blankets. Morgan took a last look at Shyrock, swung up onto the buckskin.

"I'm going up to the head of this cañon and around, kid. If they come, give me three shots as fast as you can. I'll be back."

The boy grinned up at him, curly hair gleaming wetly. "OK, Morg. Don't let anybody pull a Pecos swap on you."

Morgan touched his hat brim and turned the buckskin up. He kept to the timber all the way, moving slowly and watching the opposite ridge. The cañon finally boxed up against the mother mountain, and Morgan crossed its head through a dense grove of firs to reach the opposite spur ridge. He got his rifle out and rode with it tucked under one elbow. The sun was losing itself behind the main hogback of the Absarokas. There was a last tide of its crimson light flooding the cañon, and then it was gone, leaving everything in sudden chill shadow.

He was within a few hundred yards of the place from which they had dropped off this ridge into the spur cañon when he swung off the buckskin and tethered it to some scrub growth. Slowly, carefully he began to circle, stopping every few feet to study the timber all about him, never leaving cover, never exposing himself to the ridge behind him. It was a stalk that took infinite patience. Evening darkness lay through the timber with the texture of soot when he finally found what he wanted.

It was the print of one boot, where rocks formed a natural cover overlooking the cañon. Although Morgan searched the surrounding area carefully and thoroughly, he could find no other prints, no other sign. It filled him with a grudging admiration for a man who could build such an ambush and leave so little sign. It took a hunter of supreme skill. That one print had been a mistake, and the man probably did not even know he had left it. What made it singular was the imprint of a star that the heel of the boot had dug into the earth. Morgan guessed that it was made of metal, like the taps some boot makers put on the toes of their boots, to keep them from wearing down.

129

He mounted again and turned on down the ridge, trying to pick up sign of the man's horse. He came into sight of the main valley without finding it. He pulled his buckskin to a halt on the last height of the ridge before it broke off into the valley floor. He was just above the tops of timber covering the bottomlands, and the sooty darkness gave him the barest hint of the ranges lying on the other side of the valley, shadowy and unreal, folding away like billows of smoke to be lost in the cerements of night. The smell of sulphur hung heavily on the air and a chilling wind whipped vindictively at his hat brim and he realized that a deep shivering had gripped his body.

VI

They did not get started for the Double Arrow before night. At first they tried to ride on either side of Shyrock and hold him up. But he kept passing out. Finally Morgan lashed their sougans over his pommel to keep the horn from jabbing him, and tied him forward onto this. He had spells of consciousness during which he gave them directions.

They followed the Yellowstone River southward, crossing it several times. Finally the Absarokas broke abruptly, creating Smoky Pass, a tortuous notch winding deviously upward through the main watershed and cutting through the highest peaks to bring them out on a great plateau on the eastern side of the mountains. Shyrock guided them to a trail that ran steadily northeast till it reached a great drop-off. The moon had risen, and Morgan could see by its light that they stood at the top of a cliff that ran eastward as far as the night would carry the eye. A deep valley lay below the cliff, running northward for several miles before it came against the spur ridges of the Absarokas again. Shyrock had come to, and stirred feebly on his padded blankets.

"You're looking northward toward our line shack," he said.

"This is Medicine Rim. It runs due east for twenty miles, almost to Chinook. Best drift fence in the world. Our cattle can't get over it and King's stuff won't jump off. It's kept the two herds apart like a stone wall. Just keep following this trail, now."

A night hawk was whimpering somewhere in the sky. The wind mourned softly through the wind-stunted juniper matting the plateau. The trail led east for a while along the rim and then turned south, crossing the tableland. There seemed to be a gradual descent, and the timber became heavier. Finally the plateau began to drop off in great glacial benches. The trail shelved down sheer cliffs and twisted through exposed bedrock of gray granite. They pinched through a notch walled with grayish quartz that shone in the moonlight like dirty glass. They emptied from the lower end of the notch to find themselves at the base of a high wall. The wind whined down the notch behind them and buffeted against a stand of poplars that stood a few feet out from the wall, lifting their resinous scent in a swirling tide that swept against Morgan as he led into the trees. The trail ran through this grove and out onto another flat covered with the frosted foliage of dogwood.

Ahead Morgan saw a pole fence and beyond this the Double Arrow buildings, backed up against the bowl of a huge granite cirque that had been ground out of solid rock by the action of an ancient glacier. There were three hip-roofed barns and a house with a pair of wings that sprawled haphazardly over the flats. They rode the fence till they found a poor man's gate. Morgan had to dismount to open this. Then they went on to the house, pulling up by the long stone porch.

"King!" Morgan called.

Several front windows were open, letting light stream out onto the porch. Through these they heard the scrape of movement from within. The door was flung open but nobody appeared there.

131

"Who is it?" King asked, from one side.

"Morgan Banning. I've got a wounded man with me. We want to borrow a wagon to take him on to the Keyhole."

Another door was opened down by the barns, throwing a streak of yellow light across the ground. Morgan guessed that was the bunkhouse. Tom Law called from there: "It's all right now, Charlie."

King's long-legged silhouette moved into the doorway. He had no coat on and the weight of his body filled out a dark wool shirt heavily. His long black hair had fallen down one side of his coppery face. He brushed it back with an impatient sweep of a hand as he stared at Morgan. "What happened to the redhead?" he asked.

"He got shot over on the Yellowstone," Morgan told him. "He's bad, King, and your place had the closest wagon."

"Send a wagon over to the Keyhole? They'd never bring it back."

"Don't be a fool, King."

"Don't call me a fool, Banning."

"The man's hurt bad," Morgan said impatiently. "You know you'll get your wagon back. Oakland isn't that small. It'll take you about ten minutes to hitch one up. How about getting Shyrock in where he can rest and have something hot?"

"He'll get enough rest in the wagon," King said, and turned to go back in.

"King."

It was just the one word from Morgan. The tone of it checked King, and turned him back. Morgan got out of his saddle and walked up the steps till he was facing the man on the porch.

"This man is hurt," he said, in a trembling voice. "A dog would help him if he could. Ten minutes on a bed and a cup of coffee might mean the difference between making it or not."

"I'll give you a wagon. That's all."

"No, it isn't. We're coming in."

"No you ain't, Banning," said Law, from behind.

Morgan made a half turn to see the man standing at the foot of the steps. Rideout had come up with him and stood farther back. The dim light made old leather of his rough face. His thumbs were tucked into his gun belt, and his eyes were on Eddie.

"Get down off the porch," Law said. "Charlie don't like strangers in his house."

Suddenly Morgan could take no more. The fight and the exhaustion of the long ride had worn him too thin. These two men had pitted themselves against him since he had first reached town and he could contain himself no longer. It seemed as if all their antagonisms swept up on a hot tide of rage that he didn't even try to check, and he threw himself bodily off the top step at Law.

Law tried to jump back and draw, but Morgan smashed into him before his gun was out. He rammed a vicious punch to Law's belly as he went heavily against the man. Law doubled forward and staggered back. Morgan let his own impetus carry him after the man, smashing him across the face before his body went into Law again. This blow knocked Law off his feet, and Morgan could barely keep himself from falling with the man.

Standing above Law, with the air going in and out of him in great gusts, Morgan saw that Rideout was frozen, his gun half pulled. King had made some aborted move up on the porch, but was stilled now. It was Eddie's gun that held both of them. The kid was resting the weapon on the silver-plated horn of his saddle, grinning thinly. "You should come to Texas," he told Rideout. "We'll give you some lessons."

Law rolled over with a groan. He turned his face up to Morgan. It was the color of putty and was twisted sickly. Morgan

133

wiped his hand down the scar Law's gun had made on his face up by the Doubloon. "Get up," he said. "I'd like to do it again."

A rancid anger pulled Law's lips back against his teeth till those claw tracks dug deeply at the corners of his mouth. He looked at King, as if waiting for something. But King did not speak. Finally Morgan turned away, still breathing heavily, and walked to Shyrock's horse, untying him and lifting him down.

"Help him," Eddie told Rideout. The big buckskin-clad man looked at Eddie's gun, then grudgingly came over to help Morgan get Shyrock up the steps. King stood to one side. His face was graven deeply with a whipped frustration. Morgan saw that flickering play of violent little lights running through his eyes, but he made no move as they went by him.

"Law," Eddie said, "you go hitch up a wagon. If you aren't back here with it in ten minutes, I'm coming after you. I'd be happy as a spotted pup to finish what Morgan started."

It was a cold-country house, built solidly and tightly, reflecting a barren simplicity. There was no paneling on the walls; from floor to ceiling it was of great unpeeled logs, the firelight glittering dully across the scabrous bark. The only rugs were two buffalo robes before the hearth. There was a blazing fire in the stone fireplace, filling the room with the pungency of wood smoke and the syrupy reek of hot pitch.

They lowered Shyrock onto a sagging couch with hide lacings for springs. Then Morgan stepped back and looked around the room for a cover. He saw none, and neither Rideout nor King made a move to help. In a bitter defiance, he bent and swept up one of the buffalo robes, throwing it over Shyrock. The man was barely conscious. Pain sucked in his cheeks and compressed his lips till they were white around the edges.

When Morgan turned from the couch, he saw that an Indian woman had entered the room. She was short and fat and swarthy. Her hair was parted in the middle and braided and the

134

part was viscid with vermilion paint. She wore an elk-hide dress with curious open sleeves, decorated across the breast with bear claws. She stood utterly quiescent, her jet eyes focused on none of them, yet seeming to include all of them.

Morgan saw a knot of muscle bunch up across the heavy angle of Charlie King's jaw. His voice sounded as if someone was throttling him. *"Nun we,"* he said. She made no move, only lifted her eyes to look at him. His voice raised. "Get out, I said. Get out!"

"Icahpe ku," she said without moving.

King's boots made a violent scrape against the bare floor, but, before he completed the movement, he checked himself. His eyes slid back toward Morgan without ever reaching him. They fluttered with a guilty look. Then he looked once more at the woman. She met his gaze enigmatically. His eyes dropped to the floor and his chin sank into his neck till the coppery flesh formed pale furrows with the pressure. The woman's moccasins lifted a faint scratching from the spur-splintered floor as she came over to the couch and knelt beside Shyrock. King followed her all the way with his eyes, an artery throbbing heavily in the cup of his collar bone. His hands were closed tightly and the restraint he was putting on himself was a palpable thing. The woman unbuttoned Shyrock's shirt and took away the crude bandage Morgan had made. Once more her eyes raised to King.

"Icahpe ku," she said again. She had a deep man-like voice.

King made a small sound in his throat without answering. The woman rose and waddled from the room through the same door by which she had entered.

Eddie dragged his spurs through the front door, his gun still in his hand. "Law's hitching up a team, all right," he said.

Morgan nodded at him without answering. "We have to get the coffee, too?" he asked King.

King was silent so long Morgan thought the man did not mean to answer. He stood with all his weight settled heavily against the puncheons, staring intensely at the floor, as if lost in his dark thoughts. Rideout had taken up a position by the fireplace, a couple of feet from King, and was watching his boss closely. Finally, without lifting his eyes, King said: "Rideout, put some coffee on."

Rideout shot a narrow glance at Morgan. His eyes were yellowed by the jaundice of hostility. "I ain't rustling grub for any Keyhole. . . ."

"I said get some coffee!" shouted King, and hit him.

It was a backhand blow. It smashed Rideout back against the fireplace at an angle. He rolled helplessly down the rough cement and then upended to hit the corner in a heap. King had not moved from where he stood to do the whole thing.

Rideout came up out of the corner into a crouch, a dazed pain filling his leathery face. He shook his head and then lifted it slowly till his eyes met King's. Morgan could see the hate fill them. But Morgan could see King's eyes, too. Those violent little lights turned them to glowing coals. Morgan did not think he had ever seen so much concentrated violence reflected in a man's eyes. Rideout tried to meet it with his own anger, but he could not. King did not speak again. He stood there with his whole body trembling visibly, staring at Rideout till the man dropped his eyes, and got awkwardly to his feet. He halted there, eyes moving back up to King's once more. This time it did not last as long, and Rideout turned to limp toward the kitchen.

King watched the man till he disappeared into the kitchen. Then, without looking at Morgan, he walked stiffly to one of the hide-seated chairs and flung himself down in it, long legs sprawled out before him, staring into the fire. His chin sank deeply onto his chest, creating those furrows in the flesh of his neck. The breath made a deep and guttural sound as it passed through him. That was the only noise in the room.

Morgan glanced at Eddie, and saw that the boy's mouth was parted in amazement. Suddenly King spoke.

"How did he get shot?"

Morgan shifted restlessly, irritable with tension and weariness. "Over in the Yellowstone country. We went after a drift of Keyhole stuff."

King stared into the ruddy flames. Then his lips pulled back off his teeth. "And you called me a fool."

"What's over there, King?" Morgan asked.

"Why ask me?"

"I thought maybe you'd know. Have any of your men ever been hurt following a drift of cattle over there?"

King put a hand carefully on each wooden arm of the chair, turning his face squarely up to Morgan. "What are you implying, Banning?"

"I'm just asking you a straight question, King."

King's lips flattened against his teeth. "As a matter of fact, one of my men was lost in Yellowstone, about a year ago. And I've lost as many cattle over there as Oakland or any other outfit."

"Then why did you want me out of Chinook Basin so bad?" asked Morgan.

King settled his weight heavily back in the chair, his eyes dropping to the fire once more, and he did not answer.

"Did it have to do with Eddie's interest in Nora Oakland?" asked Morgan softly. He saw the little pucker of muscle run along the coppery angle of King's jaw, but once more the man did not respond. Finally Morgan said, more softly: "You had Tom Law tailing us in Chinook a long time before Eddie even saw Nora."

Morgan saw something run through King's face. The man

started to look up. There was a sibilant scrape of moccasins from the kitchen. A new surge of anger turned King's face the color of mud. The man looked quickly back at the fire, sinking his chin, deep and hard, against his chest, fixing his eyes upon the flames as if seeking the strength for his restraint there. The squaw came across the room carrying a bucket in one hand, clean cloth in the other, and chewing industriously on something. At the bed, she went to her knees and tore a strip of cloth to wash the crusted blood from Shyrock's wound. After this, she spat what she had been chewing into her hand. It was a blackened pulpy mass that she proceeded to rub into the wound. Shyrock stirred, groaning, but she held him.

"Morg," Eddie said sharply, "stop her. . . ."

Morgan checked him with a wave of his hand, staring at the woman. "King, what's she doing?"

King's voice was tight and unnatural. "That's *icahpe ku*. It'll heal your man quicker than any doctor can."

"That's crazy," Eddie snapped. "Don't let her do it, Morg."

Morgan watched the woman with slated eyes as she made a compress out of the sheeting and bound it on with a strip that went around Shyrock's body. "I think it'll be all right, kid," he said.

The *jingle* of Rideout's spurs brought him into the room with a pot of steaming coffee and a tin cup. He poured the cup full and handed it to the woman.

"Got any whiskey?" Morgan asked.

King hesitated, then jerked a thumb toward the kitchen. "Get the bottle in the cupboard."

Rideout put the coffee down and went for the whiskey. He brought it back, uncorking the bottle, and doused a generous slug into Shyrock's coffee.

The woman held Shyrock's head up while Morgan tilted the cup to his lips. He took too big a drink at first and burned his lips. But at least it brought him to full consciousness. He drank the rest in little sips, licking his lips and sweating, and then dropped heavily back onto the couch.

Morgan poured another cup of coffee and handed it to the boy. When Eddie had finished, he had one himself.

King did not speak throughout this. He sat sprawled in the chair, that hair fallen down over one side of his face again, coarse and black as the mane of a horse. The firelight glistened across the surface of his half-lidded eyes as he stared into the flames.

When Morgan was halfway through his coffee, the wagon *rattled* around the front, jerking King's head up from his reverie. "There's your rig," he said. "You can go now."

Morgan deliberately finished his coffee, seeing the anger slowly fill King's face. The man rose in one lithe motion that took him up out of the chair and a pace away from it. Morgan was reminded of a great cat. He put the cup on the mantle, and Eddie helped him get Shyrock on his feet. The squaw stood enigmatically by the fireplace, watching them get the man out onto the porch. King followed, making no effort to help. Law had forked hay into the bed of the wagon to make it soft for Shyrock. Eddie and Morgan got the man up over the dropped tailgate. Then they hitched their horses behind, and Eddie climbed in to wrap the man in the blankets, while Morgan walked around to drive.

King and Rideout and Law had bunched themselves in front of the steps, at the head of the wagon. As Morgan put his hand up to catch the side of the bed and climb into the seat, King spoke. "Did you get the cattle back from Yellowstone?"

Morgan turned to look at the man over his shoulder. "No."

"Are you going after them again?"

"I don't know."

"You'd be a fool to try."

"No cattle," Rideout said, "no trouble."

"Is that a threat?" Morgan asked.

Those somnolent lids had drawn together, hiding whatever lay in King's eyes. He took that quick little breath, running the tip of his tongue across his upper lip in a darting motion. "Take it any way you want," he said.

VII

For Shyrock's sake, they had to drive with painful slowness, and it was well into the early hours of morning by the time they reached the cut-off on the Chinook road that led to the Keyhole. From this point it was about as far to the ranch as it was to town, so Morgan sent Eddie on into Chinook to get the doctor while he turned the wagon down the road to Keyhole. That way Shyrock would not have to bear the double trip back to the ranch from town after the doctor tended him.

Again it was the slow rattling drive over the bumpy road, with Shyrock groaning in the back and the stars gleaming from a sky like black satin. Morgan dozed more than once, to be brought awake by a jolt. The sky grew milky with dawn. Then the sun made its bright explosion on the peaks of the eastward mountains. The road wound around the gentle slope and came abruptly into sight of house and barns and corrals.

He turned in the upper gate, and down the cut-off that passed the kitchen. Janice must have seen him from there. She called for him to pull up, and then came hurriedly down the side of the house from the kitchen door. Her hair was swept up carelessly and held by an ivory comb, leaving wisps of it blonde as corn curling against the stove-heated pink of her neck. She was not yet fully awakened and her eyes had a sleepy childish look to them that made her seem younger. Shock erased that, however, and brought a heavy shape to her lower lip, with her first sight of Shyrock in the bed. By the time Morgan had told her what happened, the sound of their voices drew others. Drift stepped from the bunkhouse and walked uncertainly this way, rubbing sourly at his cropped hair. The front door was opened, and Nora came out in a quilted robe, sweeping her long auburn hair back over her shoulders.

"Shy was shot over on the Yellowstone," Janice told her. "We can't put him in that windy old bunkhouse."

"Of course not," Oakland said, coming out behind Nora. "We. . . ."

"I'll fix one of those big rooms upstairs," Nora broke in. "He'll stay here till he's well. Drift, hurry up, we've got to get him off this wagon. Janice, go open the windows in the corner room and let some air in. Come on now, Morgan, don't just sit there. . . ."

Morgan stepped out of the wagon, surprised at her assumption of authority. Drift broke into a reluctant trot to the rig. As he came close, Morgan saw how bloodshot his eyes were. The red-headed man was half-conscious and muttering deliriously to him, but he could give them no aid by now. They had to carry him as a dead weight up the stairs.

Nora had already gone up before them and was throwing back the covers of a big tester bed in the upstairs chamber. It looked as if it might have been the room of Oakland's wife, with marble-topped tables and a delicately framed mirror, and Wedgewood and other bric-a-brac scattered haphazardly on the shelves. Morgan helped lower Shyrock onto the bed, and then stepped back.

"Janice," Nora said, "pull that table over near the bed so we can put his water on it. Drift, when you get him in bed, go down and fill this pitcher. He can have one of your shirts, Dad. His is ruined."

Morgan had the impulse to be amused, at first, by her bustling officiousness. But this soon faded. He saw behind it a mature command of the situation that he would not have looked for in Nora. At last she turned to look at Morgan. "You can go downstairs and get something to eat if you want," she said. "There's nothing more you can do here."

He nodded and turned to go out. Drift was coming back up the stairs with a pitcher of water and met Morgan at the top. Morgan tried to go around, but Drift stepped across his way.

"What were you doing in Yellowstone?" he asked.

"A cut of cattle drifted through," Morgan told him.

Drift came closer, till the pitcher was touching Morgan. The mottled scars on the man's cheeks grew livid as the blood darkened his raw-boned face. His words came out on a stertorous breath, reeking of cheap whiskey. "Listen, Banning, Shyrock was one of my men. He didn't want to go, I know that. Who're you to step in this way and . . . ?"

"Drift," said Janice from behind Morgan.

Drift's bloodshot eyes snapped off Morgan's face and over his shoulder toward the doorway. Then they fluttered with a guilty expression. Morgan had seen the same expression in a little kid caught stealing apples. Janice moved to their side, catching Drift's arm and pulling him gently around Morgan.

"Take it on in, Drift. You know you can't afford to cause any more trouble."

He sent one more look at Morgan, lips tight against his chipped teeth. Then he turned away from Janice sharply, jerking free of her hand, and went into the bedroom. The woman watched him disappear with a troubled darkness in her blue eyes, then she gave Morgan the corner of a self-conscious glance, and turned to go down the stairs. He followed her to the kitchen.

It was a comfortable place, big and roomy, with an immense O'Brien stove standing in one corner, the tile frieze on its front cracked and faded by heat and time. Janice slid the coffee pot atop one of the burners, and then *clanged* open the cast-iron door to stoke up the fire. Morgan took a seat at the big round table. He slid his hat off and put it on a chair beside him, running his hand wearily through his close-cropped black hair. Then he put elbows on the table and leaned heavily against them, letting the warmth drain the tensions of the night from him. His face in repose became somber. The hint of that droll curl almost disappeared from one end of the long lips; the lids dropped till most of the kindling expressions in the eyes were hidden. He watched the woman that way, a big man who had acquired the animal capacity for complete relaxation when he got the chance.

"Oakland was right," he said. "You have a strange power over Drift."

She started pouring buckwheat cakes on the griddle. "Perhaps I understand him."

"Perhaps he's in love with you."

She glanced at him with suddenly wary eyes. "Do you think so?"

"I often think a man and a woman are talking about two different things when they use that word," he said.

"Some men," she murmured. "Some women."

"Are you in love with him?"

Her chin lifted defiantly. "Is it any of your business?"

He smiled slowly. "You wouldn't be so touchy about it if you weren't. Does he go on a bender like that often?"

Her deeply drawn breath held a weary resignation. "Very well. So he was drunk last night."

"I guess most men take a drink now and then. When did he really start hitting the bottle? Before he rode into Yellowstone with Laramie, or after?"

She wheeled sharply toward him. "Why do you ask that?"

"Don't you know?"

143

"I don't know what Drift found over in Yellowstone, if that's what you mean."

"Then he did find something?"

She continued to stare at him, eyes dark with trouble. Then, still holding the pancake turner, she came around the table. She put one hand on his arm, leaning toward him. The scent of her was a mingled freshness of flour and milk and healthy flesh.

"Morgan," she said in an intense voice, "don't stay here. You've seen what it is now. They might have killed Shyrock."

"Who?"

"I don't know. I told you I don't know. None of us do. Only you can see what it is now, hanging over this basin. It gets into everybody who stays here."

"Is that why Drift hits the bottle?"

She shook her head in a deep helplessness. "Morgan, I can't tell you. . . ."

"Is that why Charlie King doesn't want anybody on his place?"

A vague surprise robbed her face of its helplessness. "You were on King's place?"

"That's where we got the wagon," he said. "I don't see why King keeps that squaw housekeeper around if he's so ashamed of his Indian blood."

"That isn't his housekeeper," Janice said. "That's his mother."

He leaned back in surprise, staring up at her. Then the rush of comprehension came. All the strange tension between King and the squaw was explained. In that moment he knew a deep pity for the man.

"King's father was a white trader up here in the early days," Janice said. "He married that woman. He used the Indians badly. When she wouldn't leave him, the tribe drove her out."

"That's why King has to keep her there," Morgan murmured. "Hiding her. Ashamed of her."

"Yes. The father's dead. There's nowhere else she can go." Janice drew her hand off his arm, frowning at the expression in his eyes. "I suppose it is rather pathetic, isn't it?" He did not answer, still staring up at her. She waited a moment, then bent forward. "Morgan, you don't want land in a country filled with this trouble. It's ugly trouble. Believe me. You've seen how ugly."

"Are you asking me to go for my sake . . . or Drift's?" he asked. He saw her eyes widen, and knew he had struck home. He smiled easily. "I don't think you have to worry about another fight between Drift and me, Janice, if that's why you want me to leave."

At that moment there was sound at the door, and Nora's voice. "I'm sorry," she said stiffly. "I didn't mean to interrupt."

Janice pulled back sharply, a flush tinting her cheeks. "You didn't interrupt anything."

She looked at Nora a moment, then her eyes fluttered away, and she turned to the stove. Morgan was surprised again that this whole scene should be in control of the younger woman.

"You're brother's back with the doctor," Nora said.

There was an undertone of accusation in her voice. It made Morgan feel guilty when he knew there was no reason for it. He leaned back in the chair, vaguely irritated at being caught between the obscure motives of these two women, waiting for Nora to speak again. She did not, and in a moment Eddie came *rattling* his spur chains down the hall.

Nora left and the two men ate breakfast without much talk. When they were on their last cup of coffee, Oakland came to the door and invited them into the living room.

"Sawbones is still working on Shyrock," he said. "I'd like to have a little talk before you go down to the bunkhouse for some sleep."

The living room reflected more attentiveness than Charlie King's. There were mahogany panels covering the walls head high, and the rest of the way the logs were peeled and polished. The chairs and sofa were framed by carefully matched steer horns, with handsome hide-covered seats. Eddie lowered himself into one of these near the flagstoned hearth, gazing in admiration at the stuffed head of a mountain sheep above him, its great horns curving majestically above the mantel of Manitou marble.

"Now this is what I call an outfit." The boy grinned. "Think we'll ever have a spread like this, Morg?"

"What I have to offer might start you in the right direction." Oakland smiled. He eased himself into a chair opposite Eddie, squinting one eye painfully. He bent over to tug off his right boot, and then leaned back with a pleased sigh, studying Morgan through half-closed eyes. "So you went over into Yellowstone," he said at last.

"And got shot at," Morgan answered. "Is that what you wanted to happen?"

The tips of Oakland's lips tucked in with that smile so akin to Nora's. "You old fox. You knew what was going on all the time."

"I figured you had something more in your mind than just running cattle when you hired us," Morgan said. "You hoped some beef would drift into Yellowstone. You even hoped we'd run into trouble."

"When you whipped the whole bunkhouse crew, I was pretty sure you were the men I wanted."

"But you wanted to be real sure. You wanted to see how we acted under fire."

"Partly," Oakland admitted. "A bunkhouse fight and a gunfight are two different things. But I also wanted you to see exactly what you were getting into, over there. All the talk in the world won't show you what one ride into Yellowstone will. But now you've seen, and, from what I got out of Shyrock, you're even better under fire than you were in a bunkhouse. So I'll lay my cards down. I'll give you double wages while you're working on it. I'll give you a bonus of five hundred apiece if you find out what's going on over there and stop it."

Eddie grinned broadly up at Morgan. "That's a lot of fodder, Morg. We could buy the Doubloon and stock it to boot."

"What's wrong with your law?" Morgan asked Oakland.

"County seat's in Cody, fifty miles away. The sheriff came over when Laramie was killed, and a couple of other times when we had trouble. But he couldn't find nothing. We've tried every other way we could think of. Even pulled every man we could spare off our outfits and rode into Yellowstone a couple of times. But we didn't find a thing. We couldn't stay away from our spreads long enough to cover much territory, and we can't ride over there in those numbers every time a drift of cattle goes through. We even got a detective up here from some Denver agency. He didn't do any good, either."

Morgan stared at the floor. In his heart, he knew he did not want to involve himself or Eddie in it at all. The pattern was too much like that of the things that had ruined their plans so often in the past. Yet he knew Eddie was still too interested in Nora to pull out.

"Let me think it over," he said.

Oakland grunted assent, pulling on his boot. "Don't take too long. Winter'll be coming soon. You won't be able to do much in the mountains then." He rose. "Think I'll go upstairs and see how Doc Ashland is getting on."

Eddie remained in the chair, studying Morgan, until Oakland was gone. "You're not going to do it, are you?" he said.

Morgan shook his head miserably. "Is this what we wanted, Eddie?"

"I know what you're thinking," Eddie said. "Everything you warned me about is coming true. If I hadn't chased after Nora, we wouldn't've gotten mixed up in this."

"I didn't say that. . . ."

"You're thinking it. And you aren't going to take Oakland's offer." Eddie stood up, hitching at his belt. "That's all right with me. I told you I was tired of being dragged around behind an old mare."

Morgan grabbed his arm. "Eddie. . . ."

The boy didn't try to pull free; his eyes met Morgan with a strange plea. "You're wrong about Nora, Morg. I guess it started out like those other girls. But it's different now. She's *the* girl."

"You've said that about every one you ever kissed."

"I mean it this time. I'm serious."

Morgan chuckled wryly, clapping him on the back. "I know, I know."

Eddie shook his head angrily. "You always take that attitude. You'll find out. Where is she?"

"Somebody went out back for water," Morgan said. "I heard the kitchen door slam."

Eddie headed down the hall toward the kitchen. Morgan watched him go, the smile fading from his face. He could almost feel the thing closing about them, tighter and tighter. It left him in a bleak mood. He was about to leave when he heard somebody come down the stairs and half turned to see that it was the doctor. Ashland was a tall man deeply stooped through the shoulders. A lifetime of caring for the sick of this hard country had made a weary etching of his face. Although his eyes were red-rimmed from lack of sleep, a twinkle of latent humor lit them as he saw Morgan.

"Couldn't do much for Shyrock. That black root you put on will work wonders on a wound. Where did you learn an Indian trick like that?"

"Charlie King's mother did it," Morgan said.

"Oh." Ashland pursed speculative lips. "I see." He pulled a

pipe from one pocket of a blue serge coat that hung like a sack from his shoulders. He hunted through his other pockets for a match, muttering to himself.

Morgan took out one of his matches and scraped it on the mantel, stepping over to the doctor. "Are you the man who made Jinglebob's teeth?"

"Thanks." Ashland drew on the pipe in short sucks. "Yeah. Dentist, doctor, undertaker, midwife. Whatever you want."

"Did Jinglebob come to you for a new set?"

"New set? He hasn't even paid for the old teeth yet. Never saw a man throw his money away like that cook. He's borrowed six months ahead on his pay all the time."

Morgan shook out the match. "I guess that's why he hasn't come to you. Could you make him another set if they were paid for?"

"The old ones were vulcanite. Twenty dollars for that."

Morgan pulled his wallet and peeled off two tens. Ashland took the money with a pleased grin.

"How did he bust his choppers?"

"Ran into a bunk post. Been reflecting on his cooking ever since. Whole crew has the bellyache. I figure it's worth the twenty."

"Pick them up in a couple of days." Ashland chuckled. "I hope you stay around, Banning. You're the first cash customer I've had in twenty-nine years."

As the doctor left, Morgan heard a door upstairs open, and saw Nora come from Shyrock's room onto the stairway.

"I thought you were out after water," he said.

"That was Janice," she told him, coming down. "Did Dad get you to stay?"

"I don't know yet."

She smiled wistfully. "Still hold it against me, don't you? If it hadn't been for me, you and Eddie wouldn't be involved in this at all."

He shook his head. "I told you it wasn't personal. I never blamed the girls. I never even blamed Eddie, I guess. It's just the way he is."

She walked across the room to him. "Where was it before El Paso?"

"New Mexico."

"What happened?"

"We got some land on desert entry. Already starting to stock it up. There was a fast bunch around Roswell. One of them had a daughter. . . ."

"And you told Eddie it would only cause trouble."

"I guess I did try to keep him from seeing her. Nobody was too sure where her folks got their money. Ran fancy horses and gambled a lot in town. Seeing the girl so much, Eddie couldn't help being identified with them. Then her brother and dad were caught rustling and strung up. Whoever was connected with them had to get out of the country to save their necks."

She gave him a wry smile. "You're comparing us with rustlers now."

"You know I'm not."

Nora caught his arm sympathetically. "Of course I do. I understand, Morgan. I can see the parallel here. You want to put down roots pretty bad, don't you?"

He stared at her, realizing that his mind was not completely focused on what they were saying. It had something to do with the shimmering lights in her hair. He heard his answer coming almost automatically. "I wouldn't want to count the times I've tried to put down roots."

She was studying his face closely. "You were meant to have them. Some men were made to wander. I think Eddie's more like that. But not you. I think you could build something worthwhile if they'd give you a chance." She shook her head. "I don't blame you for not wanting to get mixed up in this."

It was the scent of her, now, seeming to envelop him, sweet and fresh and perfumed. It was hard to bring the thought up, although it had been there for some while now, even harder to concentrate on the words. "Tell me truly, Nora. How do you feel about Eddie?"

"He's handsome," she said. "Exciting. We have so much fun." Then she gave a little shake of her head, dropping her eyes momentarily. "But I don't love him. Not yet, at least. I guess he's made me tell him that a dozen times. He's so impetuous."

"You say not yet. Do you think there's a chance you may grow to love him?"

"I don't know." She looked back up at him, eyes confused. "When I'm near him, I think there is. But when I'm away from him. . . ."

She trailed off, searching his face, as if seeking help there, and he spoke in a low voice. "I guess I've never really been in love, Nora, so maybe I haven't a right to say this. But I always thought, when a person did fall in love, they'd know it way down to the bottom, without any doubts or confusion or questions."

"I always thought that, too," she answered softly. She put her palms against his chest. Her voice was like velvet in her throat. "When I'm with you, Morgan, I'm not confused."

The blood began to throb at his temples. He felt a tremor run through his body. Her eyes shone with an intense plea.

"Morgan," she almost whispered, "please don't go. . . ."

He felt his arms going around her, pulling her up to him, and his lips blocked off her words. And with her body straining to his, he knew why his mind had been unable to concentrate on what they had been saying, he knew why he had felt that unaccountable depression whenever he had seen Nora and Eddie

151

together. She was not just another of Eddie's girls. He could not compare her with the others at all. He had wanted her all along without realizing it. Perhaps he had hidden it from himself through loyalty to Eddie. But now he realized it. He could hide from it no longer.

Finally her lips slid off his and down over his cheek until her face was buried in the hollow of his neck. Then he heard the small sound from the hallway, and looked aside to see Eddie, standing there.

"I guess that was as good a way as any to break up Nora and me," the boy said.

Morgan felt Nora pull slowly free of him. His own mind seemed helplessly blank. He saw the pinched tightness in Eddie's face. He saw how the eyes were squinted, like a man in pain. He felt himself hold one hand out.

"Eddie. . . ."

"Never mind, Morg." The boy's breathing sounded strained. "You got what you wanted. I'm going. Only it isn't with you. I'm going alone."

Eddie walked clear to the door and opened it before Morgan found it in himself to move. He reached the door as Eddie went down the steps, calling after the boy again. But Eddie would not turn around. He started to follow farther, then checked himself, knowing the boy's moods, knowing it would only make things worse. He stood miserably there in the doorway, watching Eddie walk up to the stables. At last he turned back to Nora. He stared at her a long time before he spoke.

"I think he would have laughed if he'd found me doing that with the others," Morgan said. His voice had a hollow sound. He shook his head helplessly, frowning at the floor. "He told me it was serious this time. I had no idea it went that deep, between you."

There was a torn look to her face. "Not between us, Morgan.

I told him I didn't love him."

Morgan's eyes sought her help. "Do you think he's really in love with you?"

She drew a deep breath. "This morning, when he got back with the doctor, he asked me to marry him."

VIII

Reaching the bunkhouse, Morgan found it deserted. He walked in, disconsolately sailing his hat onto a bunk post, and sat down in one of the rickety chairs by the table. Nora had tried to tell him it was not his fault that Eddie had gone. Yet he could not help blaming himself. He felt like a fool for having been caught by the boy kissing her. He felt an insidious sense of guilt that no logic would banish. It all seemed so twisted inside. His realization that he loved Nora should be a fine, shining thing. But it was so muddied by what had happened. And yet, could it have been any different? If he had really believed Eddie was serious about the girl, would that have made any difference? It might have kept him from kissing her, if he had stopped to think. But that was the point. He had not stopped to think. There had been no thought of hurting Eddie in his mind; there had been no other thought. It had been utterly spontaneous. He had simply realized he loved her and had kissed her.

He ran a hand tiredly through his hair, trying to see a way out. He kept telling himself Eddie would be back tomorrow. They could work it out.

"Morgan," O'Toole said. "I'd give a year's pay if I could do that."

Morgan looked up in surprise to find the Irishman standing in the doorway, snapping his flowered suspenders with his thumbs. Then Morgan saw that he had been rolling a cigarette without realizing it.

O'Toole came in and sat down across from Morgan, placing

his derby carefully on the table. Then he took out his makings and tried to build a smoke with one hand. Tobacco spilled all over the table.

"You get your thumb in the way," Morgan said.

He rolled one for the man, showing him how. Then he leaned back in the chair, sinking into his own troubled thoughts again, hardly aware of the Irishman who sat across from him sucking down the cigarette as fast as it would burn so he could start rolling another one. He finally got it down to a stub and dropped it exultantly, taking the makings out once more. At this moment, Nations came in and went over to his bunk and started putting together his bedroll.

"You must be thinkin' hard again," he observed sourly. "Enough smoke rings in this room to string on a stick."

Morgan looked up to see the gray circles of smoke floating over his head. Then O'Toole cackled triumphantly.

"I got it," he said. "I got it."

"Now pick it up and lick the edge."

"Hot damn! It came apart again."

Nations finished his bedroll and began stuffing his war bag. "Old man wants me to get up to Crazy Horse Ridge quick and keep any more cattle from drifting into Yellowstone," he said. "I told him right out I wouldn't go down in that country after them."

"Does he want me to go with you?" Morgan asked.

"Maybe later," Nations answered. "Old man figures you were too played-out right now for another long ride." He laced up his bag, eyes somber. "I told him right out I wouldn't go down in that country." He shouldered his bedroll and tucked his war bag under one arm and pushed through the door. A lonesome wind skittered dust into the room. Then the door shut behind Nations. Morgan went over and lay down, tortured by his thoughts. O'Toole was still trying to roll a smoke one-handed when Morgan finally dropped off to sleep.

He awoke with a dull headache and a bad taste in his mouth. The Irishman was gone. The room was steeped in dusky shadows. He got up and went out to the water trough, sloshing water over his face. He found an old towel and was standing inside the open door, wiping his face, when he saw Janice coming through the evening dusk from the big house. She had an apron on over her calico dress, and dough powdered one arm to the elbow. She came to the door and stopped, a strange expression darkening her blue eyes.

"Why did Eddie go to town?" she said.

Morgan realized that Nora had not told Janice anything. "He'll be back later," he said. "Did you want somebody in particular?"

"You, I guess," she said ruefully. She stepped closer, grasping his arm. "Drift hasn't shown up all day. Oakland's in a lather. He's talking of firing Drift. I think Drift's in town. If you could only get him back before it's too late."

He studied her a moment, then said: "I think I could help you more if you told me all you knew."

He saw her face begin to close up. "But I told you . . . I don't know anything."

"You never did tell me when he started drinking."

"It was after he and Laramie rode into Yellowstone," she said. "A few months after. I told you about that. Laramie got killed. Drift barely made it back alive. Laramie was his best friend here in the basin."

"Are you trying to blame that for Drift's breakdown?"

She shook her head, staring at the ground. "I've known Drift a long time, Morgan. He was a fine man. In this whole valley there isn't a better man with cattle. He wanted to have an outfit of his own someday."

"And you with him?"

Her head seemed to sink deeper. "I've tried to get him to talk, tried to find out what happened over there in Yellowstone. He won't tell me. He's changed so. . . ." She trailed off, knotting the apron up in her fingers.

Morgan put his hand an her shoulder.

"I'll see what I can do."

It was night when he reached Chinook. The kind of night that always filled him with a strange restlessness. There was a hot dryness to the air, the smell of parched dust lingering over everything. His horse was nervous, shying at the slightest thing. Sound came in muffled splashes. The *tinkle* of a piano in a saloon. The quick *rattle* of boots down a plank walk. A husky laugh from a dark doorway. And the wind was there, as always, coming out of the high passes like the fitful voice of a tired child, skipping aimlessly down the street, rattling a heap of papers with a peevish kick.

The warmth of the night had drawn people onto the streets, and they were clustered along the sidewalk in gossiping groups, the glowing tips of their cigarettes winking and darting like fireflies in the soft darkness. Morgan saw Hell Kitty and Drift's sorrel cutting horse both hitched at the rack before the Hoof and Horn. He stopped there, finding within himself a strange reluctance to face Eddie. As he dropped his reins over the cottonwood rack and stepped up to the sidewalk, his eye was caught by a man silhouetted against the yellow rectangle of a store window farther down. There was no mistaking the narrow frame of Tom Law.

Morgan felt the break in his stride, and then pushed irritably on into the time-honored smells of the saloon. The sawdust on the floor emanated the damp reek of spit and spilled whiskey; the air was stale and blue with tobacco smoke. There were half a dozen townsmen at the bar. Morgan saw Dr. Ashland and Duncan Innes, the land agent. The bartender stopped polishing a glass and glanced automatically toward the rear. Morgan had already seen it. Eddie and Drift were playing poker at the last table. Eddie was facing the front, and put down his hand of cards as Morgan began walking toward them.

"Can't you leave me alone?" he said tightly.

Drift turned to look at Morgan with drink-fogged eyes, but Morgan ignored him. "Why don't we talk it over, kid?" he said. "It always straightened things out before. I didn't know how you felt. . . ."

"I said leave me alone!" Eddie's voice broke, and he slid his chair back with its legs shrieking against the floor. As he rose to swing around the table and lunge past Morgan, Drift reached out to catch his arm. "What were we talking about?" he asked. He was looking up at Eddie with bleary eyes, and his head kept wobbling back and forth like a sleepy child's.

"You know what we were talking about," Eddie said thinly, trying to jerk away. "Leave me go."

Drift would not release him. "Did I tell you anything?"

"Damn right you did! Will you leave me go?"

"Forget it."

"I will not. I'm going over there. If you haven't got the guts to, I sure have." Eddie finally tore free, wheeling momentarily to Morgan. "And no mother hen's comin' after me again! When are you goin' to get that through your head? You and I are quits."

He swung around Morgan and walked out the front door. The raucous *squeaking* of the batwings hung on the air as they slapped back and forth after he had passed through. Morgan watched them dully until they had stopped. Then he turned back to find Drift with his head buried in his arms on the table. Morgan shook him by the shoulder.

"What did you tell him?"

Drift swung out an arm trying to push him away. "Lemme be. . . ."

Morgan caught his hair, lifting his head up with a jerk. "What did you tell him? He said he was going over there. Were you talking about Yellowstone?"

This brought Drift's head around toward Morgan sharply. A strange light had dissipated the drunken glaze in his eyes. He lunged away from Morgan in a violent effort to get free. "You keep this up and you'll get your face stomped in."

Morgan pulled him back. "What about Yellowstone?"

With a hoarse sound, Drift wheeled out of his chair, coming up so violently it spilled from beneath him. His lunge knocked Morgan backward. The next table caught Morgan across the hips, almost taking his feet off the floor. Drift staggered after him and caught him there before he could recover, swinging a haymaker at Morgan's face.

Morgan blocked the blow on an elbow. "Didn't you get enough in the bunkhouse?" he panted.

Drift tore his arm free to strike again. "That's exactly what I'm going to stomp you for."

Morgan blocked the second blow against an upthrown arm, grappling with the man. As drunk as Drift was, it was like trying to hold a bull. Fighting to tear free, Drift almost upset both of them.

"What good would it do?" Morgan grunted. "You'd still have to face it after you're through."

That stopped Drift for a moment. Breathing gustily, he let his great weight sag against Morgan, pinning him to the table. "Face what?" he said.

"What you're drinking to forget."

"I ain't trying to forget anything."

"You've probably licked most of the men in Chinook these last two years," Morgan said. "Did that help you forget it?"

Drift stared at Morgan with a drunken grimace on his face. Something was working turgidly in his fogged eyes.

"It would take something big to make a man like you go to pieces," Morgan said with soft insistence.

"I ain't going to pieces," Drift said savagely, trying to tear free and strike at Morgan again.

"You'll still have to face it," Morgan panted, fighting him. "Licking me won't help any more than drinking does. You'll be sober tomorrow. You'll still have to face it."

Drift stopped fighting again. A whipped look slowly took the anger from his eyes, and Morgan could see that at last he had gotten through to the man. Drift made an inarticulate sound deep in his throat, trying to pull free, and this time Morgan released him.

The man swung heavily around, headed for the door. But he tripped over the upset chair and would have fallen if he hadn't caught at the edge of the table. He swayed there a moment, then dropped into Eddie's chair. Only then did Morgan see how tensely the line of men at the bar were watching. The barman laughed shakily.

"Take it easy with him, will you?" he asked Morgan. "I don't want my place wrecked."

Morgan picked up the overturned chair and set it down beside Drift. The man's fumbling hand had knocked his glass off the table. With a disgusted sound, he grabbed the bottle and took a drink. Then he set the bottle down before him, staring moodily at it.

"You're right," he said. "Nothing helps. Not even this."

"You've really got something on your soul," Morgan said, in a voice too low to reach the others.

"Go 'way," Drift said dully. He took another deep drink, a silvery film forming over his eyes.

"It must be bad," Morgan said.

Drift stared foggily at the table, weaving his head from side to side. "Damn right it's bad," he said thickly. "Ruin this valley, that's what it'll do. Nobody knows how bad. Won't have no valley left. No Keyhole. No nothing."

Morgan bent toward him intently. "What is it, Drift? Do you know what's happening over in Yellowstone?"

A savage expression filled the man's face. It turned so dark the scars across his primitive cheek bones became chalk-white. For a moment, Morgan thought he would come out of the chair again. Then the foreman sank back, staring beyond Morgan. "Yellowstone," he said. His voice was barely audible. "Who knows what's going on over there?" His body began to tremble. It took Morgan a long time to realize that he was chuckling. There was a sort of subdued hysteria to it. He took another drink. He drained the bottle, and then flung it from him to smash against the base of the wall. He had quit laughing now. "Damn it," he said. His lips formed a drunken sneer. "Damn it." He leaned forward to put his elbows on the table again. One of them missed, sliding off the edge, and his head slowly sank down till the side of his face lay against the table. Morgan reached across and shook him. He could not arouse the man. He turned to the bartender.

"Sawbuck. Help me carry him to his horse?"

It was near midnight when Morgan got back to the Keyhole. Bright moonlight made an etching of the buildings. Fence shadows formed inky stripes across the undulation of the fields. Morgan came in the back way, leading the foreman's cutting horse with Drift slung face down across the saddle. He dismounted at the barn and had a hard time sliding off the man's heavy body. By the time Morgan got him on his feet, Drift was struggling feebly.

"So bad there ain't goin' to be no Chinook," he babbled.

The man could not stand alone, so Morgan shoved him back against the fence and let him slide down to a sitting position. He heard a rustling sound behind him, and wheeled to see Janice coming around the corner of the barn.

"I've been watching for you," she said, hurrying toward them. She stopped before Drift, a look of helpless compassion on her face. "Why did you bring him up here?"

"He's been babbling. I thought he might start a row if I tried to get him into the bunkhouse. You said Oakland was about ready to fire him."

"You aren't going to let him sleep in the barn," she said.

"Maybe we can sober him up a little."

Morgan went in the barn and found a bucket, and then came out again and went along the fence till he reached a water trough. He scooped half a bucketful and went back to Drift, tossing it in his face. Janice winced instinctively. Drift grimaced, sputtered, then sank back against the fence, water dripping off his chin. Morgan had to douse him twice again before he came around.

He lifted his head, staring blankly at them. Understanding crept dimly into his face. He dropped his eyes, wiping water from his mouth with the back of his hand. He shifted around to get up. Janice bent to help him.

"I ain't no baby," he said angrily, shaking her off.

A hurt look darkened her eyes, and she stepped back. He grabbed an upright and gained his feet with great effort, wheezing heavily. His shirt was sopping wet and water still dripped off him to form puddles in the dusty ground. As he reached his full height, another figure came around the barn. Oakland's voice reached them querulously.

"Janice, why are you always off somewhere when I want a cup of coffee? Nora said she saw you coming up here. What's the matter, anyway . . . ?" He broke off as he came near enough

161

to see Drift. He came to a halt a few feet away, jamming his hands uncomfortably into the pockets of his Levi's. "Drift," he said, "I told you what would happen the next day you got drunk on my time."

"I just went in to get a little drink," Drift said.

"And what about that bunch of saddle stock you'd cut out for Goddard?" Oakland asked acidly. "O'Toole thought it was the string the blacksmith shod the other day. He turned them all out to pasture."

"O'Toole should have known better."

"How could he, when you weren't here to tell him? Goddard was due back in Cody tomorrow. He couldn't wait around all night while we caught up that bunch again and weeded them out. He called the whole deal off." All the anger seemed gone from Oakland now. He just seemed sorry about the whole thing. "I can't put up with it any longer, Drift. I'll have to give you the sack."

"Please," Janice said. "Give him one more chance."

"I've given him too many already," Oakland said. "This isn't the first time he's cost me a good chunk of money. I'm sorry, Janice."

Drift rubbed his fingers roughly through the blond stubble on his jaw, leaving pale tracks in the flesh. "I guess it's been coming a long time," he said bitterly. He looked at Morgan, a thin rancor giving his eyes a yellowish hue. "Why don't you make this Arbuckle your ramrod? He'd really turn it into a high-heel outfit." He spat disgustedly and walked down the meadow toward the bunkhouse. Janice glanced at Oakland, tears shining in her eyes, and then hurried away toward the house.

Oakland shook his head. "I feel like a snake."

"I don't think Janice really blames you," Morgan said. "I guess you've put up with a lot."

162

"These last two years I have," Oakland said. "Drift was a good man before it started." He looked up, squinting shrewdly at Morgan. "I hear you had a fight with your brother."

"I'm hoping he'll cool off and come back," Morgan answered.

"I was afraid you might be leaving, too," Oakland said.

"I haven't forgotten about Yellowstone, if that's what you mean."

Oakland nodded. "That's what I mean."

They parted, and Morgan walked slowly back to the bunkhouse. He was reluctant to go in, but he knew it had to come sooner or later. O'Toole and Tony Raines sat dismally on their bunks, watching Drift making up his bedroll. They both glared at Morgan, and he stopped just inside the door, intensely uncomfortable.

As Drift pulled an extra pair of boots from beneath his bunk, Jinglebob came in the door. He held out a greasy sack, his toothless gums turning the words mushy. "I put some huckydummy up for you."

Drift pulled the drawstrings tight on his war bag and tucked it under his arm, picking up the boots. "I'm not hungry," he said.

"Better take it," Raines told him. "You won't taste huckydummy like that anywhere else."

Drift stared at the gross cook, then a slow grin spread his lips across broken teeth. "You old tub of leaf lard," he said. "Drop it in the boot."

Jinglebob stuffed the sack in the boot with a pleased grin. As Drift turned to go, O'Toole stood up, taking the chip of rock from his pocket and holding it out to Drift. "It's a piece of the Blarney stone," the Irishman said. "You'd better kiss it for luck."

"You old women sound like I was going to a funeral," the foreman said gruffly. "I'll see you in town every Saturday. We'll have bigger drunks than ever. Now get out of my way and let me drift."

He passed Morgan with a single sour glance, and was gone. Jinglebob waddled over to a bunk and sat down heavily, staring blankly at the wall. O'Toole took a chair at the table, absently plucking the makings from his shirt pocket. He had the tobacco in the paper and had started rolling it with one hand when he realized what he was doing. He swept the whole thing to the floor. "One hand," he said disgustedly. "Who the hell wants to do it that way!"

Morgan slept poorly that night, haunted by a vague sense of guilt. He awoke the next morning to the sound of grumbling men and the acrid taint of wood smoke on the air. With the rest of the crew out at the line cabins or getting ready for fall roundup, O'Toole and Raines were the only ones left at the home ranch. They had already gone to breakfast by the time Morgan was dressed. As he stepped from the door of the bunkhouse, he could hear Jinglebob's grumbling voice coming from the cook house.

"Cornmeal mush for breakfast. Think I was a baby or something. Sop and taters for lunch. I used to eat a whole cow, bones and all. . . ."

"Man at the pot," Raines said.

"I ain't at the pot," Jinglebob snapped. "Git your own coffee. Brown gargle and boggy top for dinner. I'll starve, that's what I'll do. I'll have so much slack in my skin I can use the folds for extra war bags to carry my possibles in."

Morgan was reluctant to face their hostility, and prolonged the wait, rolling himself a cigarette by the bunkhouse. As he moved around the corner to get out of the wind and light up, he saw Nora angling down from the big house. The breeze plastered her light gingham dress against the youthful curves of her body. Her hair was pulled back over her ears and tied behind her neck with a ribbon. There was an eager freshness about her that lifted something poignant into his throat. She stopped before him, half smiling.

"You and Eddie get it thrashed out?"

"He didn't come back," Morgan told her.

The humor left her face; she reached out to touch his arm. "And you're blaming yourself."

He frowned at the ground. "Who else is to blame?"

"Me."

He shook his head, meeting her eyes. "I don't blame you."

"You're trying not to," she said. "But you can't help blaming me. I can see it in your eyes. You were afraid of this from the first. You told me that very first night. You didn't want him to get mixed up with a woman."

"I didn't think it would come out quite this way."

"Morgan, how can you blame either of us? We didn't do it deliberately to hurt Eddie. You didn't know he felt so deeply about me."

"I've tried to tell myself so," he said. "I've tried to tell myself we have no control over something like what happened to you and me."

She came closer, still touching his arm. "And now that it has happened?" He felt himself pull away from her. She let her hand drop off, an intense hurt darkening her eyes. "Will he always stand between us?" she said.

He shook his head miserably. "I can't help it, Nora. This was the first time in Eddie's life. He'd played around so much before, I didn't think he would ever really fall in love. I guess neither of us knows how much it hurt him."

She was looking deeply into his eyes. "I think you do," she said. "And I think if he only understood how it really was, he'd forgive us."

165

They were silent for a moment. The breeze skipped across the compound, ruffling the ribbon in her hair. Then its sound was drowned by the *drum* of hoofs on the road. They both turned to see Nations coming in on his little bay. He rode through the gate at a run and hauled the lathered animal up by the snubbing post, swinging off and coming toward them at a half run. His saddle-leather face was haggard with the strain of a long ride; his shotgun chaps were gray with dust.

"I thought you'd want to know quick, Morgan," he said in his nasal voice. "Eddie stopped off at the Crazy Horse line shack for grub. I couldn't stop him. He went over into Yellowstone."

Morgan heard Nora make a small choked sound. It was the only thing he was aware of in that moment. Finally he realized he had dropped his cigarette. Habit made him grind it out with a heel, although he was hardly aware of that. His voice had a pinched sound. "Why?" he said.

Nations settled wearily against the ground. "From what he said, it was something Drift told him. I couldn't get any more out of him. All he could talk about was showing you. He said no mother hen was going to cut in on it this time. What'd he mean, Morgan?"

Without answering, Morgan turned back into the bunkhouse. He got his old wooden-handled Remington off the bunk post, strapping it on. He slipped into his patched ducking jacket, and then turned and began putting his blanket roll together.

Nora came in hesitantly, standing at the head of the bunk. There was a strained look on her face. "I guess I can't stop you," she said.

"Do you want to?" he asked thinly. She did not answer. She stood by the bunk post, hands knotted together, biting her underlip. Morgan started lashing up his bedroll with swift jerks. His voice had a sharp, metallic sound. "Did he take that pass over to the park?" he asked Nations, who had followed Nora in.

"I guess so," Nations said. "It was night when he left. He was singing that song. The sound of it headed south toward the pass."

Nora sounded choked. "Funny he'd be singing."

"Not like he was happy," Nations said. "Like something you'd do without thinking. That last verse over and over. 'My brother got killed in a big stampede, now I've drawed aces and eights.' "

"It was such a strange song," she said in a small voice. "What does that last verse mean, Morgan?"

Morgan was still lashing up his bedroll, and his mind was filled with so many other things he hardly knew he spoke. "Funny you wouldn't know about that up here. Wild Bill Hickok was holding that hand in a poker game when he got killed in Deadwood. . . ." Morgan broke off, still bent over the bedroll. He realized he had never thought of it in those terms before.

"Yeah," Nations said. There was a strange look on his face. "Ever since, it's been known as a dead man's hand."

IX

Nations rode with Morgan as far as Crazy Horse Ridge. They drew rein in the pass to rest their animals a few minutes. Morgan dismounted and eased the cinch on the buckskin, staring somberly down the tumbled mountains to the great valley beyond. It seemed as if he had stood here in another time, another life.

"I ought to go with you," Nations said.

"You don't want to."

"Nobody wants to go down there. I ought to."

"I couldn't ask you to. It's my fault Eddie went alone. Somebody has to stay here with the cattle."

Nations tugged his hat down against the force of the wind. "I'm sorry for what I said in the bunkhouse."

Morgan was still staring off down the pass. "What was that?"

"You know."

"You mean about the dead man's hand?"

"Yeah. I just wasn't thinking."

"Forget it."

Morgan pulled the latigo tighter through the cinch ring, tucked its end in, climbed aboard. He lifted his hand to his hat brim in good bye, then started down the steep pass.

It was not hard to pick up Eddie's trail. It was the only fresh sign leading into the valley. It was almost evening by the time Morgan reached the river. He crossed its marshy bottom lands till the tracks turned northward along the water.

Autumn filled the country with a tomb-like silence. Only the chatter of magpies broke the quiet, dying again as suddenly as it had come. The grass was curled and dry and the horse's hoofs crushed it and lifted it like dust into the wind. The air seemed filled with that dust. It covered Morgan's face in a gritty mask, stinging his eyes, crawling down the back of his neck. His horse was spooky, shying at little things, and it made Morgan jumpy.

It was almost dark and he was threading his way through some ragged poplars when the animal began snorting and balking and staring off toward the west. Looking that way, Morgan had the sense of shadowy movement in a mat of twisted juniper higher on the slopes. He brought the horse to a halt, staring through the dusk. It was some time before he realized his hand had dropped to the stock of his saddle gun. He saw no more movement, and finally decided it was his own nerves. It was getting too dark to follow Eddie's sign without taking a chance of losing it, and it looked as if the gathering clouds would hide the moon.

He found a ford and crossed the river, hunting for a campsite that would give him cover and the advantage of height. He finally found a spot up against a rock face with an open meadow falling away before it. He was afraid to build a fire. It was a miserable, lonesome meal of cold biscuits and jerked meat he had gotten from Jinglebob. It got freezing cold later on and he huddled, shivering and sleepless, in his blankets for half the night, with his horse spooking and snorting on the picket rope.

He was up at dawn, on the trail again. It led him ever northward along the river, through the bottom lands where elk fed belly deep in the marshes and young ducks swam in ordered platoons on the stagnant backwaters, waiting for the first storm to send them south. The dryness of late August was in the air, and half a dozen small forest fires had broken out on the upper slopes, filling the sky with a buttery haze. When the wind changed to sweep that away, it brought the smell of sulphur to him making his horse snort peevishly. It made him remember Shyrock's words: *You're in a helluva country, Morgan. You'll wish you'd never come.*

It was near noon that he found the other trail. It was of one shod horse, mingling with the prints of Hell Kitty, following it for several miles, and then heading east back into the Absarokas. It did not look as fresh as Eddie's sign, yet it was hard to be certain. Some of the grass was still pressed down along the trail, but he could not be sure whether Eddie's animal had done it, or the other one. It filled him with an uneasy tension.

Eddie's trail left the river where it looped and took a short cut across a rocky ridge. It was here in the talus that Morgan lost the tracks. He circled for an hour. He could pick up the back trail but he could not find where it started again on the other side of the ridge. His circling had taken him back up into the mountains, and a grim desperation was beginning to fill him, when he saw the stain in the sky. He stared up over the feathery yellow-green tops of the lodgepole pines, thinking that it was another forest fire. But something pushed him up the slope, where the lodgepoles stood so densely the sun did not

reach the forest floor. He topped a ridge with the wind booming through the trees above him and found that he was overlooking a park tucked secretively into the folds of these nameless
mountains.

There was a skin teepee at the bottom of a rock-studded
meadow. Ratty ponies grazed on picket ropes and a naked child
ran squealing after a chattering squirrel and a pair of Indians
sat at the fire.

Morgan dropped cautiously down through the timber till he
was near open ground, then dismounted. He thought of taking
his rifle, but dismissed that. He hitched his horse, paused a moment at the edge of timber, then walked boldly into the open,
hands held high with the palms outward.

The child stopped running, staring at the white man with
owlish eyes. Neither of the Indians rose from the fire. The only
movement was the Winchesters in their laps. They both shifted
till they were pointed at Morgan. He continued to walk up to
them. He had no idea what tribe they were, what their language
was. The tall one nearest him had a porcupine roach in his hair,
a collar of black and white skunk fur around his neck. His body
was almost completely hidden by the matted buffalo robe,
worked richly in red and yellow quills. Only his bare ankles
showed, shining like old copper in the sun. The other man was
short and stocky, with a deep gash across the bridge of his nose
that had healed to a white scar. He, too, was wrapped in a robe.
They stared silently at Morgan as he stopped before them, and
he could see the suspicion sharpening the planes of their dark
faces. Finally the tall one held up one hand.

"*Hohahe*," he said.

Morgan nodded. "Speak English?"

"*Wanbli K'leska*," the short man said. He stared at Morgan
with glittering eyes, saying nothing more. It lasted so long that
Morgan was going to make another try, when the tall one

abruptly turned toward the teepee, calling: "Tasina!"

In a moment, an ugly old woman waddled flat-footed from the lodge with a long clay-bowled pipe in her hand. She handed it to the taller man with a buckskin bag of tobacco. Lighting it, he conveyed to Morgan that he should sit down. When Morgan was cross-legged on the ground, facing them across the fire, the Indian pointed the pipe to the east, allowing a puff of smoke to rise toward the sky.

"*Tunka sila le ayahpe ya yo,*" he said.

He repeated this at the other three points of the compass, then ceremoniously handed the pipe over. Morgan understood the rudiments of the peace pipe, and did the same thing, without speaking.

They were watching him strangely now. Their faces were so wooden that it was hard to read any expression in them. But it seemed as if the suspicion was gone. Perhaps it was the eyes. They seemed to be studying Morgan intently, glittering with an indefinable speculation. He handed the pipe to the shorter man, trying not to reveal the tension that gripped him. He heard the woman moving around behind him somewhere. It made the skin on his neck crawl. Then she came into his field of vision again, herding the child into the teepee. The second man finished with the pipe, and put it in his lap, waiting for Morgan to speak.

He began trying to convey his questions by drawing in the earth. It took him a long time to make the Indians realize he was asking if they had seen Eddie. At last the shorter man turned to look at the other, who seemed to be the leader of the two. He nodded, and the one with the hacked nose got up and went over to the teepee. He rummaged through the gear at the door and finally lifted out a belt of great silver *conchas* that they must have traded from some Navajo. He carried this over to one of the buffalo saddles on the ground near the fire. He glanced at Morgan with a secretive look tucking his eyes deeply into his cheeks, and then carefully laid one of the *conchas* against the saddle. Morgan nodded slowly. The words left him in a whisper.

"Silver-plated."

Morgan came in sight of Yellowstone Lake near sunset. He drew rein on the ridge of the slope that dropped off to the lakeshore, staring down at the vast body of sun-burnished water that stretched away like a coppery mirror to the haze-shrouded mountains beyond. Even at this distance its rank and marshy odors were freighted on the wind, and he could see the peevish burst of steam from an underwater geyser near the shore. The Indians had guided him here by a map drawn in the dirt and by sign language. They had conveyed to Morgan that the day before they had seen Eddie near the lake where it was shaped like a thumb. It gave Morgan a lost feeling to have that gap of time between himself and the boy.

He pressed his horse down to the lake, following its rim till he reached the thumb-shaped bay. He found the sign here just before nightfall, the trail of shod hoofs with that feather-edge shoe Hell Kitty wore on her right rear hoof to prevent brushing.

He ate a cold dinner, waiting tensely for the moon to give him light. When it came, he pushed on, around a shore covered with stately lodgepoles that filtered the moonlight through in an eerie tide, past pools of bubbling mud that set the weary horse to fiddling again.

Suddenly there was a sound like the hiss of a gargantuan cat. The horse screamed wildly and reared up, almost pitching Morgan off. From one of the pools a stream of boiling water was shooting twenty feet into the air. Morgan fought to quiet the horse, but some of the steaming water splashed on its rump, setting the beast off again. He gave the horse its head and let it race in a dead run away from the boiling pools. The smell of their sulphur still filled the air when he finally drew the animal in. It was shuddering like a frightened child, its coat marbled with dirty yellow lather.

It took him an hour to pick up the trail again. It led him through the night, away from the lake, into steep mountains. Near dawn, a milky haze began to fill the trees, turning them to ghostly spires. At first he thought it was the morning fog, coming up off the river. Then the sound of that angry *hissing* reached him, and he broke into an open meadow and saw to his south another geyser. It was much bigger than any he had yet seen, throwing its column of boiling water high into the air, to dissipate and settle like a mist over the timbered slopes.

He passed through this mist with a grackle setting up a wild cackling off to his left somewhere. He was almost across the meadow when the bird stopped. The horse began to snort and fight the bit. These were signs a man came to know.

Morgan drew the horse into the trees and stepped off, pulling his Henry from its saddle scabbard. The Indians were in his mind again. Or perhaps it had only brought them to the surface; he knew they must have been at the back of his mind all the time. He was remembering the speculation in their eyes, the secretive look that had come to the one with the gashed nose when he laid the silver *concha* against the saddle. Their first suspicion had been allayed too quickly. They had been too willing to give him the information he wanted. Morgan realized he should have watched his back trail more carefully.

Then he saw the motion. His rifle raised in his hands. His eyes ached from trying to follow it in the weird mist. Slowly the motion took ghostly shape. It seemed to be coming from the timber across the meadow. Farther away, the *hissing* of the geyser was dying down. The mist began to lighten. Then the shape resolved itself. The tension washed out of Morgan, leaving only the fluttery sickness of reaction in his stomach. It was a mule deer, picking its way daintily down the slope. Rutting season gave the rusty red of its summer coat a glossy sheen. The buck stopped to rub some velvet off its antlers against a juniper. Morgan watched it out of sight, still unwilling to give up. The grackle did not start again. The timber was achingly quiet.

With great care, Morgan circled the shallow valley, but he found no sign except that of the buck. Finally, although he was not satisfied, the urgency in him pushed Morgan on. He dropped out of the valley and reached a river, dammed to shimmering pools by beaver. The winter's store of cottonwood had already been cut and stood poked in the mud like so many sticks, waiting for the time when the ice would hold the beaver under.

A roaring filled the forest now. The slopes were gradually steepening to form a narrow cañon through which the river flowed, crashing over rocks that turned it to frothing whitewater. There was a game trail up the cañon wall, and Morgan took this. Behind him, the geyser erupted again, throwing humid fog through the timber to join the mist rising off the roaring rapids. As the trail rose higher above the savage water below, Morgan turned in the saddle, unable to shake off that feeling of being followed. But he could not see far in the mist. He rounded a turn and brought his horse up sharply where the ledge had been swept away by a rock slide. He felt his eyes drawn down that slide toward the river, fifty feet below.

There was a sand spit down there, a point of beach over which the slide had spilled into the river, and, through the shredded mist hovering over the rapids, Morgan saw the horse lying on that beach, half buried beneath the rocks and débris of the slide. Part of its rigging was visible. The silver mounting on the saddle shimmered dully in the haze.

X

The brittle winds of autumn seemed to have swept Chinook clean of life and movement. Wheel tracks scrawled silvery scars against the empty street's hoof-powdered dust. The splintered planks of the sidewalk ran for six blocks without echoing the passage of boots. False fronts and wooden overhangs etched a sharp pattern out of the sun-bleached sky, and the dust-filmed buildings seemed to shoulder more closely together than before, as if seeking mutual protection against the blasts of coming winter. There was a pair of cow ponies at the hitch rack before the Hoof and Horn, but their utter lack of movement made lifeless statues of them. A spotted hound scuttled across the street and disappeared in an alley. Its furtive motion only seemed to intensify the emptiness it left behind.

Morgan Banning had never seen the town so deserted. He pulled his beaten buckskin to a halt at the head of the street, settling in heavy defeat against the saddle. The horse stood with bowed head, its hairy coat stiff with dried sweat, its snout briny with lather that had not been wiped off in three days. Morgan himself looked as beaten. His Levi's were gray with dust and blotched with mud and there was a big tear across one knee. Two inches of scrubby black beard filled the hollows of his gaunt cheeks, and his eyes were red-rimmed and feverish. His mind seemed unable to cope with a problem as simple as what he should do next.

Three days of riding lay behind him. There were great blank spaces in which he could remember nothing. He had slept on the way back. He knew that. But he did not know when. He had eaten. But he did not know what. His whole being seemed crushed beneath the weight of a terrible apathy. He could not seem to hold one clear thought in his mind more than a few seconds. He became aware of stirrings in the street. A pair of men he did not recognize stepped from the general store. One was filling a pipe and talking to the other, but they both kept sending Morgan furtive glances. The barber came from his shop with a broom and started sweeping the sidewalk. An idler appeared from the hotel lobby, picking his teeth. He was more open about staring at Morgan.

Suddenly Morgan realized what they were all doing. They had been waiting for him. They knew why he had gone. Word must have spread from the Keyhole. And now they knew why he had come back. There was something repellent about their morbid curiosity. The stir they brought to the street was like the furtive scurrying of rats.

He gigged his horse on down the street. What could he do now? The simple, obvious things. Get a room. Clean up. Eat. Sleep. He probably needed sleep more than food. Yet he could feel a need for none of these things. Perhaps a drink would help. He suddenly wanted the scalding fire of rotgut whiskey to clear the cobwebs out of him, to burn life back in.

He turned his horse in at the Hoof and Horn, not even noticing the brand on the other animals there. He dismounted stiffly and went inside and was halfway to the bar before he recognized the men standing there, turned toward him. The large chamber was unlit, and in the gloom Charlie King's face was a dark enigma. Tom Law stood beside him, a glass held halfway to his lips. Morgan was vaguely aware of Dr. Ashland and Duncan Innes, the land agent, sitting at a poker table in the rear.

"Heard you went into Yellowstone," King said. "Did you find your brother?"

It was as if the man's voice released all the pent-up fury and bitterness and grief that had lain beneath Morgan's apathy all the way back. He heard the sudden sharp beat of his boots against the splintered floor. He saw the bartender's mouth open in some protest. Then he was up against King, grabbing the man's coat with both hands, and jerking him up against the bar.

176

"You know I found him. You know he's dead. . . ."

Law swung around King to hook Morgan's elbow, trying to spin him away from King. Morgan tore free, and then smashed Law across the face with a wild swing of his arm. The blow knocked the man back into a chair. It spilled with him, and he went down. Morgan had not released King with his other hand. He wheeled back to thrust all his weight against the man as King tried to lunge outward. He jammed his forearm across King's throat, bending him back over the bar. His voice was wild and broken.

"You know I found him. That rockslide wasn't any accident. Tell me it wasn't any accident."

Morgan felt another hand on his arm, and started to strike out again. But it did not try to pull him away. It was merely a warm, insistent pressure. Dr. Ashland's voice was in his ear, soft and soothing. "Let him go, Morgan. You're not thinking straight, son. How could he know what happened? Come away, now. Come away."

It was the soft insistence of Ashland's voice, rather than the words, that finally seeped through the red haze in Morgan's brain. He stared down at King's face, twisted into a grimace with the pressure of that forearm against his neck. He suddenly found himself wondering what he was doing here. Everything was so nightmarish, so out of joint. That one burst of fury seemed to have left him spent of emotion. Dully he relinquished his grip on King's coat, pulled his arm off King's neck.

The half-breed straightened up. His breathing went in and out of him in stertorous gusts, and there was a whipped look on his face.

"Let it go, King," Dr. Ashland said. "Morgan's not in his right mind. He's been riding all the way back with that on his soul. He isn't responsible."

King pulled his coat straight with a jerky movement. There

was an intense restraint to the way his chin was sunk against his neck. It left coppery furrows of flesh about his jaw. His body was trembling visibly. Repressed violence ran its guttural thread through his thick voice. "You'd better get him out of here, then," he told the doctor. "Under any other circumstances, I think I'd kill him."

Morgan felt the doctor pull him around. He saw that Tom Law had gotten to his feet and was leaning back against the table, and noticed in a detached way the hate in the man's eyes. Like a sleepwalker he allowed Dr. Ashland to lead him out of the saloon and across the street and up the rickety outside stairs to the doctor's office above the general store, a pair of stuffy rooms filled with the penetrating reek of carbolic acid.

"First thing you'd better do is sleep," Dr. Ashland told him. "There's a bed in the back room."

Morgan stumbled through the door into the other room and dropped onto the sagging cot without even removing his clothes. The doctor threw a couple of old Army blankets over him; he was asleep before the medical man left the room.

Morgan awoke by degrees. His first awareness was of a foul taste in his mouth. Then of his body aching all over. Finally of voices in the other room. It took him a few moments to recognize the voice of Carradine, the government inspector.

"I'm going to be in Cody through the winter. If anything comes up, you double-check on it before you let them wire me."

"I know tick fever when I see it," Dr. Ashland told him. "Half my patients around here are animals. I'm probably a better veterinarian than I am a doctor."

Carradine thanked Ashland and said good bye. Morgan swung his legs off the bed and groggily gained his feet, crossing to open the door into the other room. For the first time he noticed how musty and cramped it was, almost filled by the roll-top desk and examination table and a pair of rickety chairs. The doctor was silhouetted against the dust-filmed panes of the single barn-sash window that lit the room. His smile etched a million wrinkles into his gaunt face; he tilted his head at one of the chairs.

"Better sit down and take a stiff one. You look like you're about to buckle in the middle."

Morgan lowered himself into a chair, accepting the drink the doctor poured for him. He took it neat, and then leaned into the chair, tilting his head over its back and squinting his eyes shut, letting the fiery warmth of the whiskey spread through his grateful body.

"Guess you heard the inspector leave," Dr. Ashland said. "From what he said, you just got under the wire with that trail herd. Secretary of Agriculture's slapped a quarantine on all southern cattle. I thought the Bureau of Animal Industry would have the thing licked by now. They've been working on it since 'Eighty-Three. Claim protozoa are the intracellular parasites causing the thing. . . ." Ashland broke off, peering at Morgan. "You ain't listening."

Morgan straightened his head, pinched the bridge of his nose between a thumb and forefinger. "I'm sorry. I guess I'm not much good for talking."

"I thought prattle might take your mind off it. Maybe it'd be better if you got it off your chest, Morgan."

Morgan set his glass on the table and leaned forward to place his elbows on his knees, staring at the floor. "Maybe you're right. I'll have to face it sooner or later. I couldn't face it for three days. All the way back I just couldn't think about it. Like I was riding in a daze. It all seemed to boil over when I saw King."

"You needed something to strike out at. You'd been riding

back for three days with that on your soul. It was a natural re-action."

Morgan shook his head. "I guess I've had something on my mind about King from the first. He had Law watching Eddie and me from the first night we hit Chinook. Then Law and Rideout jumped me in the Absarokas."

"King's tried to scare more than one suitor away from Nora," Ashland said.

Morgan looked up at him. "Do you honestly believe it was no more than that?"

Ashland pursed his lips, frowning at Morgan. "You want to connect King up with what's happening in Yellowstone?"

"The man who shot Shyrock left one print behind," Morgan said, straightening up in the chair. "A star on the heel of his boot."

"A boot maker down in Cody does that. Like metal taps on the toes to keep them from wearing down. You could find a dozen men around here with boots he made."

"All with stars?"

Confusion shuttled through Ashland's face. "No." He pursed his lips. "The boot maker claims he has a different design for each pair of boots. That sounds impossible to me."

"You ever see the bottoms of King's boots?"

"I never had occasion to." The doctor snorted. "He must wear more than one pair anyway. It just doesn't add up, Mor-gan. What would King be doing over in Yellowstone? We haven't had any rustling in a long time. No known crime big enough so's a man would kill to keep it a secret. King is suffering as much as any other man. He must have lost a lot of cattle over there. You don't see half the Double Arrow stuff on the upper ranges you used to. He'll go bust just as quick as the rest of them if we keep losing beef over there and can't get it back."

Morgan was frowning as he looked out the window, remembering the hidden park tucked away in those nameless mountains, the skin teepee, the enigmatic faces. "How about Indians?"

"That's more logical. There's always a few bronco Sioux getting off the reservation. Yellowstone's holy to them, you know. No Indian ever liked white men tampering with his gods."

Morgan swung around to meet his eyes. "And Charlie King's half Indian."

Ashland hit the desk. "Damn it, Morgan. You forget King hates his Indian blood. I hold no brief for the man. He's gotten a raw deal here, but he's got a wild streak in him. It isn't only his Indian blood. His father was wild. King would have that streak in him if he was white or red. But you can't go condemning him just for that. You needed some way to let off steam when you came back, and he was the only man in the room who'd ever antagonized you. Look at it this way. You're on Oakland's side of the fence now. Who would be the villain if you were on King's side?"

Morgan nodded rueful acceptance. "I guess you're right. It's all in the point of view."

Ashland drummed on the desk a moment, studying Morgan. When he finally spoke, his voice held a husky compassion. "You actually found Eddie?"

Morgan's lids drew together till his eyes were hardly visible. "He was underneath the rock slide. I dug him free and buried him out there. I didn't see any point in bringing him back. This wasn't any more his home than Yellowstone. I covered the grave with rocks so the wolves wouldn't get him. . . ."

He trailed off, staring at the floor, and Ashland let a space go by before asking: "Did you find any sign around the slide?"

"Nothing. And I looked. Believe me, I looked."

Ashland drew a deep breath. "You see what you're up against. Those slides are a natural thing. They happen all the time. I've treated several men who got caught in them." He paused, as if

Les Savage, Jr.

waiting for Morgan to speak. Then he nodded toward the washroom. "Why don't you clean up? You can use my razor. I got your extra clothes from your blanket roll when I put your horse in the livery stable."

Morgan washed and shaved and changed clothes. Then they went downstairs. He was surprised to find that it was almost noon. He had slept eighteen hours through. The doctor turned west along the main street. The white false fronts of the buildings reflected the sun brightly, as if trying to retain the last heat of summer, but there was an undeniable chill to the air that even midday could not dispel. Morgan pulled his hat down to block off the glare and sided the doctor moodily down the walk.

As they passed the Land Office, they heard the scrape of a chair pushed back, and the hurried sound of boots. Duncan Innes appeared in the doorway, halting them with his call. He came on out and put a hand on Morgan's arm.

"I was sorry to hear about your brother, Morgan. I mean it," he said.

Morgan dipped his head in acknowledgment.

Innes hesitated, then went on: "I thought I'd tell you, the final release on the Doubloon has come through from the East. The place is yours anytime you want to sign the papers."

Morgan stared past the man, thinking of the long years he had dreamed of this moment. "Thanks, Innes," he said.

The man waited, as if expecting something else. When Morgan said no more, Innes glanced quizzically at Ashland. Something passed between them.

"Well," Innes said awkwardly, "I'll see you, then."

After he had gone, and they were walking on down the street, Ashland said: "A man often reveals himself as much by what he doesn't say as by what he does. You didn't tell Innes you'd get the papers. Does that mean you aren't going to buy the Doubloon?"

182

"I don't know." Morgan frowned helplessly. "I just can't seem to feel anything, Doc. I did for that minute in the Hoof and Horn. I guess I wanted revenge. It must have been working at me all the way back from Yellowstone and I took it out on King. But now I don't even feel that."

"I'm glad," Ashland said. "Wanting revenge in a reaction like that is natural. You've got to blow off somewhere. But I always thought it would take an essentially small man to really let revenge become a driving motive."

"Small or big, I can't feel it. I should want to get even for Eddie somehow. I should want to stay here and find out for sure what happened to him. But I can't seem to get my hands on anything. It's like fighting cobwebs, inside and out. I feel so empty."

Ashland looked at him closely. "Are you saying you have nothing to stay in Chinook for?"

"I don't know." Morgan shook his head dully. "I just don't know anything, Doc."

The first snow came that night. It was not born on storm. It came softly, banking up along the curbs and at the bases of the buildings and hiding the squalor of rutted streets and can-littered alleys. Morgan awoke with the chill of it in his hotel room and swung out of bed and walked to the window and looked out on a white world. He thought of it falling out there on Eddie's grave and it made him feel lonely and cold.

He went through the motions of dressing and shaving automatically, and then went downstairs for breakfast. He was not hungry and only had black coffee and doughnuts. Up to now his apathy had kept him from thinking of the Keyhole. But he knew he would have to face it sooner or later. He had a deep reluctance to go back there. It was the same thing that had made him ride into town, instead of turning off to the ranch on

183

his return from Yellowstone. The motive then had been more obscure, but it had been the same. He didn't want to face them yet, to talk with them about it. The crew, Janice, Oakland had all known Eddie so much better than had anyone in town. And yet it was more than that. He found it hard to admit to himself. It was Nora he really didn't want to face.

He left the café and walked restlessly down the main street, Mackinaw collar turned up against the chill, hands buried in his pockets. The wind was wet with the tenuous odor of fresh snow. The wheels of an early-morning wagon had cut through to the mud, leaving scummy brown channels in the alabaster mantle of the street. He was beyond the hotel, with no destination in mind, when he saw the rider come into the street from the west on the dainty little bay with the jet-black points. He felt his whole body pivot with the impulse to turn into the nearest doorway, and checked it, disgusted with himself.

Nora saw him and brought her horse down the two blocks at a trot. She had a heavy cloak over her jade-green riding habit, and the wealth of her auburn hair was wound in a tight coronet to accommodate the ear-flapped cold country hat she wore. She pulled the bay in with the breath steaming from its pink nostrils. She looked down at Morgan with tears in her eyes and a deep compassion on her face.

"You've heard," he said.

"Duncan Innes was by last night. He told us. Morgan. . . ."

She broke off helplessly, the tears soundlessly brimming over and rolling down her cheeks. He realized she wanted to get down and reached up to help her as she swung off the animal. Then she stood facing him, so close they were almost touching, her face tilted down and her eyes closed for a moment.

"I thought I'd cried it out last night," she said. She caught his hands, opening her eyes to look at them, gripping them tightly. "I wish I could say something, Morgan."

184

"I know how you feel," he said in a low voice. "The less said the better. It's still too close."

She threw up her head to look at him, brushing the tears from her eyes with a mittened hand. "I guess you're right . . . Innes said the Doubloon was clear. When are you moving in?"

"I don't know."

Her eyes darkened as she saw the expression on his face. "Maybe you aren't moving in."

"I can't say, Nora. I've got to think it out."

"Eddie's still between us, isn't he?"

He shook his head miserably. "Please, Nora. I don't know what's inside me now. It's so vague and mixed up."

"You should have come back to the Keyhole instead of here. You're one of us. You didn't want to face me, did you, Morgan? Why not admit it? We've got to talk it out sooner or later. You still blame yourself for what happened to Eddie. I think you blame me, too. You feel that we sent him out there to die."

He shook his head in a vague torture. "Nora, I don't blame you. . . ."

"Might as well admit it," she said. "It's in your face. Every time you saw me, touched me, thought about me, it would be in your mind, it would stand between us. If I hadn't kissed you that day, Eddie would be alive right now."

XI

It was too cold to remain outside long, after Nora had gone. Morgan could not face the confinement of his room. The only place left was a saloon. He bought a beer at the Hoof and Horn and took one of the tables next to the wall. He did not drink much of it and it soon grew flat, and then he sat there staring at nothing and thinking of nothing, that strange apathy pressing him down.

The saloon was not busy at this hour. A couple of townsmen

drifted in for a drink, sending Morgan their tight stares. The pale shafts of sunlight coming through the front door slowly swung around on the floor till it was afternoon. There were more men at the bar. There were a dozen cigarette butts around Morgan's chair. Finally he realized how late it had grown and was about to rise when one of the men detached himself from the crowd and walked over to the table.

"I'm Roger Bardine," he said. "Down Cody way. I hear you're taking over the Doubloon. It isn't stocked, is it?"

"The Eastern owners let the courts dispose of the stock when Dodge disappeared," Morgan said.

"With this new quarantine law, you won't be able to bring any feeders up from Texas," Bardine said. "I've got a thousand double-wintered whitefaces I'd like to sell, if you're interested."

Morgan stared at the half-empty beer glass, trying to reach a decision. This was another consideration he had been unwilling to face. He knew he would have to let Innes know soon about the Doubloon. And if he took it, he'd need stock.

"Sit down, Bardine," he said. "We'll talk about it."

Bardine dragged up a chair, slacking into it. "Did you know Dodge?"

"No, but from what I gather, the Doubloon is sort of a jinx spread."

"In a way," Bardine admitted. "With this trouble in Yellowstone, nobody's wanted to buy it. Being so close to the park, a lot of Doubloon cattle are bound to drift over there. I understand Dodge had lost so many head in Yellowstone he was about to close his books anyway."

"That's what's happening to a lot of the outfits around here," Morgan said absently. "Half the hands won't even follow a drift into Yellowstone. The ones that do run into trouble. You ever been over there?"

"Oakland gathered a bunch of us to ride over in force. We

186

didn't dig up anything except a couple of Sioux and a lot of saddle sores."

Morgan frowned at him. "Was one of the Indians a short, bowlegged man with a gash on his nose?"

"That's right. You've seen them?"

Morgan was looking past Bardine. "Yes," he said. "I have."

That was the way it went. Bardine wanted too much for his cattle. Morgan wouldn't commit himself. He turned the talk back to Yellowstone and found out some more he hadn't heard before. It did not add up to anything, but he automatically tucked it away for future reference. Later, Dr. Ashland joined them, and a game of poker started. They broke for supper, and then went back to the cards. A man from Meeteetse sat in. He got to talking about Yellowstone, too. Morgan prodded him and picked up a couple more things he had not heard. The game broke up late, and he slept through till 11:00 A.M. the next day. He wandered around the town till afternoon, got a haircut and shave, found himself in the Hoof and Horn again after supper. Bardine was still there and other cattlemen drifted in and out during the evening. There was another game with Dr. Ashland sitting in and Morgan letting the talk swing around to Yellowstone again. Near 10:00 P.M. Tom Law came in and got a drink at the bar. He watched Morgan from there, the overhead lights making black pools of his cavernous eye sockets.

"That's one of King's men, isn't it?" Bardine said.

Dr. Ashland was studying his hand with pursed lips. "Yeah. Wonder what he's doing in town on a week night. King's short-handed as it is."

"Did he ship any beef this year?" Bardine asked.

"Not for two years," Dr. Ashland said.

Bardine shook his head. "They're still trying to squeeze him out, aren't they? How did they block him off?"

"It's funny," Ashland said. "Oakland claims they haven't put the pressure on that way. King could ship if he wanted." He put down two cards glancing at Morgan. "You want to keep your eye on Law. I don't think he's forgot that time you knocked him down in here."

Morgan smiled thinly. "He's got more than that to remember."

They played till after 11:00 P.M. and the game broke up. Law was still at the bar when Morgan left. Dr. Ashland and Bardine had remained at the table for a last drink. The street was an empty black chasm between the dim false fronts. The only light came from the windows of Innes's Land Office, a block down on the other side of the street. Their twin yellow streamers fell across the splintered sidewalk and were swallowed by darkness. A spotted hound was nosing a garbage pail in the alley siding the Hoof and Horn. He scuttled away as Morgan passed.

The wind came in noisy gusts, carrying a chill that made Morgan pull up the collar of his Mackinaw. He reached the alley between the general store and the hotel. Halfway down this alley was an outside stairway that led to the second story and was a nearer route to Morgan's room than the one through the lobby. Night's cold had already formed a thin crust on the slush, and Morgan's boots made a *crackling* sound, breaking through this, as he stepped off the sidewalk and turned into the alley. It took him abruptly out of the wind, and it suddenly seemed very quiet. He was almost to the dark mouth of the covered steps when a faint *creak* of wood reached him.

He stopped sharply, peering into the thick darkness till he could make out the vague form of a man, stepping out from the stairway. Then he heard the muted *clatter* on the sidewalk behind him and the sharp *crackle* of snow crust, as a man stepped from the sidewalk into the alley's entrance. Morgan half wheeled that way, to see a man silhouetted against the light of the Land Office across the street. The man's hat brim made a fluttering sound against his face. Then it stopped, as he stepped into the alley, out of the wind.

Morgan took two quick steps to the rear, till his back was up against the wall of the hotel. He started unbuttoning his Mackinaw to get at his gun. The man at the stairway was about ten paces to his left, and had started moving in. The one at the end of the alley was about the same distance from his right, and had never stopped.

"Law," Morgan said. There was no question in his voice. "I didn't think you'd be able to let it go." Neither man answered. The only sound was that of their boots *crunching* through the crust. "Or is it something else?" Morgan asked softly. Again they did not answer. Each of them was only about five paces from him now. He raised his voice. "All right. I've got my hand on my gun now. Take another step and you aren't getting out of this without a shooting."

Both of them stopped abruptly. He could barely see them. There was a moment of intense silence in the alley. The wind was whipping through the street but it sounded very far away. Then Law spoke, and from the position of his voice Morgan knew he was the one who had come in from the street.

"Maybe we didn't aim to get out of this without a shooting," he said.

"Then you won't get out of it without a killing," Dr. Ashland said from behind Law. "If you start shooting, Law, I'm going to empty my gun in you."

Morgan felt tension flatten him harder against the wall. Again there was that silence, thick as cotton in the alley, while the wind whipped at the buildings out in the street. Finally Dr. Ashland spoke again: "If that's Rideout, you and him both come out here. I saw your horses down in front of the livery stable. It shouldn't take you long to get out of town."

After another long hesitation, Morgan heard Law stir. "Keep

this in your mind, Banning," he said. His voice trembled with anger. "The doctor won't always be around."

"You'd better go, Law," Ashland said.

Rideout moved around Morgan and joined Law and they walked toward Dr. Ashland. Morgan felt his whole body sag with the tension washing out of him. There was the fluttery nausea of reaction in his belly. He heard the *clatter* of their feet as the two men stepped onto the sidewalk.

"Thanks, Doc," he said.

Ashland came down the alley toward him. "Forget it. I always take special care of my cash customers."

Morgan could not help smiling. "I didn't know you carried a gun."

"I don't. I borrowed Bardine's. Law left the saloon about two minutes after you did and I figured what he had in his mind."

"Are you sure it'll be safe for you to walk home now?"

"We'll wait till they leave town," Ashland said. There was a silence, and Morgan sensed the man looking at him intently. "I wonder what Bardine would do if he knew you were just leading him on?" Ashland said at last.

Morgan felt a tug of surprise. "Leading him on?"

"Oh, you've convinced yourself you're doing business. You're a man who's going to buy an outfit and you need stock. So you talk to a man from Cody who has whitefaces to sell, or a man from Meeteetse. But after a while, the talk always swings around to Yellowstone. I've seen it happen two nights, Morgan. That's all you're really interested in, isn't it?"

Morgan let out a long breath. "I guess so, if I'd only face it."

"And yet, are you really interested in that?"

It struck home, and Morgan shook his head miserably. "I don't know, Doc. It's like fighting cobwebs. I've tried to tell myself I should stay here. I'm not convinced Eddie's death was accidental. I've tried to tell myself I should feel some need of revenge. He was my own brother. But everything I feel is so jumbled. I can't find out anything for certain about Yellowstone. I haven't a shred of evidence to prove Eddie was murdered. You can't want revenge against a rock slide. I'm like a clock that's running down."

Dr. Ashland put his hand on Morgan's shoulder. "I don't think Law and Rideout will be in town again till Saturday night. King certainly can't spare them from the cattle. It's likely they did this on their own. I think it would be safe for you to take a ride. Why don't you go out to the Doubloon tomorrow? Maybe you'll find your answer there."

Morgan rode out of Chinook the next day. Although the first snow had melted in the flats, it still remained in the higher peaks, banking up on either side of the road and clinging in great white patches to the sides of the mountains.

He reached the glacier near noon, and pulled up his laboring horse. He did not know how long he sat there, looking down at the Doubloon. The green fields were sere and brown now. There were still banks of snow up against the barns and the house, and a section of fence had fallen down since he had seen it last. He noticed these things indifferently. He was remembering all that he had felt upon first seeing the place. He was remembering the fulfillment of some deep need within him. That fulfillment was no longer there. Remembering the sense of infinite peace, as if he had at last come home. That peace was not there. Remembering the stilling of restlessness and vague longings he had known during all the wandering years of his youth. They were no longer stilled. He looked down on the Doubloon and could feel nothing. And he knew now why the doctor had sent him up here. Ashland had seen what was happening to him more clearly than he had.

Morgan turned his horse around, finally, and rode back. He

reached the cut-off to the Keyhole to find Janice Wickliffe wait-ing there in the wagon with the red rack bed. He checked his horse, unable to feel surprise.

"I was in town shopping," she said. "Doctor Ashland told me you'd gone to the Doubloon." She bent forward slightly, to peer at his face. "Did you find what you wanted, Morgan?"

"I guess I did," he said dully.

"And now you're leaving."

He glanced at her. "Does it show that much?"

"You're a man who's lost everything, Morgan, and you show it." She gathered her sheepskin coat about her, sitting straighter. "I can understand the Doubloon not meaning anything to you any more. A big part of that dream was Eddie. Too big a part. But what about him? Don't you want to find out who killed him?"

"Don't you think I've tried. . . ." He broke off, sagging in the saddle. "Why do you say *who*, Janice? He was caught in a rock slide. That's all I know. I've tried to find out more, even though I have nothing to go on. I'm fighting shadows. You can't keep that up forever."

"It's come around full circle, hasn't it?" she said. "This only justified what you saw coming from the very beginning. You tried to stop Eddie with Nora. It had always caused trouble before. And now everything you feared has come about."

He dropped his eyes. "I suppose that's the way I feel. It's like some kind of cycle has been completed. It's like I had no control over it from the start. I was brought up here for this to happen, and now it's over with, and it's time to go. There's nothing to keep me."

"Nothing?" she asked.

He forced himself to meet her eyes. "You're thinking of Nora."

"She told me how you feel," Janice said. "You blame yourself for Eddie's death. You're wrong, Morgan. You didn't have anything to do with it. You were all simply caught in circumstances over which you had no control."

"Ashland tried to tell me the same thing," Morgan said. "It doesn't help. I feel that way and I can't help it."

"You have no right to blame yourself," she said. "Do you know where Eddie had been that day just before he came in and found you kissing Nora?"

"Out back, I guess. I thought Nora had gone for some water."

"I'd gone to get the water," Janice said. "Eddie found me at the creek. Before he went back, he told me your reaction to Oakland's offer. He said you blamed his romance with Nora for dragging you into this mess. He knew you wanted to pull out and he didn't think you were going to accept Oakland's proposition. Eddie said he wasn't even going to argue with you. He was going over into Yellowstone alone."

He stared at her in surprise, the implications of that beginning to stir in him. "You're not just telling me this?"

"Of course not," she said. "Don't you see . . . you're not to blame for his going over into Yellowstone. He would have gone whether he found you kissing Nora or not."

He frowned at the ground, unwilling to accept such a simple way out. His sense of guilt was too deep.

"I suppose it's going to take you some time to accept the fact that you're not to blame," she said. "You see it with your mind, but you still feel responsible. I'm not going to argue with you about it. I don't think you can leave Chinook Basin anyway."

He raised his eyes. "Now what do you mean?"

"Nations told us what Eddie said before he left the line shack for Yellowstone. He was going to find something that threatened the whole of Chinook Basin. . . ."

"Eddie got that from Drift when Drift was drunk," Morgan said.

"And you don't put any faith in the babblings of a drunk?"

"It's obvious what Drift meant," he said. "This quarantine keeping feeders out of the north even makes it worse. The outfits around here aren't able to ship fresh stock in. The cattle they have keep drifting into Yellowstone and they can't get them back. It's going to bust everybody."

"Do you really think that's what Drift meant, Morgan?" she asked. He tried to meet her gaze, but could not keep the confusion from his eyes. "You know you don't," Janice said. "It's something more than just the loss of cattle. And if it threatens Chinook Basin that much, it threatens Nora, too. Can you ride away and leave that hanging over her head?"

XII

It was long after dark when they got back to the Keyhole. Lamp-light made fuzzy squares of the bottle windows in the bunk-house. Janice pulled up to the barn and Morgan swung off to open the door and light a bull's-eye lantern. They had led his horse back-hitched to the tailgate, and he unsaddled the animal and unhitched the wagon team and found empty stalls for all three. He was forking hay and Janice was up front filling a tin with corn for the horses, when they heard a shout from outside. Morgan put the fork down and joined Janice at the door. The front door of the main house was open, spilling light out over the porch and into the compound. The gangling figure was silhouetted in this, coming jerkily down the steps and shouting hoarsely: "I never had anything to do with the Chinese navy!"

Nora appeared in the doorway behind, carrying a pitcher in one hand. "Shyrock, come back here, you'll catch your death of cold."

Shyrock was veering across the compound, shouting at the top of his voice. Nora ran down the steps after him, trying to catch up. The bunkhouse door opened and Jinglebob burst out in his nightcap and long underwear.

"Nora!" he shouted. "Throw it on him. It's the only way you can wake him up."

"I can't!" Nora cried angrily. "He'll catch pneumonia."

"You've got to. Throw it in his face."

"I can't. I just can't."

"I never worked for the Chinese navy!"

Shyrock was halfway to the barn, with Nora running after him, by the time Jinglebob reached them. He took the pitcher from Nora and jumped after Shyrock, catching him and emptying the pitcher in his face. The man came to a halt with water streaming down over his head and shoulders. He shook his head vaguely, blinking around him. Finally his eyes focused on Nora. He spat water disgustedly.

"I never thought they'd ring you in on this, too, Miss Nora."

"Shyrock, you were having nightmares."

"I never have nightmares. I might have expected this from them knot-heads in the bunkhouse. I never thought I'd see the day you. . . ."

"Chinese navy, Shyrock."

"I never had anything to do with the Chinese navy. It's bad enough when an outfit plays a joke like that on a well man. But when he's sick in bed with a bullet. . . ."

He trailed off, aware of Morgan and Janice, coming down toward him. He shook his head again, splattering water on everybody. "Morgan," he said, "they told me you left."

"I came back, Shyrock."

"For good?"

"I don't know. You better get inside and take off those wet clothes."

"Look what they done to me, Morgan."

"They won't do it again."

"They sure won't. Not with you back." He turned belligerently to the others. "Did you hear that? Morgan's back. You better not do that again. You remember what happened in the bunkhouse. Him and I can lick the whole crew."

"All right, Shyrock, all right," Janice soothed. She must have seen what was passing between Morgan and Nora, for she spoke quickly to Jinglebob: "Help me get him inside. If the doctor hears what happened, he'll scalp us."

When they were out of earshot, Nora moved slowly toward Morgan, holding his eyes with hers. "I didn't have anything," she said. "When I thought you were gone for good, I didn't have anything left." Her head was thrown back, her parted lips glistening. He knew she was waiting for him to take her into his arms. It was natural that she should expect it, natural that she should think he would not return unless there was nothing more to keep them apart. Yet Eddie still stood between them. The picture of the boy was in his mind, bringing its insidious threads of guilt that he could not yet dispel. The frustration of it made his voice brittle.

"Did Janice tell you what Eddie told her at the creek?"

Nora nodded, the expectancy still in her wide eyes. "That he was going over into Yellowstone whether you went or not. So you really aren't to blame."

"But I would have gone with him."

"How do you know? Maybe he wouldn't have told you. You know how impulsive he was. He might have gone alone anyway. He figured you had decided not to."

He shook his head helplessly, eyes squinted tightly. She saw it, and settled back slowly, a bitter disappointment in her face.

"He's still between us."

"A man doesn't lose something like that in a minute, Nora. It's all so mixed up inside me. Janice said I would see, in time."

She tried to smile, but tear shine glistened in her eyes. "I'm willing. Just having you here is enough. We'll give time a chance."

Morgan went on down to the bunkhouse after he left Nora.

Jinglebob had not returned from the big house yet, and all the other men were evidently out with the cattle. Morgan was half undressed when the fat cook waddled in. He stopped by the table, frowning uncomfortably.

"I guess you know how we all feel about Eddie."

Morgan nodded. "Thanks, Jinglebob. I know how you feel."

"I guess you don't want to talk about it," the cook said. "How about something good? Like my new teeth." He grinned broadly, revealing gleaming dentures. "Doc Ashland said you'd paid for them. You ought to see me now. Steaks is nothing. I got to have something real tough. I been chawing all the bunk posts down just for practice." He chuckled till his belly shook. "You're really a man to ride the river with, Morg. The bunch of us was set to throw you in the Pecos after that fight. Now all you gotta do is teach O'Toole how to roll a smoke one-handed and you'll have the whole crew on your side."

"There's still Drift," Morgan said.

Jinglebob sobered. "Yeah. Drift."

"Where do you suppose he's gone?"

"We sort of expected him to take up with King, just to spite Oakland."

Morgan let that run through his mind and merge with the other thoughts that had been working at him since he had returned here. It had to do with the main reason he had come back. He would find the answer to nothing by sitting out the winter on the Keyhole. There was only one place he would find the answers.

He finished undressing with this in his mind, and turned in. He slept heavily and woke to the prodigious grunting the effort of dressing always drew from Jinglebob. He rolled out to pull his clothes on, and was almost finished when Oakland pushed open the door. He showed an unusually sober face, coming over to Morgan and putting a hand on his shoulder.

197

"I'm sorry the ruckus didn't wake me up last night. I would've welcomed you back then. I just want to tell you I felt terrible about Eddie, Morgan. I felt as bad as if he'd been my own son."

Morgan dipped his head in thanks. Oakland squeezed his shoulder, then went over and sat down, easing his foot out of a boot. "It's sure hell when a cowman can't wear the footgear he was born for," he said. He rubbed at his foot, studying Morgan for a moment. "What now?" he asked finally.

"Yellowstone," Morgan said.

Oakland's frown held furrowed reluctance. "Why don't you wait a little while? The crew'll be back. I'll make a couple of them go with you."

"Do I have that much time?" Morgan asked. "When does the bad weather start?"

"Not for a couple of weeks down here," Oakland said. "You might run into anything on top."

"Then I'd better get over the ridge while it's still clear," Morgan said.

"I guess you're right." Oakland pulled on his boot, frowning at the floor. "Morgan, why don't you wait till next year?"

Morgan grinned thinly at him. "You're not going soft on me, are you?"

Oakland stamped his boot down angrily. "Damn it, when I first made that proposition, you were a stranger. Now I'm sorry I did it. I'd go with you myself, but an old man like me'd be more hindrance than help."

"Same goes for a tub of leaf lard like me," Jinglebob said. "I'd wear my horses out before we reached the ridge."

Morgan stood up, his jaw growing heavier. "You know it's no good waiting. If I'm going to do it, I'm going to do it now."

Oakland started to lift his hand in protest, then settled back, staring at that outthrust belligerence in Morgan's jaw. He drew a resigned breath. "Why don't you go up to the house, then, before you leave? I think Nora has something for you."

Oakland stayed behind when Morgan went up. Nora was waiting alone in the front room, her pig-tailed hair giving a fresh, little-girl look to her face. She held up a pair of fleece-lined gloves.

"How did you know I'd have any use for these?" he said.

"When I first saw that you were back, I thought it meant Eddie was no longer between us. When I realized that wasn't true, I knew the real reason you'd come back. You won't be free till you find out what really happened over there, will you?"

"Will any of us?" he asked.

"No," she said in hollow resignation. She handed him the gloves, then held onto them, looking up into his face. "Morgan, before you go, will you do something for me? Whether Eddie is standing between us or not, will you kiss me, before you go?"

It stayed with him all the way up into the Absarokas. The feel of her body in his arms. The salt taste of her soundless tears on his lips. Her arms straining around his neck in their passionate plea, although she never put it into words, for she must have known how useless it would be to ask him not to go. It had been like tearing something out of him and leaving it behind, with the pain still somewhere deep inside, as he rode into the brooding mountains.

It had taken them a couple of days to push the cattle up to Crazy Horse Ridge, but driving beef was always a slow process, and he figured a man alone could make it in less than a day to the pass, if he rode hard. It had been clear when he started, but now black clouds were beginning to pile their mordant billows up over the northern ridges. He rode the buckskin he had used before, and led a spare and a pack horse, loaded with two weeks' supply of grub Jinglebob had gathered for him. The animals were blowing heavily in the chill as they labored upward. The snow had not melted on these higher slopes. It lay like skin over the meadows, and the squeaking *crunch* of the horses' hoofs, breaking through the crust, was always with him. He passed through a stand of timber, swimming with the wet pungency of pine needles, and pulled out among the rock faces of a ridge where the wind's spiteful gusts spattered loose snow against the horses. Breath steamed from the blood-red nostrils of the animals and hung like clammy mists in the air after they had passed. They were working so hard by the time he neared the narrow trough of the pass that he halted in the shelter of some junipers to let the beasts blow. Staring at the mountains beyond, he was struck by how much the snow changed them.

When he had first seen them, their bleak rock faces, their saw-tooth peaks, their awesome cañons had filled him with the sense of titanic power and violence, of a past filled with savage happenings on a plane incomprehensible to man. Now that was all gone. It was hard to conceive of anything having happened in such a white silence. The mountains looked stilled, as if they had stood this way during all time, untouched by the world.

Snow *creaked* beneath him as he heeled his animals forward once more, pushing up toward the last ridge between him and the pass. A hundred yards farther on he came across the prints. They had been made sometime this morning, for no new crust had formed over them. They were too big for a deer. The animal had been traveling fast, for there was a little heap of snow kicked up behind each foot. It might have been an elk. But elk would be moving down out of the mountains to their winter feeding-grounds, and these tracks were headed up. He found himself bending out of the saddle to see whether the hoofs had been shod or not. But the snow was too deep and soft here to record anything so faithfully. Somehow he was remembering those tracks he had come across in Yellowstone, crossing Eddie's trail, and what he had found later.

He shook his head irritably. Why was he so jumpy now? The time for that was on the other side. With a last apprehensive look around, he pushed on toward the ridge. He topped it and was almost swept out of the saddle by the force of the wind. He had been cut off from its direct blast by the crest, and hadn't realized how it was building up. He had to lean against it, protecting his eyes with a hand, to see anything ahead.

The gale was howling down the bleak trough of the pass, sweeping talus and shale off rocky upthrusts in stinging gusts, whipping snow up out of the drifts till it filled the air in a feathery curtain. The black clouds seemed enormous from here, sitting on the peaks directly across the pass, piling higher with each minute. Morgan realized he could not get down into Yellowstone before the storm hit. If these blizzards were anything like a Texas norther, he'd better seek shelter quick, he told himself.

The Crazy Horse line shack was across the pass and about two miles north, the nearest place he knew. His horses were whimpering dismally and constantly shifting their weight in search of a more solid foothold in the treacherous snow. He started dropping down the slope once more, when some fluttering motion above caught his eye. He drew rein, staring up there. His mind went back to those prints on the other side. Then he stared into the pass. The timber was spotty on the way down. He would be exposed for long stretches. There was a tingling foreboding in him he could not ignore.

He pulled his animals back into dense timber, hidden from above, and hitched them by a trio of lodgepoles and a huge snow-banked boulder. Then he got his Henry out of its saddle scabbard and started to work his way upward. It seemed to him the motion had come from timber line. He took a circuitous route that would bring him behind the spot. He climbed out of timber and into the brutal rock faces above. The wind slammed relentlessly at him, making so much noise he could hear nothing else. He got above the spot where he thought he had seen movement. He searched the rocky shoulders of granite below him, the timber below that, but could see nothing. Then he moved carefully down to hunt for sign. If there had been any, wind-driven snow had covered it. He was so cold now he was clenching his teeth unconsciously to keep them from chattering.

Finally, finding nothing, he went back to the horses. He reached the three lodgepoles and the boulder, half covered by snow now. He halted ten feet away, staring at the trees. He knew he could not be mistaken. The position of trees and the rock was too distinctive. Yet the horses were not there.

In a moment of thoughtless panic, he floundered through the snow into the timber, looking for sign. He wiped viciously at the snow caking his face, straining to peer through the thickening darkness. He realized it was more than darkness. It was falling snow. The storm had started.

He tried to check the panic knotting his stomach. He'd be lost if he let it get to him. There was no use trying to follow the horses in this. If they had broken loose, they'd probably drift with the storm. But he couldn't follow them far without losing his sense of direction. He couldn't see farther than a hundred feet ahead of him now. The only way he could keep his bearings was to follow timber line. With a sick reluctance in him, he turned back the other way.

He was able to follow timber line to the steep slope that formed the south wall of the pass. He had to leave the trees here, and work down the face of the slope. He would take the river as his next landmark. The wind swept snow against him like a great cottony fist that never ceased its buffeting blows. His feet were numb and he had to keep incessantly wiping snow from his eyes. Then his feet struck a rock face beneath knee-deep snow and he was pitched downward, losing his rifle. He had the sense of rocks tearing at his face, of branches kicked against him, of his fingers clawing for handholds. A sharp blow on his head stunned him. Then he struck something soft and feathery and sank deeply. Filled with a suffocated claustrophobia, he began to fight like a wild animal seeking release from a trap. He gained no ground. He felt himself sinking deeper. The air seared his lungs. Panic was a clawing rat in his belly.

With a great spasm of will he stopped himself. He sagged into the sucking snow, so drained by the wild battle that it was pain to breathe. He'd only kill himself this way. He was already so exhausted he could hardly move. If he kept this up, he wouldn't be able to go on even if he did get out. He couldn't fight the whole mountain—and after this came the other thought, a crazy thought born of desperation—if a man belonged, he didn't have to fight. He would be taken care of. He didn't have to fight. And Shyrock had said he belonged. He had felt it himself. That strange sadness, bringing him so close to the land.

It helped, somehow. As crazy as it was, it helped. He was still sinking into the deep drift. That insidious panic welled up in him again. But he had the strength to fight it now. He wouldn't be suffocated, he told himself. A man's breath formed an air pocket in the snow. It would only finish him to fight. It would only drain him of what little energy he had left. He didn't have to fight. He belonged.

As he sank deeper, he found it was no struggle to breathe. It had been the panic giving him that sense of suffocation, not the snow. Then his feet found something solid beneath him. A rock ledge. On his hands and knees, clearing the snow out ahead of him, he followed the ledge down. It took him to the bottom of a gully; the gully pinched off, and he climbed out of the deep drift.

He lay there, gasping like a fish out of water trying to regain his strength. It came slowly. A drowsiness crept over him. He knew how dangerous this was, and made himself move. He kept going downslope, fighting icy rock faces till the gloves Nora had given him were torn to shreds, floundering through drifts, feeling the vitality slowly drain out of him. At last he found the river, frozen over at the narrows, and crossed it. The trip up the steep north wall of the cañon was a dim nightmare. He found timber line at last and worked his way northward, tree by tree, fighting an unending battle against wind-driven snow. Sleep was the danger now. He knew an overpowering urge to give way, to lie down in the soft white snow, to drift off.

He struggled against it all the rest of the way. Finally he had the sense of being at the edge of a precipice. The emptiness below seemed to suck at the blanket of snow. He felt his way downward till he reached icy rocks, where no snow would cling, and realized he was at the lip of the cliff that ran like a bowl above the line shack. He could see it curling away into the whiteness on either side of him.

He did not know how much longer it took him to find the way down. There was no clear thought left to him. Only that crazy little idea coming back time and time again—if a man really belonged, he'd be taken care of.

Finally he was down off the cliff. He sought the upward slant of the meadow. He realized he was crawling and stood up again. Each movement was like lifting a great weight. He finally reached the base of the cliff and followed it around to the right till he reached timber. Then he moved from tree to tree till the vague form of the shack loomed before him. He went toward it with hands outstretched. He walked right into it and fell to his knees. He crouched there a long time, feeble as a baby, trying to find the strength to rise. Then he realized he was up against the door. He climbed to his feet, tried to shove it open. He didn't have the strength. Then it was swung open abruptly, almost pitching him in. He caught himself on the frame, blinking his eyes at the man who stood before him. It was Charlie King.

XIII

The battering of the blizzard made the cabin mutter and groan like a human in pain. The fire's ruddy light washed out to tawny shadows in the far corners of the room. The cracked glass bowl of the hurricane lamp reflected Charlie King's face in a grotesque illusion. His nose looked prodigious and twisted off to one side; his right eye was twice as big as his left; his lips held a warped leer.

"Better?" he asked.

Morgan had stripped off his sodden Mackinaw and gloves and was standing over the fire. His back was to King, but he could still see that reflection of the man's face in the lamp bowl. "Lots better," he said.

"You were lucky to reach the shack," King said. "A man's usually finished up here when he loses his animals in a storm like this."

"Is he?"

There was a moment of silence. Then King's boots scraped against the splintered puncheon flooring. His face faded from the lamp. Morgan turned to his left, till King came into sight on that side.

"What were you doing over here?" Morgan asked.

"Cut of my cattle drifted down off Medicine Rim," King said.

"I thought there wasn't any way cattle could get down off that cliff."

"There was an old Indian trail. We blasted it out a long time ago. A slide closed it up again some time this fall and we didn't run across it till today. Cattle were bound to find it sooner or later."

King moved behind Morgan in the other direction. It took him out of Morgan's vision again. Still facing the fire, Morgan turned the other way till he found King's face in the cracked bowl once more. He saw King's eyes on the lamp. The man must have realized how Morgan had been keeping him in sight. King smiled sardonically. "What makes you so jumpy?"

"Am I jumpy?"

King frowned at him in the lamp bowl. Then he wheeled abruptly and walked over to a bunk. It removed his reflection from the glass again. Morgan turned around to face him. King had taken a blanket off the bunk, and he threw it at Morgan.

"At least strip off the rest of those wet clothes. We'll rig a line with my dally rope. Then we'll have what's left of my coffee and beans."

Morgan unbuckled his gun and hung it on a bunk post. He did not move away from it while he pulled off the rest of his clothes. He had never seen King wear a six-shooter. Now all he could see in the room was a rifle that looked like a Remington-Keene, standing against the wall in its rawhide scabbard. He noticed that it was not within reach of King's bunk.

"Why did you waste your time on one drift of cattle?" Morgan asked, pulling off his pants. "Oakland would have picked them up in his spring roundup."

King stared bleakly at him. "You still don't know how it works up here, do you? I'd never see that bunch again. They don't miss a turn, Morgan. Any way they can cut into me." His eyes grew veiled, as he saw the puzzled expression on Morgan's face. "I know it's hard for an outsider to believe. You've got to see it work. You come from Texas. What do they think of 'breeds down there?"

"It's always been bad near the border," Morgan said. "A 'breed's pretty low on the scale."

"Like a dog?" King asked thinly. He took an uneven breath.

"How do you feel about it personally?"

Morgan let the man see exactly what was in his eyes. "What do you think?" he asked.

King studied him. "I think you dislike me personally, but not because I'm a 'breed."

"You'll have to admit you haven't been friendly."

King got up and scooped a coiled dally rope from his gear in the corner, tying one end to a bunk post. "You're thinking of Law and Rideout," he said. "They got out of hand. I didn't tell them to beat you up."

"Why were they on my tail in the first place?" Morgan said. "Somebody tried to give me the impression that was your way of discouraging any outside interest in Nora. I can't quite believe that."

King walked across the room, paying the rope out. "You were going to work for Oakland. Isn't that enough?"

Morgan frowned at him as he climbed on a chair to tie the other end of the rope to a rafter. King finished and climbed down, looking at that intense frown on Morgan's face. "I told you it was hard for an outsider to understand."

Morgan shook his head. "Maybe you're right."

"I suppose you know now who that woman in my house was."

"Is that why you didn't want Eddie and me to come in that night with Shyrock?"

A little muscle puckered in King's jaw. "You're thinking I'm pretty snaky, being that ashamed of my own mother." He turned and began to pace. "That's how it is, Morgan. It's funny what it does to a man. I shouldn't give a damn what people think. But it gets to be a habit. You get to fighting back without even thinking. It's like being in a corner and they're coming at you from every side." He made a savage gesture with one hand. "As long as I had a little shoestring outfit, it was all right. They'd play poker with me in town. Buy me a drink. Maybe they wouldn't invite me in their homes or let me mix with their women. But they'd treat me human in town. Then I started getting big. They couldn't stand that. They couldn't stand a damn' Indian getting big."

"I understand you haven't shipped any beef out in two years. Is that part if it?"

King stopped pacing to give him a sharp look. "I'll be shipping again," he said finally. He began to pace once more. His movements held the restrained violence of a caged cat. His voice rose to a savage note. "They'll never pinch me off. You'll see the day they accept me. I'll sit in their parlors and drink their whiskey and talk to their women like I was a human being. . . ." His bitter voice broke off suddenly. He stood a foot from the far wall, staring at it. His long black hair had fallen down one side of his face and he brushed it back with an impatient gesture, drawing a ragged breath. "Cabin fever must be getting me," he said. "I never did like being cooped up."

He finally turned to glance at Morgan, as if to gauge his reaction. Morgan could see an anger in the man's eyes that he had let himself go so far. King wheeled impatiently to his gear and pulled out the coffee and food.

Morgan hung his clothes on the line to dry, and drank coffee and ate beans while wearing nothing but the blanket. By the time they were finished, the clothes were dry, except for the Mackinaw, and Morgan dressed again. The warmth of the fire and his own exhaustion were making him unbearably drowsy.

He turned toward his bunk and had taken a pair of steps before he realized he had turned his back on King for the first time. He halted and half turned. King was standing by the rifle. The man stared blankly at Morgan for an instant. Finally he spoke. "I guess I'll turn in, too."

Morgan watched him go to his bunk and roll up tightly in his blanket, the way a man would who had spent most of his nights outside. Morgan found himself reluctant to go to sleep. There was too much under the surface here. All the man's old antagonisms rose in Morgan's mind, all the questions that had remained unanswered. Morgan lay down and pulled his blanket over him, remaining on his side so he could see King, with the definite intention of staying awake. King's eyes were already closed and he was breathing heavily.

Morgan did not know when he fell asleep. There was a long stretch without consciousness, and then he was awake again. It was utterly dark. He tried to see through the blackness, but could make out nothing. Then a board *creaked* somewhere in the room.

"What's the matter?" he said.

There was a moment before King answered, and it did not sound as if his voice came from his bunk. "I thought you were asleep."

"I was."

"You must be a light sleeper."

"You get that way on the trail."

"Do you?"

"What's the matter?" Morgan asked again.

"Nothing. The fire's gone out and I'm just cold as hell."

King started the fire again while Morgan got up to feel his Mackinaw on the line. It was still damp, but he put it on over his clothes anyway, hoping body heat would dry it out. Then he went back to bed, shivering despite the growing warmth of the fire. He could not go to sleep again.

The storm beat at the cabin. Time dragged on. Finally the room seemed filled with a little more light than that of the fire. King was lying on his side asleep. He woke without sound or movement. One moment his eyes were closed and the next they were open, staring at Morgan.

"Don't you ever sleep?" he asked after a while.

"Do you want me to?" Morgan said.

King gazed at him for a long space. "I'd better see to that horse," he said, swinging abruptly out of the bunk.

The wind slammed snow into the room the moment he opened the door, and he leaned far forward, driving out into the storm and banging the door shut behind him. Morgan got up and replenished the dying fire. In a few minutes King came back in, stamping his feet and beating snow off his clothes.

"That shelter Shyrock built over this end of the corral doesn't help much," he said. "If that pony didn't have such a heavy coat, he'd be frozen already."

He opened his canvas-lined Mackinaw and hauled a chair up to the fire, sprawling out in it and putting the soles of his feet toward the flames. Morgan went back to his bunk and sat down. It brought the bottom of King's boot heels into his vision. He saw that they were tipped with metal, grooved in the pattern of a star. It left Morgan's mind utterly blank for a moment. His only consciousness seemed to be of those metal stars. Then, with the first shock of it gone, the thoughts began to come. At first it was the sudden ugly comprehension of all the implications. Then it was a reasonless fury, bringing a savage impulse to jump at the man, to get his hands on him somehow. It jerked at his body and King saw it and looked up. Then King looked down again, following the direction of Morgan's eyes, to those boot heels. And finally King's eyes rose a second time, bringing Morgan's with them, until the two men were staring at each other. There was no measurement to that next moment. There was an expression on King's face Morgan had never seen there before. It was as if the knowledge he had read in Morgan's eyes swept all need of pretense from the man. He stared at Morgan an instant more, his face filled with a savage acceptance of all the implications in those starred boot heels. Then he jumped out of his chair, catching it in one hand and flinging it at Morgan.

Morgan tried to roll out of the way and grab his gun from its holster hanging on the bunk post. But the chair caught him in the face, smashing him back in the bunk. Half blinded, he had a shadowy impression of King jumping for that rifle against the wall. Morgan threw the chair off and came out of the bunk again. King tore the Remington-Keene from its scabbard and started whirling back toward Morgan, snapping the finger lever down. Morgan yanked his six-shooter from its holster and hit the hammer with the palm of his hand. The explosion rocked the room, but it was a snap shot. The bullet drove through the wall a foot to one side of King. The man checked his whirling motion sharply, not quite facing Morgan. He had his rifle cocked, but it was still pointing at the side of the room. Morgan stood with the back of his legs against the sideboard of the bunk, his hand trembling over the hammer of his gun. He blinked stinging eyes, trying to get a clear vision of the man.

"Drop it," he said. "I really meant to hit you."

King's lips pinched so tightly there was a ridge of white flesh around them. For an instant, Morgan thought he would whirl on around anyway. Then he let the rifle down to the floor.

"Kick it over here," Morgan said.

King complied, and Morgan stepped over to unbar the front door. The howling gale swept snow across the room in a blast, powdering everything. Still covering King, Morgan picked up the rifle and hurled it as far as he could outside. A few minutes in that and it would be useless. He slammed the door and stood with his back against it, staring at King. His whole body was trembling now, in reaction and restrained fury. His voice sounded strangled.

"So you meant to do that all along," he said.

King's face was a mask. "Did I?"

"You were waiting for a chance ever since I came in. You were after that rifle last night when I woke up."

"Was I?"

"You left those starred prints behind when you bushwhacked us over in Yellowstone. Didn't you know that till just now?"

"A lot of men up here have that on their boots."

"You didn't know it till now." Without realizing it, Morgan was bending toward the man. "But when you saw me staring at your heels, you realized what it meant. You knew what I knew and you couldn't cat-and-mouse me any longer." He drew an uneven breath, trying to settle back. "And my horses. They didn't break loose. You cut them loose. I don't even think you were over here after a drift of cattle. You were following me ever since I left the Keyhole. You were waiting for me to start into Yellowstone."

King's voice was brittle. "I don't have anything to do with Yellowstone."

Another tremor shook Morgan's body. "It's funny," he said, "I'd almost convinced myself I was a big man. Doc Ashland said only a small man would want revenge."

King read what lay in Morgan's smoldering eyes. "You told me yourself a slide killed Eddie," the half-breed said. "You'll never prove different."

"All the proof I want is what I've seen today."

"You won't shoot a man in cold blood."

"Won't I?"

The edge of hysteria in Morgan's voice changed the expression in King's face. That pucker of muscle ran through his cheek. Then a fatalistic calm filled his eyes, widening them faintly, and he settled himself against the floor as if to meet something. Morgan realized his left hand was still held stiffly over the hammer of his gun. He lowered it with a jerky motion, and waved his gun at King's bunk.

"Go lie on your belly," he said.

King frowned at him, then reluctantly complied. Morgan got the rope down and moved over to the bunk. King flopped over on his back, those savage lights flaring in his eyes.

"I can just as easy hit you on the head and do it while you're knocked out," Morgan said.

King's anger drained the blood from his face till it had a putty hue. Slowly he rolled back on his belly. Morgan tied his ankles together, and then bent his knees till his feet were pulled up against his hips. He ran the rope up around the man's neck, and then brought it back and tied his hands. That way, every tug on the rope would choke him.

Then Morgan went back and sat down in the chair. There were so many black and ugly things moving inside of him he didn't know exactly what he felt. There was something unreal about sitting so calmly across the room from the man who had killed his brother. It seemed to reverse reality and illusion. The violent impulses in him were the reality. His physical presence in the chair was the illusion. He should be answering those impulses. There was a simple animal logic to them that made anything else seem foolish. And yet King had been right. He couldn't shoot the man in cold blood. Despite the feeling that he was betraying Eddie, he could not wreak any sort of vengeance on the man like this. It left the whole thing hollow and aborted and deeply frustrating. He finally realized he was shivering, and saw that the fire was dying.

King had turned his head with great difficulty till he could look at Morgan. "How about some wood on that fire, at least?" he said.

"We'll save it till it gets dark," Morgan said. "I'll want to see you all night."

King's eyes thinned to mocking slits. "Going to be a long storm, Morgan. Think you can last it out?"

"You'd better hope I can. If I break first, I'll be thinking of Eddie."

"What if you fall asleep first?"

Morgan did not answer. Finally King turned his head the other way, as if for relief from his cramped position. Morgan was shivering again. His belly sucked at him with its emptiness. He was so jumpy every small *creak* of the storm made him start. Finally he got up and heated some snow water and drank it. But it only bloated him and its warmth did not last long. He was getting sleepy now, and he stayed on his feet, pacing back and forth, to keep himself awake.

The afternoon passed, with hunger and cold and his own frustration making him increasingly irritable. At last it grew so dark he had to light the fire to see King. Its warmth made him unbearably drowsy. He went back to the chair, sitting in it so he would fall if he went to sleep.

He didn't know how many times he was jerked awake just before he pitched off onto the floor. Once it was a strange scraping sound that seemed to wake him. He caught himself, straightening up. King was staring at him. The cabin was filled with the storm's complaint. The frame *creaked* and the rafters *groaned*. The door *rattled* loosely whenever the wind slammed at it.

"Sounds like it's easing up a bit," King said.

Morgan did not answer.

King's eyes narrowed to those mocking slits again. "What happens when it's over, Morgan? You haven't got anything for the law. A lot of men have stars on their boots. It was just cabin fever that made me jump you here. We'd been cooped up a long time."

"I don't know what happens," Morgan said thinly. "You just aren't going to get another chance at me in this place."

"No?"

214

Morgan looked at him sharply. Then he went over and tested the ropes. They were still tight. He put more wood on the fire without turning his back on the man. He paced a while. Finally he went back to the chair. Again he fell asleep, and was jerked awake. The sounds of the storm seemed more subdued. He shifted his body, sinking heavily into the chair. Then there was a long blank space, and, when he came awake, he was not falling. The fire had died, but it was light enough to see. Dawn. He must have shifted so that he did not fall, and he had slept for several hours. King lay on his side, face toward Morgan, eyes closed.

Shivering with cold, Morgan went to the door. It opened inward, allowing a heap of snow to spill across the room from a drift that had piled against the portal. The snowfall had stopped, but the wind was blowing hard, kicking up great white gusts that filled the air in powdery banners and then sifted back onto the three-foot mantle of snow that covered the downsloping meadow. Morgan was stiff and aching with cold, his fingers so numb they seemed glued to the gun he still held. He started to shut the door when he heard the *creaking* sound behind. He whirled to see King lunging out of the bunk toward the axe in the corner, frayed ropes trailing off him. In that last instant Morgan realized what the scraping sound last night had been. The half-breed had rubbed those ropes against the sideboard till they were worn through.

King reached the axe before Morgan got his gun up. Morgan's thumb was so cold it would not hook around the hammer in time. In desperation, he slapped at the hammer with his other hand.

But King had already heaved the axe. The blow of it threw Morgan back and knocked the gun from his hand as it went off. He was slammed into the door so hard it stunned him. Only then did he realize the blade had not struck him. It had gone

215

over his shoulder, sinking into the door, and it was the handle that had struck his arm and knocked him backward. Before he could tear free, King lunged into him, smashing at his face.

Blinded by the blow, Morgan heard King pull the axe free. Morgan twisted aside as King struck. The axe hit with a shrieking crash, going into the crack between door and wall and severing the upper hinge. The door sagged outward with Morgan's weight, twisting on its bottom hinge. Morgan could not help falling back with it. He had no purchase to roll aside as King brought the axe back for another blow. All he could do was use the sagging door for leverage. He thrust his whole weight against it and brought both feet off the ground to kick out at King.

It knocked King backward. But the force of it was too much for the weakened door. Its bottom hinge tore free. The door fell out, spilling Morgan with it. He rolled off onto his hands and knees, pawing snow from his face. King had regained his balance and was coming out the door with the axe upraised. Morgan dived at the man.

King couldn't shift his weight to strike before Morgan hit him. He toppled heavily onto the fallen door with Morgan on top. Sprawled flat, King tried to swing the axe out to the side and strike. Morgan lunged up on one knee and stamped at King's arm with his free foot. He felt his sharp heel drive the man's wrist into the door with a *crunch* of bone. Pain twisted King's face and his hand opened spasmodically from around the axe handle. King tried to twist over and grab it with his good hand. Morgan caught his arm, heaving him away. They rolled off the door into a deep snowbank. King came on top and raised up on Morgan, smashing him in the face.

Dazed by the blow, Morgan jackknifed a leg till his shin was against King's chest. Then he straightened it, throwing the man off. King tried to roll over and get up, but Morgan lunged after him. They went waist deep into a drift, slugging at each other.

The snow dragged at Morgan like a great weight. The men were fighting the snow as well as each other now. One of King's blows got through and knocked Morgan off balance. He felt himself floundering back into the snow with King on top. He was pushed down till all he could see was the white stuff. His mouth was full and he was gagging. With the panic of suffocation filling him, he began thrashing wildly. His only thought was of escape.

With King battering at him and kicking him, he finally managed to burrow away like some animal in a blind search for solid ground. He found the rocky side of a gully that took him up out of the drift. He heard King coming after him. He turned to face the man and back-peddled halfway up the steep slant of the gully and then jumped feet first down on King. His boots struck the man's chest with a sodden sound. It knocked King back into a drift and Morgan was on top of him. He smashed at the man, knocking his head brutally back. King twisted around and floundered away through the snow till he was free. Then he fought to his feet and wheeled on Morgan as Morgan came wallowing after him. Morgan rushed into the half-breed, slamming a blow at his belly. King gasped and doubled forward and grappled with Morgan. They were both sobbing with the violent effort of the battle now. The struggle against the snow was draining them twice as fast as the violence of an ordinary battle would.

King's blows did not have the force to knock Morgan away. Morgan realized his own blows were as feeble. He had no measurement of the time they floundered back and forth through the snow, grappling, slugging, flailing at each other. His arms were like great leaden weights and every time he reached for air he thought his ribs would burst. Finally one of his wild haymakers caught King off balance. He jumped soddenly after the falling man. King rolled him off and Morgan flopped to his hands and knees five feet beyond the man. He tried to get up. His legs folded like loose rubber beneath him. He saw that King could not rise, either.

They began crawling through the snow toward each other. The sound of their breathing filled the air in painful gusts. They rose to their knees when they met, flailing at each other. Again Morgan did not know how long they fought this way, too drained to get on their feet, surging backward and forward with the snow's cottony insistence pulling them down at every shift. Finally Morgan tore free, putting the last spasm of his strength in a blow that knocked King back. He sank down. He knew he couldn't meet the man if King came at him. They both crouched there, sobbing in their exhaustion. King tried to get on his hands and knees again. He wobbled a moment, then sprawled flat on his belly. He stared at Morgan from eyes squinted and watering with strain, then turned and looked toward the shack. He began dragging himself through the snow in that direction. Morgan realized what lay in King's head. Neither of them had the strength to finish the fight. There was only one thing left.

Morgan started crawling after King. In ordinary weather Morgan might have gotten back to the Keyhole afoot, even not knowing the country. In this snow and freezing cold he knew he'd never make it without the horse. After crawling a little way, Morgan managed to gain his feet and stumble a couple of steps before his exhaustion dragged him down again. It put him ahead of King. Then King found a rocky shoulder and crawled up it to a stunted juniper, pulling himself to his feet. He staggered along the ridge of the shoulder, but it petered out before he was ahead of Morgan, and he had to come down into the snow again. He tried to throw himself past Morgan. Morgan lunged out and hammered him behind a knee; it buckled that leg and he went down.

He turned on Morgan, smashing feebly at his face. It knocked

Morgan back in the snow, and allowed King to get ahead. But the violent effort of the blow had robbed King of his last strength. He tried to stand again and couldn't. He had to start crawling once more. Groaning with exhaustion, Morgan pulled himself to his feet, stumbling after King. He couldn't waste his strength in trying to skirt the man. King tried to pull him down as he went by. He kicked the man's hand free, throwing himself in a last burst at the corral a few feet ahead. He went full length into the drift piled up against its gate. Here he turned, brows hedged with snow. King crawled to him and came up off his knees.

Morgan grappled with King, and heaved him backward. He crouched there, breath coming in feeble gasps. Then King came back. Again they grappled. Again Morgan threw him off. Again they crouched there, like a couple of whipped animals, staring at each other. With a sob, King tried to come at Morgan once more. But even his arms would not support him in a crouch, now, and he went flat on his belly in the snow. Morgan sagged back against the corral post, limp as a rag doll. "You'll never get the horse," he said in a broken voice.

Morgan did not know how long King lay there, trying to gain the strength to rise. The heat of the violent effort left Morgan and the sweat grew cold and clammy beneath his clothes and he began to shiver uncontrollably. Finally King raised his head, and slowly fought his way to hands and knees. Morgan thought he meant to try again. But defeat engraved his face deeply. He stared a long time at Morgan. Then, without speaking, he turned and began to crawl back down the slope.

It was a painful thing to watch his terrible exhaustion. He could not rise till he reached the first tree. It took him a long time to pull himself to his feet there. He turned to glance back at Morgan. Then he stumbled into the forest, almost pitching over on his face before he reached the next tree. Morgan felt a little strength returning now. He didn't have much doubt that King would get out of it alive, on foot, where he couldn't have. There was a difference between them. King knew the country. And he was half Indian.

Finally Morgan crawled over to the doorway of the cabin. It took him a long time, pawing through the drifts, to find his six-shooter. But he didn't give up till he found it. Then he pulled himself to his feet at the door frame and staggered inside, fumbling for a match in his pocket. He didn't think he had ever wanted to be warm so badly in his life.

XIV

Morgan did not leave right away. He wanted to see if it meant to blow again before he started. And he knew he had to give himself a chance to recover from the fight if he meant to have enough strength to make it. There was a throbbing ache all through him from King's blows; he could not draw a deep breath without wincing from the pain of battered ribs. He was torn by a recurrent nausea that kept him wanting to lose food he did not contain.

He did not want to waste his strength putting the door back up so he stoked up the fire and sat as close to its heat as possible. He did not know how long he had been there when he heard the sound outside. He jerked around in the chair, thinking it was King. But the man who stepped into the doorway was not King.

He was tall, over six feet, a snow-crusted buffalo coat hiding his big frame, its matted collar turned up about his neck. His Levi's were filthy and blackened with grease, and his boots had rawhide soles tied on with thongs. His face was half hidden by a blond beard just grown out of the stubble stage, and his cheeks were blackened with charcoal as a protection against snow blindness. It was the scars, showing whitely through the charcoal, that identified him for Morgan.

"Drift."

The man's voice held sardonic mockery. "I never seen a fight like that."

Morgan frowned at him. "You saw?"

Drift came in through the doorway. "When this blow first started, I was lucky enough to reach a cave up north of here. It slacked off this morning about three, and I figured the line shack would be a safer place to sit out the rest of it. I was up on the cliff when the two of you come busting out the door. Cabin fever get you?"

Morgan studied Drift's face carefully as he said it: "No. King was trying to kill me. Like he killed Eddie."

The surprise filling Drift's face seemed genuine. It faded slowly before a narrow-eyed skepticism. "I heard what happened to your brother. How do you know King did it?"

"The man who shot Shyrock in Yellowstone had stars on his heels. King has the same thing. He followed me from the Keyhole the other day to kill me."

"That wouldn't stand up in court," Drift said. "I've seen cabin fever make tigers out of mice." He beat snow off his buffalo coat, staring around the room. "Doesn't look like you have any grub left."

Morgan started to speak sharply, then checked himself. "Four strips of bacon in two days," he said, settling back in the chair.

Drift turned back out the door and disappeared. In a moment he showed up again, hauling a pair of horses into view. He tied their reins to one of the broken hinges and from the pack on one animal extracted sacks of flour and coffee, a frying pan, and a buckskin-wrapped package the size of a ham. He walked in and put these on the table and unwrapped the package. It was a haunch of venison.

"Shot a buck a while back," he said. "Meat's kept good this

cold weather." He sliced the venison into steaks while Morgan made coffee and biscuits. Morgan was ravenous, and ate half a steak before the edge was off his hunger. Then he poured himself a second cup of coffee and leaned back in the chair. There was an indrawn tightness to Drift's face, and Morgan knew he was still thinking about what they had said.

"Somehow I got the idea you meant to sign on with King when you left," Morgan said.

"The hell with King."

"So you just took off for the mountains."

"Nowhere else to go."

"Why didn't you clear out completely?" Morgan said. Drift stared at the table, without answering. "Janice?" Morgan asked softly.

Drift put his knife and fork down, and his breath left him in heavy defeat. Finally he nodded. "I tried to get her to go. She wouldn't leave the Keyhole."

"And you couldn't leave her. You said it was something bad, going on here. It would ruin the whole of Chinook Basin. You were afraid it would hurt her, too." Morgan frowned at him. "But you didn't tell her what you knew."

Drift swept his empty tin plate off the table with a savage gesture. "I couldn't tell her. Anybody that knows is marked."

"Is that why you were drinking?"

Drift got up abruptly, almost upsetting his chair. He walked to the door, staring out so long that Morgan thought he did not mean to answer.

"It gets a man," he said suddenly. "I thought it wouldn't get me. I was tough. I could lick any man in Chinook. I'd never been afraid of nothing before. But it ain't like licking a man. It's something you can't see. You can't get your hands on it. But it's there all the time, blowing down your neck. It's been two years since Laramie and me took that ride into Yellowstone. It's been with me all that time."

"What did you find in Yellowstone?"

"They got Laramie. They got my horse and I had to walk back and I barely made it alive. I thought that was bad. I didn't know what bad was. You ever been marked before? Waiting to be cut down. Every time you step out the door. Every time you ride home alone. They tried twice. Last time was six months ago." He wheeled slowly, a bitter look to his eyes. "Two years. That's how long I've been waiting. That gets a man."

"I guess it does. I guess most men would do worse than drink. But why, Drift? What did you find over there?"

"You'll be marked if you know."

"Don't you think I'm already marked?" Morgan asked softly.

Drift stared at him a long time. Then he came back and sat down. "Laramie and me had trailed this drift of Keyhole stuff over into Yellowstone," he said. He was looking beyond Morgan. "Up past the lake. Up in the mountains. Then this cañon. Like a big slice in the ground. So steep nobody could get down. All filled with bones. Cattle bones. Hundreds of cattle."

Morgan frowned at him. "You're not trying to tell me that's where all these cattle go that drift into Yellowstone?"

Drift shook his head. "I don't know what it meant. Some of the skeletons still had meat on them. Others were bleached so white you'd think they'd been there a hundred years."

Morgan settled back into his chair. "And that's all you have to go on?"

"Ain't that enough?" the man asked savagely. "All you have to do is see that cañon, Morgan. It's up there where the geysers never stop steaming and you can hear the mud bubbling all the time. It's like somebody opened up a window and gave you a look at hell. You know how ugly it is then. And if it's big enough so they'll kill a man to keep it secret, it's big enough to ruin the basin."

Morgan stared into Drift's eyes. The insidious implications of what the man had seen began to exert their pressures against him. He rose, trying to shake the eerie feeling loose. "If it's so bad, why have you kept this to yourself?"

"I said a man was marked if he knew. When I had to walk out of Yellowstone that time, it was Dodge who found me up in the Absarokas, half dead. He took me back to the Doubloon and kept me there till I was strong enough to get back to the Keyhole. I told him about the cañon. A week later he followed a drift of his Doubloon cattle into Yellowstone and never came back. I couldn't bring that on anybody else. If it'd do any good, I might have told. But how would it help? A cañon full of bones. All it does is mark a man to know. It got Eddie, didn't it? I was a fool and spilled it to him while I was drunk and it got him. And all for what?"

Morgan shook his head, frowning at the fire. "All those cattle wouldn't just drift into that one spot."

Drift was studying him narrowly. "I've gone all over it, too. A thousand times. So somebody drove them there. Why?"

Morgan faced him. "If it keeps up, it'll ruin the basin, won't it?"

"You're thinking of King again."

"What more could he want than to wipe them all out?"

Drift shook his head. "The cattle from this basin drift into Yellowstone over a line fifty miles long. King's only got a small crew and his own herds keep them busy. It'd take an army to pick up all those drifts and drive them to that cañon. It just ain't possible."

Morgan saw the logic of that. "What other answer is there?"

Drift was looking out the door, a haunted expression in his eyes. "I knew a man once that had been around the world. He told me things like that. He said in Africa the elephants have a graveyard. Nobody knows where it is. The elephants go there to die. For thousands of years they've been going there to die and nobody's seen it yet. I bet you'd find a lot of bones there."

"Now you sound like an Indian," Morgan said impatiently.

"Then you tell me the answer," Drift said.

Morgan paced restlessly across the room, trying to shake loose the eerie spell of it. Drift saw the expression on his face.

"Now you know what I mean," the man said. "You know it's there and you know it's something ugly but you can't even touch it."

Morgan turned to him. "You're wrong. It's King."

Drift shook his head wearily. "King isn't the only one up here with boot heels like that. If you found the sign when they got Shyrock, why didn't you find it with Eddie?"

"The landslide wiped all the sign away."

"Then why didn't King try to kill you over there, too?"

"I was a day behind my brother. King was already gone. He tried to kill me here, didn't he?"

"The man's part Indian. Get them mad and they'll murder you for nothing."

"You might as well go back to the bottle."

Drift's head jerked up angrily. "Now what do you mean?"

"You're hiding from it again," Morgan said disgustedly. "King's the one, but you won't face it. I could understand you running away from something when you didn't even know what it was. I didn't think you were the kind to run from something you could get your hands on. You should have left the country in the first place. Janice wouldn't have a man like you anyway."

Drift rose slowly, the scars across his cheeks turned livid. There was a wild flash in his bloodshot eyes, and for a moment Morgan thought the man meant to jump at him. But he could see it working through Drift's face, obscurely at first, then more palpably. It allowed him to see just how much Janice meant to the man. There was a strange pain in Drift's voice. "Did she tell you that?"

"Did she have to? It would take a lot of man for that kind of woman, Drift. Do you think you measure up over a bottle?"

Drift stared at him for a long moment, then spoke gutturally. "Suppose I do face it. Suppose King is the one. What good does that do us?"

"It gives us something more to work with. Always before, everybody was looking over in Yellowstone. Why don't we start at the other end? Why don't we start with Charlie King?"

Drift studied Morgan's face a long time. Then he grinned. It came slowly, and his broken teeth made it ugly, and what humor it held was grudging. But it was a grin. "Why don't we?" he said.

XV

They stayed that night at the shack, and started before dawn toward Medicine Rim. They reached it in the afternoon, traveling eastward along the base of the rocky cliff till they found the trail. As King had said, a fresh slide had filled the space left by former blasting, about halfway up. It was treacherous going, and they had to lead their horses most of the way.

Reaching the plateau, they crossed it southward till it began shelving off in those glacial benches. Instead of taking the trail down through the benches they turned east along the rimrock till they came to the great bowl-shaped hollow of the granite cirque. Three hundred feet below them, backed up against the cliff, were the Double Arrow buildings. Snow still mantled rooftops and lay in blue-shadowed drifts against walls. Morgan and Drift hitched their horses out of sight, and then huddled down behind a stretch of rocks. After an hour of watching, they saw a man emerge from the cook shack and kick his way through a foot of snow to the bunkhouse.

"That's Haycroft, their cookie," Drift muttered.

"I guess there'll be a lot of them I don't know," Morgan said. "King must have pulled his crew down from the high pastures by now."

"Not so many," Drift told him. "He cut his crew down a couple of years ago."

Morgan frowned at him. "How can he do that? If he hasn't shipped any beef in two years, his increase should make him need even more men."

The man shook his head. "He's got a lot of natural barriers on his range. You don't need as many men to watch the drift lines that way. Not many men would stick with him anyway."

As he finished speaking, the Indian woman came from the main house and began shoveling snow off the path to the bunkhouse. And after her, stepping onto the porch, came Charlie King. Morgan felt no great surprise.

"I guess that was to be expected," he said.

"Just a little hike for him," Drift said. "You can't get rid of an Indian that way."

King smoked a cigarette, and then went down to the bunkhouse, saying something shortly to his mother as he passed her, still shoveling snow. He went into the bunkhouse and after a while came back out with Tom Law and a man Morgan did not recognize. After talking to them, King headed back for the big house, and they went to the barns. They appeared in a few minutes with saddled horses and mounted up and headed toward town.

"Ten to one King's sent them in to get some word on you," Drift said.

"We found out what we wanted, anyway," Morgan murmured. "King's back. Now we'll have to sweat it out. We'll be spotted sooner or later if we try to keep tabs on him from here, won't we?"

Drift nodded. "The crew'll be coming back and forth across here all the time, working what winter drift lines there are. There's only one route King can use over into Yellowstone from this side of Medicine Rim, anyway. I guess you and Eddie used it when you brought Shyrock back."

Morgan looked at him. "Smoky Pass?"

They got their horses and headed west. They did not follow any of the trails, for fear one of the Double Arrow hands might pick up their fresh sign. It was hard going, fighting through drifts and dense timber, struggling over treacherous stretches of talus and shale. The storm had cleared the air and there was an aching purity to the snow-mantled mountains ahead of them. They lay, silent and white, with the bold rock faces higher up standing out, black and defiant, and snow making great torn patches on the boulder-littered slopes below. The plateau gradually lifted into these slopes till it broke off into valleys and spur ridges and lost itself against the backbone of the mountains.

Drift and Morgan established camp overlooking the pass, at a spot as near to one of King's line shacks as they could get. In case a storm came up, they threw up a half-faced shelter of pine boughs, open to the fire, and started keeping four-hour watches, with one man waiting in the rocks above the pass while the other slept.

Morgan took first watch, and settled down in a scattering of icy boulders, wrapped tightly in a blanket. It was a desolate vigil. Through the afternoon and night he had two watches, and most of his consciousness was taken up with the bitter cold. Even wrapped in blankets, its intensity seemed to eat through to his very bones. He was sitting out there when dawn came, and it was then that he noticed the first change. Crouched there, with a dawn wind booming through the distant pines, with the black mountain masses rising all about him, he was touched with that same sense of poignant sadness he had known upon his first sight of the peaks. Again it gave him a feeling of great intimacy with the land, of becoming a part of its somber strength, its ageless calm. All the bitter conflict and confusion that had torn him seemed petty and trifling. He no longer felt driven by his grief for Eddie, his bitter anger at King, his sick need to end all this. Those things were still there, but they were subdued, they seemed to take their proper position in this new adjustment of his values. He felt his insidious sense of guilt for Eddie's death slowly changing. He seemed to see now the truth in what Janice had said. Eddie would have gone into Yellowstone whether he found Morgan kissing Nora or not. Janice had been right. Time was healing the wound. Time was allowing Morgan to see it in its true light. But it was more than time. It was this deep intimacy with the fundamental pattern of life that the mountains seemed to give him. He saw Eddie's death as a part of that pattern. What had happened to the kid over in Yellowstone was only the end of a cycle. The cycle had begun long ago, the first time Eddie had rebelled at Morgan's authority, the first time the kid had chased a woman. Those things in the boy's personality had contained the seeds of his own destruction. One man had no control over a thing like that. It had been a losing battle for Morgan. It was a sad knowledge. But it seemed to cleanse him. He knew, with a deep surge of joy, that if he ever got back to Nora, the boy would no longer stand between them.

Drift came out about 8:00 that morning, surly as a bear. "I threw together some cold breakfast," he said. "I'll stand watch while you eat yours." He stopped, squinting his sleep-puffed eyes at Morgan's face. "What's the matter?"

Morgan rose stiffly, pounding his gloved hands against his legs to beat out the numbness. "Nothing," he said. "Why?"

"You look different," he said.

Morgan smiled slowly. "Does it show?" he said. He looked

off toward the mountains. "Shyrock has a theory, Drift. Either a man belongs to this country or he doesn't. What do you think of it?"

Drift studied him, seeming to sense part of what had happened to Morgan this night. "I think Shyrock's right," he said. "And I think maybe you belong."

Morgan gripped his arm, feeling a warmth toward this man for the first time. "Thanks," he said simply.

"I guess we've both changed a little tonight," Drift said.

"You mean you can go back to Janice?"

"When this is over, I can," Drift said. "You done that for me, Morgan. I'm going to ride this out with you."

After that it was the waiting. Four hours on, four hours off. Drift coming through the treacherous shale to relieve Morgan. Drift going out to hunt during one of his off periods and coming back with a six-point buck. They ran out of coffee the fifth day. They finished the buck the sixth. Dark clouds built up on the horizon that same day and they prepared to make a run for the line shack. But the storm did not develop. The clouds finally dissipated and lay through the valleys in a smoky black haze. Then it was that night when Morgan was off duty and sleeping in the half-faced camp. He was awakened by a hand on his shoulder, and his first sensation was of painfully cold feet. Then he looked up at Drift's dirty, bearded face.

"He's going through the pass," Drift said.

Morgan got up, shivering with cold. He was fully dressed and in his Mackinaw. He followed Drift down to the edge of the cliffs and looked into the cañon. Three men were driving a bunch of cattle, maybe fifty head, strung out in single file through the narrow rock-walled notch. The whole cavalcade was barely visible in the darkness, and Morgan could recognize none of the men.

"It must be some of King's Double Arrow outfit," Drift muttered. "Nobody else would come through this way."

"But why are they driving the cattle over here?" Morgan asked him.

"There's only one way to find out," the other man said. "It's what we've been waiting for, isn't it? Let's drift."

The going was too rough and steep to get down into the gorge from here, so they backtracked till they found it easier going. Once into the cañon they pushed hard, catching up with the cattle just as they reached the other end of the pass and dropped into Yellowstone valley. It was coal-black without a moon and they had only vague hints of the ghostly herd moving through the bottom lands below. They struck the river and followed it northward through long stretches of cottonwood and willow that stood like shivering skeletons in the wind. Once in a while the bawling of a steer reached them. It sounded feeble and far away.

Dawn came and the mountains became visible all about them like great hump-backed monsters rising out of the milky haze. The sky was slate-colored all morning, with no sun to burn it away. Drift and Morgan climbed into the spur ridges to keep from being seen by the men driving the cattle. Keeping to the cover of the fringing timber, they crossed vast rock-studded meadows and rode through thickets spattered with the bright red and gold of frost-bitten chokecherry. There was more snow up here, and they wallowed through drifts whenever they crossed the narrow valleys between ridges.

All through the day the cattle were pushed north, raising the dust of their passage till its tawny thickness obscured the Absarokas to the east. In mid-afternoon Morgan topped a ridge and looked down into the park where he had seen the Indians. A lonesome wind swept its desolate emptiness, scattering autumn leaves over barren ground.

They never got too near the herd, for fear of being sighted.

Most of the time they kept so far away it was only a dark mass moving through the bottom of the valley. But whenever timber stood near the cattle, they closed in, and it brought them close enough to recognize the men. Tom Law rode drag, Rideout was on a swing, and Charlie King led.

They reached the lake in late afternoon, its water shining dimly in the subdued light of a day still hiding its sun. A sooty darkness seeped into the sky, and it was night again. Morgan rode in a stupor now. His horse was stumbling and beaten and he had to use spurs to keep it going. Drift's complaint was like a voice from some other world.

"Why'n hell do they have to push so hard? I never saw anybody drive cattle night and day like this."

Up into the mountains again, where the air was so thin it cut the lungs like a knife, topping a crest and finding the river and passing the first geyser sometime in the night, exploding with a dull roar and a sibilant hiss. They reached the narrow cañon and began to climb the treacherous game trail. The river was flowing too swiftly below them to be frozen over yet, and this was the only way the cattle could have been driven. They came to the landslide, and Morgan pulled up, staring down at the beach below and at the cairn of stones. Drift pulled on, to let him have those few moments. Finally Morgan gigged his horse and followed, shivering in the bitter cold.

They crossed the dangerous slide area and descended the other side. They came to the cascades formed by beaver dams, where falling water filled the night with a silken splash that never died. The sky lightened with coming day as they left the cañon and dropped into a shallow valley. From ahead came the hissing *boom* of more geysers erupting. A mist began to lay its clammy pressure against Morgan's face. It filled the air in a milky haze that hid what lay around them, although it was full daylight now. They circled until they picked up the cattle sign on the ground, and followed by trailing. Frost turned the dying grass to a shimmering silver that was splashed with the crimson pinpoints of buffalo berries still ripening in sheltered crannies. Then even this growth was left behind, and they were crossing ground burned black, with the hole of an extinct crater gaping from rocky flats. Slowly the burned rocks became streaked with luminous ribbons of blue and green and strange patches of yellow. Then they came upon the first of the mud pots, *hissing* and splashing sardonically. Soon the chuckling *hiss* of boiling mud was all about them, and the exhausted horses were spooking and fiddling and fighting feebly at the bit. Then the ground began to tremble beneath them.

Drift pulled up, staring about them. "That means the big geyser's somewhere near us," he said. "It shakes the ground like that before it goes off. We'd better be careful. Get caught in it and you'd be a boiled fish."

Groping their way through the mist, they rose to a low and rocky ridge patched with the frosted foliage of dogwood. A rising wind was shredding the mist now, and they could see the cattle sign on the ground leading them to the left, down off the slope. But as they started to follow, a feeble bawl came from the other direction. Morgan pulled up his horse. It was silent again, except for the intermittent rumble from the ground.

Then, dimly, through the torn banners of the mist, he could see the steer, standing in the shallow trough of a coulée to their right. The wind shifted and the mist closed about the animal again.

"He must have cut off from the herd," Drift said.

Morgan was still staring out into the mist, toward that steer. "That cañon of bones," he said. "Are we near it?"

"Up beyond this big geyser. Not far."

"That's where they're driving the stuff."

"I guess we've both known that."

233

"Is there any way to get down in the cañon?"

"None that I could find."

"Then we'd better get a look at this steer now."

"Take it easy, Morgan. That drag rider's liable to come back after it."

"They're driving them up here for some reason, Drift. If we wait till they run them off the cliff, we'll never find out."

There was a renewed rumbling from beneath him, and Drift pulled in his spooking horse. "Wait'll we're beyond this big one, Morgan. If that drag rider don't get you down there, the geyser will. I don't know exactly where it is and it's going off pretty soon."

Morgan shook his head. "We may not get another chance like this. I've got to find out. Cover me from here." He had to fight with his animal to force it down off the rocky slope into the bottom of the wash. The horse was snorting and whinnying beneath Morgan, and the animal's panicky nervousness began transferring itself to him. The ominous rumbling seemed to crawl through his body, twitching at his muscles, prickling his scalp.

He sighted the steer through the mist again and spurred the horse after it. The steer made a feeble attempt to run, veering back and forth, and then slowed to a trot again, and finally stopped at the base of another rocky ridge. It was Morgan's first good look at any of these animals. It was painfully emaciated, its ribs looked ready to break through its mangy hide, its snout was dripping dirty lather. He swung off his horse to make sure what it was, laying a hand against the steer's hide, finding it feverishly hot.

A new rumble shook the ground beneath his feet. His horse tossed its head, trying to wheel away. As he turned to mount, he saw a shadowy shape resolving itself out of the mist.

"This steer's got tick fever, Drift," he said.

The man pulled his horse up sharply. But not soon enough. He was visible now, and Morgan could see it was not Drift. It was Tom Law.

They hung on that last instant of surprise, staring at each other. Then they both went for their guns. Morgan got his up first. His shot made a smashing sound. It knocked Law backward like a blow. He pitched off his horse's rump and the beast bolted. Morgan had let the reins of his own animal go to draw, and the shot had caused it to start running. It was already too far away for him to catch. Law groaned and rolled over. Morgan went to him and helped him sit up, unbuttoning the bloody shirt to examine the wound.

"You're hit bad, Law," Morgan told him.

"Damn you," Law said feebly. Morgan took off his neckerchief and made a compress. "You might as well tell me about this. I can guess most of it now. These steers have tick fever. That's why King hasn't shipped out for two years. He was afraid they'd slap a quarantine on him if the fever cropped up in a shipment and they found out his whole herd was infected."

Law nodded defeatedly. "King fired all the men he couldn't trust when he realized the fever couldn't be stamped out right away. We couldn't do anything with the diseased stuff on the Chinook side. There were too many to bury. If we'd tried to burn them, somebody would have seen the smoke sooner or later and investigated. This was the only way."

"So you took a chance on infecting all the cattle in Chinook."

Law shook his head. "Medicine Rim kept it from getting into Oakland's herd. We kept close watch on our other drift lines. If that fever'd been found in any other outfit, it would have ruined King just as sure as finding it in his own cattle. He'd've been wiped out if they condemned his herds. He's mortgaged to the hilt trying to hold on while he weeded it out. . . ."

The roll of giant drums began once more in the earth. There

was a sinister *hissing* sound from a mound at their left. Staring that way, Morgan knew they had only a few minutes left before the geyser went off. He had finished his crude bandage on Law, and he was slipping his hands under the man's arms, when a shout came from out in the mist.

"Law? What was that shot?"

Before Morgan could stop him, Law answered. "It's Morgan, King," he said hoarsely. "He followed us."

The effort made blood bubble from his mouth. He choked on it, sagging against Morgan. Their bodies were vibrating to the tremble of the earth.

"Rideout!" King shouted from out there in the mist. "Go around to the south. That geyser's going off in a minute. If we don't get him, it will."

Holding Law in a sitting position, Morgan strained to see through the pearly mist. "Law is wounded, King!" he called. "We've got to get him out of here before this geyser goes off . . . !"

A shot smashed into his words. The bullet kicked black rock into the air a foot from him. He caught Law under the armpits and scrambled toward a rocky uplift, throwing the man behind this cover, and then sprawling down himself.

"King!" he shouted. "You can't do this to a wounded man! He'll boil alive!"

"That's his hard luck!" King shouted. "You're not getting out of here, Morgan! Nobody's finding out about these cattle!"

Morgan felt acid anger pull his lips against his teeth. "Like Eddie didn't find out?"

"Eddie or Dodge or any of them, Morgan."

A bitter fury shook Morgan's voice. "You killed Eddie, then, damn you . . . !"

"He was getting too close."

"You'll never beat this game, King. You can't weed that fever out."

"We can." It was King's turn for anger now. "We wouldn't have had any trouble if the government hadn't sent you in here."

Morgan forgot the sinister rumblings of the earth momentarily with this revelation. "That's why you had Law and Rideout try to drive me out at first?" he called.

"We didn't see how a trail boss could have the money to buy the Doubloon," King answered. "I was afraid the government would send somebody in sooner or later to find out what was going on here. We couldn't take a chance on you."

The ground shook in a new spasm. The subterranean thunder of it drowned all other noise. Morgan felt his body grow rigid with the impulse to leap up, as he thought this was the eruption. But the rumbling died down a moment, allowing him to hear the *hiss* of escaping steam from that mound at his rear. He got to his hands and knees, eyes squinted painfully with his effort to see through the darkening mist. If he could only get one shot at King. Just one shot. He called again, hoping to locate the man by his voice.

"If I'd been a government man, having Law and Rideout jump me would've made me more suspicious than ever."

"What else could we do? Let you snoop around and find out what we had here? Then you rode into Yellowstone with Shyrock and made us sure you were. . . ." King broke off, as if Morgan's words had finally penetrated. "What do you mean . . . if you'd been a government man?"

Before Morgan could answer, there was a fresh cannonade from beneath his feet. Trembling violently, he tried to make his voice heard above the blast.

"King, I'm coming out with Law! Damn you, he's your own man! You can't let him boil alive!"

"Come on out, then!" King bawled. "A bullet's better than boiling!"

A new rumbling drowned him out. Anger burned through Morgan. He felt his lips pull flatly against his teeth as he slipped his hands beneath Law's arms. The muscles bunched through his body to lift the man. He was shaking violently with the trembling of the earth now. As he started to pull Law up, the man's head lolled off to one side, mouth sagging open. Then Morgan saw that the eyes were open, too. Open and glassy. Morgan let him sag back, wondering how long he had been dead.

Then, with anger searing everything else from him, he pulled his gun and scrambled up over the uplift, shouting into the mist. "All right, King, I'm coming . . . !"

The rumbling was so loud now he could hardly hear his own voice. As he ran across the rocky ground, the earth was torn with a new spasm. From behind him there was a gigantic *hissing,* and a great column of steam shot its white pillar into the sky. Its heat struck Morgan's back with a clammy pressure and then the first boiling water splashed over him. He could not help shouting in pain. At the same time, he saw the vague motion before him and off to the right.

The flame of a gun made its cherry streak in the pearly mist. He felt the whipping wind of a bullet past his cheek. He answered the fire. The motion ahead of him became a man's figure. He saw it jerking as his bullets drove home. The man's gun streaked the mist with its blast again. But it was pointed skyward now. Morgan ran right on into him, shouting something he couldn't understand himself, emptying his gun at the man till he saw the mist-hung body pitching over backward.

He was only a few paces from the body, still going forward, when another shape came running out of the mist far to his left. He wheeled and squeezed the trigger. There was no shot. He realized he had emptied his gun. The other man saw him and pulled up. Before he could shoot, there was the muffled *boom* of a gun from farther away. The figure turned, firing that way. He seemed to fling a last look at Morgan, then wheeled, firing again behind him, and ran off to the south, fading into the mist. As he did so, a second figure came into sight.

"Morgan?" shouted Drift.

"Over here," Morgan said.

Drift came running toward him. "That was Rideout. I wish I could've nailed him."

Morgan began walking toward the man he had shot, realizing for the first time who it was. Within a couple of paces, King became clear to him, lying on his back. With the geyser still spouting into the sky behind them, and the steamy fog thickening on every side, the two men stood there, staring down at the dead half-breed. The unending *hiss* of spouting water made Drift's words oddly muffled.

"Want to go after Rideout?"

"Not much point," Morgan said. "Looks like King was our killer. All Rideout did was hide a few infected cows."

Drift stared down at King for a long time. "It's over, then," he said, taking a weary breath. "It's funny. Two years. Two lifetimes. And then just a couple of minutes."

Morgan knew what the man was thinking. He felt the same way himself. It had taken so long, and had caused so much pain, and had ended so suddenly. It left a hollow feeling in a man. There was no great sense of vindication. It almost seemed as if there should be more, somehow.

"Well," he said, "it's over, anyway."

XVI

They came riding out of the Absarokas and into the wedge-shaped valley, two ragged men with dirty stubble beards and eyes hollowed by exhaustion. They came riding down into the valley and onto the road and up the snake fence to the gate. And by that time somebody up at the barn had seen them and before they were halfway across the compound it was swarming with people. The whole crew seemed to erupt from the bunkhouse and Oakland and Janice and Nora came from the big house, running across the thin crust of a snow that had fallen the night before. Drift pulled up, grinning his ugly grin down at Janice. She stared wordlessly up at him, and her eyes shone with tears as she saw the change in his face. He stepped down and drew her roughly into his arms. An instant before she buried her face in his chest, she sent Morgan one glance, full of more heartfelt thanks than her words could ever tell.

Nora hung back, looking with dark and troubled eyes at Morgan's face. He got off his horse, gazing at her over the shoulders of the men as they surged around him, clapping him on the back. She saw his expression, and a shining knowledge wiped the darkness from her face. He told Oakland what had happened, never taking his eyes off Nora.

"I guess we better report it right away," Oakland said. There was a sharp fear in his voice. "They'll want to get the inspector up here."

"I don't think you'll have to worry about getting your cattle condemned," Morgan told him. "King was watching his drift lines too close. He knew any other outfit that discovered the fever would report it and ruin him."

O'Toole stood to one side, trying to look casual as he rolled a cigarette with one hand. "We'd've found the fever if any had cropped up in our stuff."

The worry seeped out of Oakland's face, and he chuckled at O'Toole. "You don't need to show off your smoke-rollin' now. Morgan won't have eyes for that till next year."

Nora sent Morgan a last, meaningful glance, and turned and

went back up toward the house. He shouldered through the men, giving Jinglebob an affectionate punch, and followed her across the compound. Neither of them spoke till they were inside. As soon as he came through the door, shutting it behind, Nora wheeled and was in his arms. There was no taste of tears mingling with the kiss now. It was only her lips, ripe and full and giving, and her body in his arms.

"Janice was right," he said. "Time took care of it. And the mountains. It seems like you can see everything in its proper place out there."

"You can if you belong. And you belong, Morgan."

"That's why I'm going to stay. I'm going to the Doubloon, Nora. Will you come with me?"

"You knew the answer to that a long time ago," she said, her voice husky. "I'll come whenever you say, Morgan."

ACKNOWLEDGMENTS

"Trail of the Lonely Gun" first appeared in *Action Stories* (Spring, 1946). Copyright © 1946 by Fiction House, Inc. Copyright © renewed 1974 by Marian R. Savage. Copyright © 2009 by Golden West Literary Agency for restored material.

"Shadow Riders" first appeared in *Zane Grey's Western Magazine* (12/50). Copyright © 1950 by The Hawley Publications, Inc. Copyright © renewed 1978 by Marian R. Savage. Copyright © 2009 by Golden West Literary Agency for restored material.

ABOUT THE AUTHOR

Les Savage, Jr. was born in Alhambra, California and grew up in Los Angeles. His first published story was "Bullets and Bull-whips" accepted by the prestigious magazine, Street & Smith's *Western Story*. Almost ninety more magazine stories followed, all set on the American frontier, many of them published in Fiction House magazines such as *Frontier Stories* and *Lariat Story Magazine* where Savage became a superstar with his name on many covers. His first novel, *Treasure of the Brasada,* appeared from Simon & Schuster in 1947. Due to his preference for historical accuracy, Savage often ran into problems with book editors in the 1950s who were concerned about marriages between his protagonists and women of different races—a commonplace on the real frontier but not in much Western fiction in that decade. Savage died young, at thirty-five, from complications arising out of hereditary diabetes and elevated cholesterol. However, as a result of the censorship imposed on many of his works, only now are they being fully restored by returning to the author's original manuscripts. Among Savage's finest Western stories are *Fire Dance at Spider Rock* (Five Star Westerns, 1995), *Medicine Wheel* (Five Star Westerns, 1996), *Coffin Gap* (Five Star Westerns, 1997), *Phantoms in the Night* (Five Star Westerns, 1998), *The Bloody Quarter* (Five Star Westerns, 1999), *In the Land of Little Sticks* (Five Star Westerns, 2000), *The Cavan Breed* (Five Star Westerns, 2001), and *Danger Rides the River* (Five Star Westerns, 2002). Much as Stephen

Crane before him, while he wrote, the shadow of his imminent death grew longer and longer across his young life, and he knew that, if he was going to do it at all, he would have to do it quickly. He did it well, and, now that his novels and stories are being restored to what he had intended them to be, his achievement irradiated by his powerful and profoundly sensitive imagination will be with us always, as he had wanted it to be, as he had so rushed against time and mortality that it might be. *Lawless Land* will be his next Five Star Western.